GL♥SS

Marilyn Kaye is a bestselling American author. Her Replica series, about a genetically altered clone (Random House USA, Hodder UK), ran to over twenty titles and was an international success. She lived in New York for many years and currently lives in Paris.

MARILYN KAYE

Marilyn Kaye

GL♥SS

MACMILLAN

First published 2013 by Macmillan Children's Books
a division of Macmillan Publishers Limited
20 New Wharf Road, London N1 9RR
Basingstoke and Oxford
Associated companies throughout the world
www.panmacmillan.com

ISBN 978-1-4472-2397-9

3 5 7 9 8 6 4 2

A CIP catalogue record for this book is available from
the British Library.

Printed and bound by CPI Group (UK) Ltd, Croydon CR0 4YY

For Ben Baglio and Richard Wilson,
and in memory of Bob

Chapter One

Sherry Ann Forrester knew the rules. Among the many social guidelines that had been drummed into her since childhood was this fixed decree: a lady maintained an air of composure, whatever the circumstances. And by the age of eighteen Sherry considered herself an expert at putting on the right face for every situation, no matter what she might be feeling.

Last year, when her name had been called as a finalist in the Miss Teen Georgia pageant, she'd been able to look simply pleased and humble rather than thrilled to bits. When she only placed second runner-up in the final round, all anyone could see was her happiness for the new queen, despite the fact that she disliked the girl intensely and believed the well-endowed baton-twirler had only won through family connections and some shameless flirtation with a judge.

Soon after that, at the funeral of her beloved grandfather, she'd presented the perfect picture of the dignified mourner, sorrowful and grieving, but still able to greet guests in the church with a sad smile, even as she fought back the urge to throw herself on the coffin and sob hysterically.

And less than a month ago, when she was declared Senior Prom Queen in the high-school gymnasium, she was able to appear completely and utterly surprised. She widened her eyes, her mouth dropped open slightly and she put a hand over her heart, as if she was overwhelmed emotionally. No fake tears though. It was just enough and not too much. No one could have guessed that her best friend, one of the vote counters, had alerted her well in advance of her imminent coronation.

And today, as she and the seven other interns were taken on a tour of the *Gloss* magazine offices, she assumed a calm air of avid interest without gaping or gawking. But there came a point when her carefully honed restraint was seriously challenged.

'And this . . .' Miss Caroline Davison, the managing editor, paused at a door. Flourishing an invisible magic wand with one hand, she turned the knob with the other.

'*This* is the famous *Gloss* samples closet.'

Sherry joined the others in a collective gasp which became something close to a shriek of pure and utter amazement. First of all, it wasn't a closet, it was a room three times the size of the largest office the interns had seen. And its contents were beyond belief.

Miss Davison had to raise her voice to be heard over all the 'oohs' and 'ahs'.

'It's where we keep all the items sent to us by designers and clothing companies in the hope that we'll feature them in the magazine. What you see before you is a good representative sample of the apparel industry.'

That was an understatement, Sherry thought. She'd call it fashion paradise. Dresses, skirts, gowns, blouses, trousers and coats hung from the rods. On the shelves lay shoes and handbags, mounds of sweaters and a large glass case containing jewellery. She tried to catch the eye of her roommate, but Donna was looking down, as if she was unworthy to feast her eyes upon such gorgeousness.

The girls spread out, and it was interesting to see who was attracted to what. Vicky, the tanned California girl with sun-streaked hair, made a beeline in the direction of a rack of bathing suits. Sweet-faced Ellen from Texas, whose dark hair was adorned with tiny matching bows over each spit curl, was clearly thrilled by a tray of brightly coloured hair ornaments, ribbons and barrettes. Sherry turned her attention to the pale blue two-piece ensemble that had adorned the cover of the March issue. She remembered considering a trip to Atlanta, to see if Rich's Department Store carried the outfit, but decided that three-quarter sleeves wouldn't be very wearable in a hot Georgia summer. Of course, that was before she knew for sure that she'd be spending the summer in New York City.

The girl with the perfectly sculpted bouffant on Sherry's right, Linda, murmured, 'Do you think they'll let us wear any of this stuff?'

And Diane, the girl on her left, whispered, 'Dibs on the blue suit.'

But any hopes they might have were quickly dashed when one platinum-haired intern stepped forward and picked up a low-heeled pump. Examining the sole, she squealed in delight

'Five and a half! That's my size.'

Linda spoke into Sherry's ear. 'Can you believe that hair?'

Sherry smiled. The girl had clearly gone overboard with peroxide and Sherry was reminded of her little sister's Bubble Cut Barbie. This girl even had Barbie's trademark sweep of black liner over her eyes and the doll's bright pink lips.

'Five and a half is the standard sample shoe size,' the editor informed

her. 'But, girls, let me warn you – this isn't a lending library. These items aren't for borrowing.'

Pamela – that was the name on the platinum-blonde's tag – sighed dramatically. 'Never?'

Miss Davison lips twitched slightly. 'Rarely, which is almost the same thing. We've been known to bend the rules on occasion, but only for some extraordinary event and with special permission. Or when you're doing something exceptional on behalf of *Gloss*. And of course the item would have to be returned in pristine condition.'

'An extraordinary event,' Pamela repeated. 'Like what?'

'Talk about pushy,' Linda murmured. 'And that skirt she's wearing!'

Sherry smiled without commenting. The skirt *was* awfully tight. And the low-cut blouse wasn't exactly office attire either.

Sherry had chosen her own first-day-at-*Gloss* outfit with care and some trepidation. Was her madras skirt outdated? Everyone back home still wore skirts like this, but she hadn't seen any madras lately in the pages of *Gloss*. She'd topped it with a navy-blue sleeveless shell, and accessorized with navy tassel loafers and a matching pocketbook. She was relieved to see bare legs in loafers on a couple of other girls, and while no one else wore madras, at least three of them had on print skirts with blouses or shells that picked up one of the colours in the print.

The editor brushed Pamela's question aside. 'I don't think we need to get into that now. We have more important things to go over today. Other questions?'

A petite redhead with a close-cropped pixie cut raised her hand. Sherry thought she too was dressed strangely, in black capri pants and a black-and-white striped T-shirt. She'd never seen anything like that in *Gloss*.

'How do you choose which items will go in the magazine?'

That was exactly what Sherry had been wondering. Why hadn't *she* spoken up? Of course, she knew why – it was because well-brought-up Southern girls didn't call attention to themselves.

Miss Davison nodded at the redhead with approval. 'That's a good question, Allison, and one of the main topics we'll be covering during your apprenticeship. We don't have time to go into this in any detail now, but I'll give you an example.' She turned to Sherry. 'Do you see that black oblong quilted handbag with the chain handle on the shelf?'

'Yes, ma'am.'

The response that revealed the region of her upbringing slipped out automatically, and she heard a muffled giggle from one of the other girls. Miss Davison smiled too, but kindly.

'You can call me Caroline,' she said.

'All of us or just Sherry?' Pamela asked.

Sherry couldn't help being amused by the girl's impudence. And the editor actually smiled.

'All of you, of course. Sherry, pass the bag to me.'

'Yes –' This time she caught herself before the 'ma'am' could slip out. 'Yes, Miss Davison – I mean, Caroline.'

She took up the bag and brought it to the editor. The woman held it aloft for all to see. 'This is a bag that was designed by the great Coco Chanel. Although it's quite lovely, we decided not to feature it in *Gloss*, since we didn't see it as appealing to our readership. As you all know, *Gloss* is aimed at the American teenager, and this bag is well beyond the means of our readers.'

'How much is it worth?' Pamela wanted to know, but the editor was distracted by the appearance of a new figure at the doorway.

'Hi.'

All the interns turned to the young man, and Sherry wasn't surprised to see some eyes light up. He was very good-looking, with blond hair, and he was as tanned as Vicky-from-California. A lazy grin revealed deep dimples. For Sherry, he brought to mind the dreamy surfer guys in all those beach movies – more California than New York.

'The new girls, right?' He addressed Caroline Davison, but his eyes rested on the younger females.

The editor's lips tightened for a second. 'The new *interns*. Everyone, this is Ricky Hartnell. He's . . .' she paused, as if she was trying to come up with some way to explain him. 'He's an office assistant.'

'*Editorial* assistant,' the boy corrected her. 'At least, I *think* that's my title.'

'We're very busy right now, Ricky,' Caroline said briskly. 'I'm sure you'll have an opportunity to meet everyone individually later.'

'Looking forward to it,' he said with a wink at the girls. 'See you around, ladies.'

'Cute,' Diane whispered in Sherry's ear.

Sherry nodded, but mentally she added, 'And he knows it.' Mama was always warning her about making snap judgements, but in this particular case she felt reasonably sure her assessment was accurate.

Miss Davison waved them out of the samples closet. 'This finishes the tour. Since you only arrived yesterday, I'm not planning to keep you here for a full working day. But keep in mind that we'll be working on a very special issue of *Gloss*, the annual readers' issue. You will be representing two million subscribers who depend on *Gloss* for advice on everything from fashion and beauty to planning for the future. It's a huge responsibility and I hope you're ready for it.'

There was a general bobbing of heads. A balding man with glasses passed by, and Caroline called out to him.

'George, could I have a minute?'

The man frowned. 'I'm in the middle of something, Caroline.'

'I'll be quick. Girls, this is George Simpson, our features editor. George, these are the young women who will be working as summer apprentices.'

His disinterested eyes swept over them. 'Who can type?' He nodded at the show of hands. 'Good. And I assume you're all familiar with the alphabet, which means you can file.'

'Mail!'

This announcement came from a tall, dark-haired boy with deep-set eyes. He wore an oversized grey jacket with 'Hartnell Publications' embroidered over a pocket, and he was gripping the handles of a cart filled with envelopes and boxes.

'Leave mine on my desk,' Mr Simpson told him.

The boy stared at him. 'I'm sorry, sir, I don't know your name. I'm new here.'

'That's no excuse,' the man barked. 'If you're going to deliver the mail, you need to know to whom you're delivering it.'

The boy flinched as if he'd been physically attacked. Caroline seemed to take pity on him. 'This is George Simpson, the features editor,' she told him. 'And I'm Caroline Davison, managing editor. All the editors' names are on their office doors, and everyone in the central room has a nameplate on his or her desk. And you are . . . ?'

Sherry could see his Adam's apple bob before he said, 'Michael Dillon.'

'How do you do, Michael. These young women are interns here at *Gloss*.'

The boy didn't meet their eyes, but he muttered, 'Pleased to meet you,' before continuing to roll his cart down the corridor.

'Well, now that we're all great chums, I've got work to do,' Mr Simpson said, and walked away.

Sherry didn't miss the withering glance Caroline gave him before turning back to the interns. 'And so do you all. Here's your first assignment: I want a five-hundred-word review of the film you saw this morning by noon tomorrow. Keep in mind that one review will be selected to appear in the readers' issue. You can stay here to work at your desk of course, or back at your residence hall if you prefer. You might want to spend the afternoon settling in, or exploring the city, and write your piece tonight. It's up to you.'

The girls dispersed and headed to the desks they'd been assigned earlier in what was called the bullpen, the large open space filled with rows of desks, where the secretaries and junior staff worked. Linda walked alongside Sherry.

'Diane and I are going to Times Square. Want to come with?'

It was one of the famous landmarks on Sherry's

must-see list, and she nodded. 'Sure. Just let me get my stuff together.'

'We'll meet you outside, in front of the building,' Linda said.

Sherry fumbled through the papers on her desk, and in the process she knocked over the pencil holder. As she bent down to retrieve the contents, the good-looking editorial assistant, or whatever his title was, appeared by her side.

'Need some help?' he asked.

'It's all right,' she murmured. Of course, a Southern gentleman would have ignored what she said and bent down to pick up the items. Surfer guy did not. But as she rose, she murmured, 'Thank you anyway.'

'You're welcome, Sherry Ann Forrester.'

She stiffened as she realized he was staring at her chest, until she remembered that her name tag was there.

'First time in New York, Sherry Ann?'

'Yes, this is my first visit,' she told him. 'And it's just Sherry,' she added. Which wasn't quite true. All her life, she'd been called Sherry Ann. But it was so Southern, to have a double first name, that she'd decided to drop the Ann for the summer.

Unfortunately the name tag had been prepared before her arrival. Not to mention the fact that there wasn't much she could do about her accent.

'Where are you from?' he asked.

'Georgia. North of Atlanta.'

'So you're a Southern belle,' he said with a grin.

Mentally she bemoaned the fact that a *Gone with the Wind* revival had taken place in movie theatres all across the country just the year before. Every girl who crossed the Mason–Dixon line was now subject to comparison with Scarlett O'Hara. Even the taxi driver who'd brought her from LaGuardia Airport the day before had reacted with a comment when he heard her speak. At the time, she'd thought it was cute. Maybe it was Ricky's cocky smile that made his remark annoying.

'No, just an ordinary girl from the South,' she said lightly.

'You don't have a plantation? With cotton fields, and slaves, and a mammy to pick up after you?' At a desk not far from hers, a dark-skinned secretary looked up sharply.

Sherry tried to keep her tone light. 'This is 1963, Ricky, not 1863. We don't live like that any more.'

'You still talk like it,' he pointed out. 'And it's cute. *You're* cute.'

She couldn't tell if he was flirting or just teasing, and she fought back the automatic instinct to thank him for the compliment.

'Excuse me,' she murmured, and stuffed the papers in her handbag.

The other interns had all taken off by then, but

GL♥SS

as she passed through the swinging doors into the hallway she spotted the blonde bombshell waiting by the bank of elevators. She knew how Pamela would be labelled back home. In a picture dictionary, she would be the illustration for a 'skag', the word of the moment for a girl with a less-than-sterling reputation. The bleached hair, the revealing top (which Sherry strongly suspected covered a pair of falsies), the way she jiggled when she walked, which indicated the absence of a girdle.

But she wasn't back home, and she was going to have to get accustomed to being around the kinds of folks she'd never known before. Assertive career women like Caroline Davison, cocky boys like Ricky . . . new people, new experiences, that was what this summer was all about.

Turning, Pamela blocked the elevator door that was about to close with her arm.

'Hey, hurry up, I'm holding this for you.'

Sherry hurried forward. 'Thanks,' she said, stepping inside.

Pamela hit the lobby button. 'So how about that samples closet? Swift, huh?'

'Very impressive,' Sherry agreed.

'I've got my eye on that purple gown with the rhinestones,' Pamela declared.

'But where would you wear something like that?' Sherry wondered. 'It's not like we'll be going to any senior proms while we're here.'

'Are you kidding? We're in New York, the most glamorous city in the world! There are millions of places to wear a gown. El Morocco, the 21 Club, Sardi's . . .'

Sherry looked at her with interest. 'How do you know about these places?'

'I've read about them, mostly in movie magazines. New York is full of nightclubs, cocktail lounges, fancy restaurants. I've made a list.'

'You really think they'll take us to places like that?'

Pamela grinned. 'I doubt it, but I'll get there on my own. Well, hopefully not completely on my own, if you know what I mean.'

'I've never been to a nightclub in my life,' Sherry confessed.

'Neither have I,' Pamela said. 'The closest thing to a nightclub in my hometown is a strip joint and a couple of bars where old guys gamble in a back room. And that's what I'll be going back to when this summer is over. So I'm planning to take advantage of what the Big Apple has to offer while I've got the chance.'

'You'll need an escort,' Sherry remarked. 'Like you said, you can't go to those kinds of places alone, can you?'

'Of course not,' Pamela agreed. 'And anyway, I gotta find someone to foot the bill. Like a sugar daddy.'

GL♥SS

Sherry tried not to look shocked. 'You mean, an old rich man?'

'Well, I'd prefer a young good-looking one,' Pamela said cheerfully. 'Did you notice that photographer at the dinner last night? He looked pretty fine to me.'

'He's got to be at least thirty,' Sherry pointed out. 'Wouldn't you rather go out with someone your own age?'

'We're in New York, the most glamorous city in the world!'

Pamela considered this. 'That Ricky wasn't bad,' she acknowledged.

'What about that boy from the mailroom?'

Pamela made a face. 'He looks like a hood.'

Sherry thought back. Maybe his hair *was* a little greasy. And he hadn't smiled at all. She wasn't sure why she'd even mentioned him.

'Besides,' Pamela continued, 'boys who work in mailrooms don't have any money. Anyway, I'm not looking for a boyfriend. I just want to have some fun.'

The elevator doors opened, and as they stepped out into the lobby Sherry was regarding her with curiosity. Who didn't want a boyfriend? This comment intrigued her and she wanted to hear more. Maybe she should invite Pamela to join her and the others on their jaunt to Times Square. But recalling Linda's comments back in the samples closet, she had a feeling the blonde wouldn't exactly be welcome.

In any case, Pamela had her own plans for the afternoon. 'Wanna go shopping?' From her handbag she withdrew the discount-coupon booklet they'd each been given the night before. 'If I'm going to hit the hotspots, I'll need something to wear.'

'Thanks, but I've got plans,' Sherry said. They walked out of the building and on to Madison Avenue, baking under the hot July sun. 'Maybe I'll see you at dinner,' she told Pamela. 'Of course, I'm referring to the dining hall at the residence, not Sardi's,' she added with a grin.

Pamela laughed. 'OK, dining hall tonight. But mark my words, we'll make it to Sardi's before the summer's over.' She strode off, and Sherry wasn't surprised to note that her hips actually twitched. The girl positively exuded confidence.

She didn't see Linda and Diane in front of the building, but then she spotted them, waving to her from across the street, in front of a drugstore. As she walked to the corner crosswalk, she barely felt her feet on the pavement. It was too hard to believe that she was really, truly walking on a street in New York City.

She'd seen images of New York of course, in photos and movies and on TV, and she'd thought she was prepared for it. But the impact was so much more than she had anticipated. How could she have known that looking up at skyscrapers would make her dizzy? How could she have imagined the cacophony of horns and the rumble of trucks, the drivers who stuck their heads out of the windows and yelled in frustration at the vehicle in front of them? From the sidewalks, the buzz of a million simultaneous conversations. Everyone seemed to be moving in accelerated motion, like they were all late for some terribly important appointment. Construction noises, drilling and hammering . . . all of it punctuated by intermittent sirens.

She joined the crowd at the corner. Even when the light turned green, she didn't want to step into the street before looking both ways. Could she trust these angry New York drivers to actually stop? But she had no choice – she was swept across with the crowd.

As she headed towards Linda and Diane, she tried to remember what she knew about the girls. Not much, really. All eight girls, including herself, had introduced themselves at the welcome dinner the night before, but their respective hometowns and interests had become a bit of a blur in her mind.

It didn't really matter. She knew instinctively that Linda and Diane were the kind of girls she would hang out with. They weren't Southern, but in every other way they fit the mould of Sherry's clique back home. Diane's auburn hair was styled in a chin-length flip, just like her own, and she wore a light green shirtwaist dress that was identical to the light blue one in Sherry's closet. And resting on the round collar of Linda's crisp white blouse was a gold circle pin very similar to the one in Sherry's jewellery box. She'd bet anything they'd both been cheerleaders at their high schools, or homecoming queens, or members of their local department store's Teen Board – popular, all-American girls, just like she was. Typical *Gloss* girls.

They were both looking a little impatient, and Linda had another reason to appear unhappy.

'I had to buy some aspirin – this noise is giving me a headache,' she said. 'Now I need something to wash them down with.'

'There's a diner over there,' Diane said, pointing up the street. They started in that direction.

'Sorry I'm late,' Sherry apologized. 'That boy Ricky wouldn't stop talking.'

Their expressions changed. 'Well, aren't you the lucky one!' Linda exclaimed. 'He's only the most eligible guy here.'

'I guess he's cute,' Sherry conceded. 'Seems kind of conceited though.'

'He's got a right to be,' Diane said. 'Didn't you catch his last name? Ricky *Hartnell*. As in Hartnell Publications. The name over the door to the building. He's the boss's son.'

'Oh.' She tried to look suitably impressed. 'Well, he's not my type. Too full of himself.'

'Don't be so quick to brush him off,' Linda advised. 'He'd be a real catch.'

'Except I'm not fishing,' Sherry told her. She tugged on the chain around her neck and pulled out the ring that had been hidden under her blouse.

Linda's eyebrows went up. 'Going steady, huh?' She immediately topped that, fingering a thin gold chain around her neck and lifting the pendant from which dangled two Greek letters.

'You're lavaliered,' remarked Sherry, impressed.

'He's a Sigma Chi at the University of Illinois,' Linda told her. 'I'll be starting there in September.'

They entered the diner, which wasn't too busy, and took seats at the counter.

'Do you have Tab?' Linda asked the waitress.

'Yeah. Three Tabs?'

Personally, Sherry would have preferred a real Coke and not this new sugar-free version, but she could just imagine the disapproving looks from the other girls. Any opportunity to avoid calories was to be taken advantage of – another rule.

'You're lucky to be already dating a college boy,' Diane said to Linda. 'You guys must be pretty serious.'

'He'll give me his frat pin next year,' Linda informed them. 'And we'll get engaged when I'm a senior. Then, when I graduate, we'll move to Chicago, where Bill will be in law school. I'll teach elementary school for a couple of years. Then we'll want to start a family, so we'll move to the suburbs. Probably Lake Forest.'

Diane made no effort to hide her envy. 'You've got your whole life planned.'

Linda nodded happily as their drinks arrived.

'University of Illinois,' Sherry repeated. 'That's a huge school, isn't it? What do you want to do there?'

Linda lowered her voice, as if she was about to reveal some amazing secret. 'I want to become the sweetheart of Sigma Chi.'

Sherry had been thinking more along the lines of what Linda would major in, but she nodded politely. 'That would be pretty neat.'

'No kidding,' Diane exclaimed. 'There's a Sigma Chi where I'm going, Ohio State. My sister's already there, and she told me that every year, when they choose their new sweetheart, the whole fraternity sings to her outside her dorm.'

Linda nodded. 'Or outside the sorority house –' her forehead puckered – 'which is something I'm really worried about.'

'Getting into a sorority?' Sherry asked.

Linda shook her head. 'Oh, I'll get into one. The big question is, which one will I choose? Bill, that's my boyfriend, he says the sweetheart is usually a member of Kappa Kappa Gamma. But I'm a Tri-Delt legacy. And my mother would just about kill me if I don't pledge Tri-Delt.'

Sherry understood. A friend back home, Tommie Lynn, had told her about legacies. If your mother had been a member of a certain sorority, you were pretty much guaranteed an invitation to join that one. Tommie Lynn had been very relieved to know that the Chi Omega chapter at the University of Georgia was one of the best sororities, since her mother had been a Chi O at another school.

Diane bit her lower lip. 'My mother didn't go to a university.'

'But you won't have any problem getting into a sorority,' Linda assured her. 'Didn't you tell me you were captain of your cheerleading squad? They'll all want you. What about you, Sherry? Do you know what you want to pledge?'

'There aren't any Greek organizations where I'm going,' Sherry told her. 'It's a small women's college in Atlanta.'

Something close to horror crossed her companions' faces.

'It's a family tradition,' Sherry explained. 'My grandmother went there, and my mother.'

Their expressions didn't change.

'But my boyfriend's going to Georgia Tech,' Sherry added. 'I'm sure he'll join a fraternity there.'

Their faces cleared. 'Oh, well, that's OK then,' Linda said. 'You'll have a social life. Is there a Sigma Chi chapter at Georgia Tech?'

'I don't know,' Sherry admitted. She could have been having this exact same conversation with friends back home. 'Y'all ready to go to Times Square?'

Diane giggled. '"Y'all" – that's so cute!'

Wishing fervently that other regions had accents as distinctive as the South, Sherry just smiled and fished in her bag for change. The girls paid and left the diner.

'There's a taxi stand across the street,' Linda pointed out.

'Oh, let's just take the subway,' Sherry urged. It was another item on her must-see list, and besides, she was on a budget. She checked her map. 'There's an entrance on the next block and Times Square is just two stops from here.'

'What do you think of the other girls?' Diane asked as they walked.

Recalling her efforts to not make snap judgements, Sherry demurred. 'Kind of too soon to tell, isn't it?'

But Linda already had formed opinions. 'Some of them don't look like *Gloss* girls to me. That platinum blonde, for example. She seems kind of trashy.'

'And the girl from Boston, she looks like a beatnik,' Diane added. 'The artsy type, you know? Probably writes poetry.'

'Which one's your roommate?' Linda asked Sherry.

'Donna. Tall and thin, long brown hair . . .'

Linda frowned. 'I don't remember her.'

'She's kind of quiet,' Sherry admitted. Actually,

Donna was more than quiet. In the twenty-four hours since they'd met, she'd barely been able to get a word out of her.

They descended the steps to the subway, purchased tokens and passed through the turnstiles. Then it was down more steps to the tracks.

Immediately Linda wrinkled her nose. 'It smells down here,' she murmured.

She was right, but Sherry was too distracted by the New Yorkers waiting on the platform to take much notice. She'd never seen so many different-looking people in one place – young and old, all shapes and sizes and colours. People who looked prosperous standing right alongside people who looked like beggars. There were people like this back home – you just never saw them in the same place. It was a lot to take in.

There was a distant but thunderous noise, and seconds later the train pulled into the station. The doors opened, and the crowd on the platform surged forward, propelling the girls into the car.

There were no empty seats, so they all clutched hanging straps as the train jolted forward. And it was too noisy to talk. But the trip was so fast it didn't matter – within a few minutes they arrived at the 42nd Street station. Once again, it wasn't necessary to make any effort to leave the train – they were pushed out by people behind them, and then up some stairs, across a platform, up more stairs and finally they emerged on to a street.

And what a street it was. Even in broad daylight, it was completely lit up, with neon signs and marquees and enormous billboards advertising everything from soft drinks to cigarettes. If Madison Avenue had been energetic, the corner of Broadway and 42nd Street was positively manic. Instinctively, the three girls linked arms as they proceeded through Times Square.

There were a lot of movie theatres, all featuring films that Sherry couldn't imagine appearing on a screen back home, with names like *Circus of Sex*, *Wild Pussycats* and *Tantalizing Teens*. They passed storefronts and businesses that made no attempt to disguise what lay beyond their doors: peep shows, topless bars, sex shops. At tables on the sidewalks, shady-looking men urged passers-by to gamble their money on card games. And in practically every doorway stood a scantily clad and heavily made-up woman. Sherry tried not to stare, but it was impossible. These women made Barbie Doll back at *Gloss* look like Little Miss Goody-Two Shoes.

'This is *gross*,' Diane whispered, and Sherry could understand her reaction. It was all nasty and seedy and disgusting. And yet, it was like passing a car accident on a road – you couldn't help but look.

A man with a pockmarked face and a creepy smile fell into step alongside them. 'Hey, pretty ladies, where you heading?'

'None of your business!' Linda snapped.

GL♥SS

He wasn't put off. 'New in town, huh?' As he linked his arm through Diane's, she let out a shriek that would have summoned the entire population of Sherry's hometown to her side. On this street, no one seemed to have heard her, but at least it sent the man away.

'I want to get out of here,' Diane wailed. 'Now!'

Personally Sherry thought she was overreacting, but she put an arm around the sobbing girl. 'C'mon, let's head back to the subway and we'll go to the residence.'

'I have a better idea,' Linda declared. 'We'll go to the Plaza Hotel and have tea. My parents always do that when they're in New York.' She went to the kerb and flagged down a yellow cab.

Sherry walked Diane to the taxi, but she herself didn't get in with them.

'Aren't you coming?' Linda asked.

'Um, no, I think I'll go back to the room and work on the assignment,' she said. 'I'll see you at dinner.'

She watched as the taxi sped away. The Plaza Hotel was another item on her must-see list, and she wouldn't have minded spending a little money on a cup of tea there. Only a few years ago, she'd read the stories about Eloise, a little girl who lived at the Plaza, to her kid sister, and she'd been just as enthralled as little Beth.

So why hadn't she felt like going with the others?♥

Chapter Two

O n the second floor of the residence, Sherry stopped in front of room 212 and unlocked the door.

For a moment, she just stood there and surveyed the room. *Gloss* had guaranteed pleasant accommodations in the letter, and the magazine had lived up to its promise. Two single beds, two desks, two bureaux, a decent-sized closet and an adjoining bathroom. The beds were covered with blue and yellow patterned spreads, the walls were painted a matching yellow, and the curtains at the small window picked up the blue colour.

It certainly didn't compare to what she had back home though – a big, lovely pink and white room that she'd never had to share. Her record player, her own pink princess phone extension, her homecoming queen crown hanging from one side of the movie-star mirror on her vanity table, and the newly added prom-queen crown on the other side. The huge picture window, with rose-patterned curtains that provided the perfect frame for the dogwood trees outside. This room had a window, but it looked out on an alley lined with garbage cans.

Glancing at the clock radio on the desk, she saw

that it was now five thirty. What would she be doing right now, back home? Playing tennis at the country club, with Elaine or Carol or Tommie Lynn? Or just finishing a game probably, since she'd have to be home and at the dinner table by six thirty. Maybe she and her tennis partner would be indulging in a sundae or a milkshake at the club snack bar, assuring each other they were simply replacing the calories they'd burned on the court.

Then home, where she might find a letter from Johnny. He hadn't been very good about writing since he left for that summer job in Washington DC, but she supposed working for a congressman was pretty time-consuming.

She remembered the day he told her about the job, the morning after the senior prom. It had been a spectacular evening. She'd worn floor-length pink taffeta, purchased for the occasion on a special shopping trip to Atlanta, with the wrist corsage of pink tea roses that Johnny presented her when he arrived to pick her up. He'd looked so handsome, in the light blue tuxedo he'd rented. They'd danced all night in the gym, which had been decorated beyond recognition with sparkling lights and streamers and balloons. In accordance with tradition, there were no curfews that night, and they'd ended the festivities at three in the morning at a fancy breakfast set up in Tommie Lynn's basement. And at some point in the early hours, when she and Johnny found themselves alone together, she'd let him get to second base for the very first time. She'd heard that some girls went all the way on prom night, she'd even heard that this was a tradition, but she wasn't ready for that. Still, she had to admit, she liked the feeling of his hand on her bare flesh, and for a brief moment she actually considered letting him progress to third base. But she controlled herself – third base would have to wait till he gave her his fraternity pin.

She was surprised when he showed up at her home at ten the next morning, early for a Saturday after such a late night. She was up – Beth, with all the typical impatience of a twelve-year-old, wanted all the details of the big event and wouldn't let her sleep late.

Opening the door to Johnny, she could see right away that something was up.

'I have to tell you something,' he said. 'My dad, he got me a summer job, working for a congressman.' He took a deep breath, and then added, 'In Washington DC.' He swallowed, and more information came out in a rush. 'I'll be away all summer. I found out last week. I didn't want to tell you right away, so we could have a great prom, but now . . .' his voice trailed off, and he looked at her anxiously.

Obviously he thought she'd be upset that he wouldn't be there for lazy afternoons by the pool at the country club, evening barbecues, day trips to the lake. But there was something he didn't know.

GL♥SS

She hadn't even told her family the news yet, maybe because it still didn't seem real to her. Months earlier, when she'd applied for the *Gloss* magazine intern programme, she wasn't even sure why she was doing it. She'd never considered journalism as a career goal. She'd never really thought about careers much at all. But for some strange reason she kept finding herself turning back to the page in her favourite magazine that encouraged readers to spend a summer in New York and learn about magazine work. And on one weeknight evening, when there was nothing to watch on TV, she'd filled out the form. Then she went through the essays she'd written for classes and picked one to submit with her application.

There was nothing remarkable about this particular essay. She'd received an A, but that wasn't unusual for her. The assignment, which had been given by Mrs Jackson, her English teacher, was to choose a holiday, any holiday, and write about its personal meaning.

Three of her classmates wrote about Thanksgiving and how they tried to be sincerely grateful for all they had. Two of them chose Christmas, and wrote the standard 'think about Jesus, not Santa' essay that you saw in newspaper editorials every December. Another friend went the patriotic route and wrote about the Fourth of July. But Sherry had written about Halloween, despite the fact that she knew Mrs Jackson was deeply religious and probably didn't approve of a holiday that was suspiciously pagan. She'd enjoyed it, writing about the one night a year when she could be someone else.

She got her A, though Mrs Jackson had scribbled a note on the paper stating that Sherry hadn't taken the assignment very seriously. But Sherry had liked that paper; it was something she'd written to please herself.

After sending off the application, she didn't entertain any fantasies about winning a place in the internship programme. *Gloss* was the most popular teen magazine in the entire country, there had to be thousands and thousands of girls who applied. She firmly put it all out of her mind and concentrated on enjoying her senior year.

When she'd received the acceptance letter, she'd read it in disbelief. And when she finally broke the news, Johnny was happy for her, relieved that she wasn't furious with him, and maybe a little envious. Washington DC was impressive, but New York! Even her normally protective parents were pleased – worried of course, but reassured when they received the letter from *Gloss* explaining that the interns would be cared for and watched over. They saw it as a marvellous little adventure for Sherry to have before starting college in Atlanta and settling down to the life she was supposed to live.

Her thoughts went back to Linda's description today of *her* plans for the future. With a few changes in names and places, Sherry could have presented the same plan, word for word. And again she wondered why she hadn't wanted to spend the rest of the afternoon with those girls.

There was the assignment to do of course. She sat down at her desk, and took the cover off her new portable Smith Corona typewriter, a graduation present from her parents.

But there was something she'd promised to do first – something she should have done the evening before, but she'd been too tired.

She opened a desk drawer and retrieved the neatly wrapped box she'd been given at the airport yesterday. She knew what it contained – all the kids in the family got a box like this when they went away from home.

Knowing her mother's taste, she unwrapped the box with some trepidation. But it wasn't too bad – the stationery set consisted of cream-coloured paper with a border of pink cherry blossoms, and envelopes in the same shade of pink. She took out a sheet and picked up her pen. Personal letters had to be written by hand of course.

In proper letter-writing style, she wrote '6 July, 1963' in the upper right-hand corner of the paper, and on the left side she put the return address: Cavendish Residence for Women, 642 East 58th Street, New York 24, New York.

Dear everyone, Well, here I am, safe and sound, on Manhattan Island, New York City.

Of course, they already knew she'd arrived safely. At the pay phone in the residence lobby, she did what people always did to avoid paying the outrageous long-distance phone charges. She'd dialed '0', asked the operator to make a person-to-person collect call to a Miss Taylor and gave the phone number of her family home.

She could hear the phone ringing and then her mother's anxious voice.

'Hello?'

The operator spoke. 'I have a person-to-person collect call for Miss Taylor. Will you accept the charges?'

Sherry could have sworn she heard her mother exhale in relief before she said, 'Miss Taylor isn't here at the moment, could you ask the party to call later?'

There was no one named Taylor living in the Forrester household, and Sherry had no idea how that particular name had come to be employed. But that was their signal, the name that was used to indicate that a family member had arrived at his or her destination, and all was well.

I know I promised to write the first night, but it was just impossible. I only had an hour to unpack, shower and change my clothes before the formal dinner. By the way, Mama, the pink dress was perfect.

They'd both been a little worried about that, not knowing exactly how dressy the welcome dinner would be. She didn't want to look too casual, but at the same time, being overdressed would have been just as great a sin. And there was the question of sophistication too. Pink might seem too young, but it was *her* colour, and *Gloss* magazine itself had declared in last month's issue that pastels were very important this

season. And looking around the table at the dinner, seeing other girls in pastel knits, she'd felt quite comfortable.

Naturally the editors looked much more sophisticated – one wore a Jackie Kennedy-style suit with a boxy jacket, and at least three of them were in terribly chic little black dresses. The men, of course, were in suits.

There were a couple of interns who looked a little odd. The petite redhead had worn a black pencil skirt and black top, which was pretty unusual. Sherry never saw girls their age wearing black. The platinum blonde had been decked out in a shiny low-cut red cocktail dress, totally inappropriate.

But by far the worst was her roommate. As a regular

reader of *Gloss,* Sherry knew beige was all wrong for Donna's sallow complexion and mousy-brown hair. The shirtdress needed ironing, and the style, while OK for daytime, hadn't been dressy enough for the occasion.

We had dinner at the famous Waldorf-Astoria Hotel, and the food was delicious! We had something called a Waldorf salad, which had apples and celery and walnuts in it. Then we had beef stroganoff – Mama, you absolutely must get a recipe for this. There were real French pastries for dessert.

After dinner we all gave our names and said something about ourselves, like our hobbies or where we came from. I'm the only girl from the South. Miss Margo Meredith, the editor-in-chief, gave a speech.

She wasn't planning to go into detail about the speech – actually, she'd been too excited or too exhausted to remember it all that well. What she *did* remember was the intimidating woman herself. She'd been editor of *Gloss* since, well, forever, and she had to be over fifty years old but she certainly didn't look it. The girl she now knew as Pamela had been sitting next to Sherry and she'd whispered 'facelift' in her ear. Maybe so, but the woman was very striking, with shiny black hair pulled back in a tight chignon. Her make-up was perfect too, almost frighteningly so – Cleopatra eyes and dark red lips. It made Sherry think of the evil queen in the Snow White movie. She wore a simple black sheath, with large gold earrings and a strand of gold beads.

She gave a sort of flat 'welcome to *Gloss*' speech, and then promptly disappeared. Her place had been taken by Caroline Davison, also a very cosmopolitan-looking woman, but not quite so intimidating, more elegantly cool, like Grace Kelly or the actress in that scary movie about the birds going wild.

Of course, we won't have much to do with Miss Meredith. Our boss is the managing editor, Caroline Davison. She seems very nice.

Her speech, however, had been a little daunting.

'I hope you all realize how very lucky you are to be here. We had over ten thousand applications for the summer-apprenticeship programme at *Gloss* this year, and you eight are the recipients of this prestigious opportunity. You were judged on the basis of the writing samples you submitted, so you must have some talent. But talent isn't enough to guarantee a successful summer here. You will have to work very, very hard. You must be disciplined, observant, obedient, very careful and, above all, punctual.'

Sherry had noticed a couple of girls squirming or looking a little uncomfortable, and she'd wondered which of those requirements scared them. She was also a little unnerved . . . she had come here expecting a fun adventure. Now it seemed she'd have to start thinking about it as an actual *job*.

All the staff we've met seem very nice. The magazine photographer, David Barnes, is soooo handsome! Honestly, he looks just like Rock Hudson. But don't worry, Daddy, he's at least thirty years old so he won't be interested in me, and I promise not to flirt with him!

My roommate is Donna, she wrote, and then stopped again. What could she possibly say about someone she knew absolutely nothing about? When Sherry had asked about her hometown, she'd only said something vague like, 'Up north.' Sherry could only guess she'd meant somewhere like Maine or Vermont. Maybe even Canada.

There was something else strange too. The other girls had dragged big suitcases into the residence, and some had also carried hairdryers and typewriters. One girl even had a portable television. All Donna brought with her was a small backpack.

Donna's quiet, and she didn't take up much of the closet space. The other apprentices seem very nice.

Nice . . . what a meaningless word. But did she really want to go into details here? How could she describe Pamela without letting her mother think Sherry would be hanging out with a slut? And describing Allison would make the redhead sound like a beatnik. Dressed in black, the boyish haircut, and that awful burlap bag she toted . . .

She moved on quickly to write about the residence hall.

GL♥SS

It's a very safe place, with a doorman on duty twenty-four hours a day. No men are allowed beyond the lobby. And there are curfews of course. We have to be in the building by eleven on weeknights, midnight on weekends. I haven't seen much of New York yet, but a couple of interns and I went to Times Square today.

She hesitated for a second, and then added, *It was interesting.* That was all she was going to tell them about that particular adventure.

At 'Gloss' today, we were shown a new movie for teens on a projector in a conference room. Now we have to write a review of it, so I'd better get to work. Kiss Beth for me, lots of love, Sherry Ann.

She put the letter in an envelope, addressed it, sealed it and applied a stamp. Then she went back to her typewriter, inserted a sheet of paper into the rollers and typed the heading in capital letters.

BEACH BLANKET KISSES
A REVIEW BY SHERRY FORRESTER

That was as far as she got before a rumble in her stomach told her it was dinnertime. She'd assumed her roommate would be back by now and they'd go to dinner together. But maybe some of the other interns would be in the dining hall.

Quickly she washed her hands, rubbed a little pressed powder on her shiny nose and added a touch of pastel pink lipstick. A massive dose of hairspray that morning had kept her light brown chin-length flip from frizzing, but she was a little worried about her bangs. Shading her eyes with one hand, she sprayed the fringe that covered her forehead. Then she fled the bathroom to escape the pungent odour of the hairspray.

Downstairs, the dining room wasn't very crowded. She went through the buffet line, selected meat loaf and a salad, and then scanned the room.

According to the Cavendish pamphlet, the residence was designed to give young single working girls a safe and comfortable home. Looking around at the tables, she tried to imagine what the women sitting there did for a living. Secretaries, she imagined. Or teachers maybe. Women waiting to meet Mr Right. She figured there was probably a big turnover of residents, as girls left to get married.

She didn't see Diane or Linda, but she did spot one of her fellow interns – Allison, the tiny redhead, still in black. She sat alone, her face buried in a book as she ate. Sherry moved over to her table.

'May I join you?' she asked politely.

Allison looked up. 'Please do.' She took one last longing look at the page she'd been reading, then she put a bookmark in and closed the book.

'What are you reading?' Sherry asked as she sat down.

'*To Kill a Mockingbird*,' Allison told her. 'Do you know it?'

'I've *heard* of it,' Sherry said carefully.

'Didn't you see the movie?'

Sherry found herself giving undue attention to the cutting of her meat loaf. 'It didn't play in my hometown.'

'It's about racism,' Allison said.

Sherry nodded.

Allison cocked her head thoughtfully. 'You're from the South, aren't you?'

Sherry nodded. 'Georgia.' And then she added quickly, 'But I'm not a racist. I'm totally in favour of integration.' As the words left her mouth, it dawned on her that she'd never said that before out loud. Back home, it was something adults spoke about in whispers, and teens not at all.

'How about interracial dating?'

Sherry was taken aback. 'I – I don't know. I guess I've never thought about *that*.'

Allison reached into her burlap bag thing and pulled out a copy of *Gloss*. She slapped it on the table and opened it to the table of contents.

'"Inter-faith dating – what's your opinion?"' she read aloud. She shook her head. 'I mean, really! Is that such a big deal? Maybe a hundred years ago. Nobody cares about that any more. This is a very old-fashioned magazine.'

Sherry didn't know what to say. A girl she knew had gone out with a Jewish boy, and her parents threw a hissy fit. So yes, for some people it *was* a big deal. Not to Allison, obviously.

'Where are *you* from?' she asked.

'Boston.'

'I guess people are more liberal there,' Sherry remarked.

'Ha. Not in *my* family.'

The way she said that, wrinkling her nose, made Sherry wonder about Allison's background. But of course it was much too soon in their relationship to bring up anything personal, so she changed the subject.

'What did you think of that movie we saw?'

'It was stupid,' Allison declared. 'Just another beach movie.'

'Well, it couldn't compare with *A Summer Place*, that's for sure,' said Sherry.

'I never saw it,' Allison said.

'Really?' Sherry found that hard to believe. It had been the number-one teen movie just a couple of years ago. 'Troy Donahue and Sandra Dee, making out on the beach? It was positively dreamy.'

Allison grimaced. 'Sounds like typical teen fodder.'

'Well, there was an adult romance too, between the girl's father and the boy's mother,' Sherry added. 'And it was based on a book. It was actually a pretty mature movie.'

'Have you seen *Jules and Jim*?' Allison asked.

Sherry shook her head.

'It's about a love affair between two men and a woman. It's in French, it's black and white and it's artistic. *That's* the kind of movie *Gloss* should be writing about. Not this squeaky-clean, unrealistic, goody-goody garbage.' She began flipping through the pages of the magazine.

'I mean, look at all this junk! How to throw a theme party. What to wear to the prom. Who's your favourite TV doctor hero? My summer at cheerleading camp. And the ads! I counted five ads for silverware patterns. As if that's the most important thing on our minds – what kind of knives and forks we want when we get married.'

Sherry's lips twitched. She didn't think this was the moment to announce her own silverware choice, 'Prelude' by International Sterling. Nor did she mention her two weeks at a cheerleading camp last summer. Instead she asked a question.

'If you think *Gloss* is so stupid, why do you want to work for it?'

'To change it,' Allison replied promptly. 'To bring it up to date, to make the editors realize that the world is changing. You know what they should include? Poetry. Articles about folk music, experimental theatre, modern dance. The civil rights movement.'

Sherry considered this. 'I guess that could be interesting,' she offered. Though not to anyone I know, she added silently.

'And all this "meeting Mr Right" junk. How to talk to a boy, should you kiss on the first date? Who needs this kind of advice?'

At least Sherry could respond honestly to this. 'Not me. I've been with the same guy for three years.'

'So you're serious?'

She nodded. 'We've talked about getting married after we both graduate from college.'

'Wow, you've planned that far in advance?'

'Kind of,' Sherry said, catching the look of disapproval on Allison's face. She supposed this kind of life wouldn't appeal to a rebel beatnik type. But she was spared any further indication of Allison's disapproval by the arrival of Pamela.

'Hey, roomie,' Allison greeted her. 'You don't look very happy.'

'And where are your bags?' Sherry asked. 'I thought you were going to shop.'

'Do you know what things cost in this city?' Pamela moaned. 'Even with the discount coupons, I couldn't afford anything.' She reached in her bag. 'I did pick up this.' She showed them a lipstick, and then, using the back of a spoon as a mirror, she applied it. In Sherry's opinion, the fuchsia pink only made her look even more inappropriate. But she admired the fancy gold-coloured case.

'Was it expensive?'

'Probably.' Pamela grinned. 'I didn't pay for it.'

GL♥SS

Sherry tried very hard not to look shocked, but she didn't do a very good job of it.

'Don't worry, I only take little things,' Pamela assured her. 'And never from friends.'

'These department stores deserve to be ripped off,' declared Allison. 'They overcharge. You better be careful though.'

'Oh, I wouldn't try to take anything like clothes,' Pamela said. She grinned again. 'I don't have a handbag big enough to stash them in. So what were you two talking about?'

'Sherry was telling me about her boyfriend,' Allison told her. 'What's his name?'

'Johnny.'

'They're going to get married when she graduates from college.'

'Really?' Pamela shook her head. 'That's tragic.'

Sherry was completely taken aback. 'Why do you say that? I'll be twenty-two. That's old enough to marry.'

'It's still too young,' Pamela declared. 'You'll be in your best years. Why do you want to throw them away?' She reached into her handbag and pulled out a dog-eared paperback book. 'It's all in here. How you don't need a husband for your best years, you just need men, and the more men you can know, the more fun you'll have.'

Sherry's mouth fell open, and Allison burst out laughing. Pamela beamed, and showed them the cover.

'*Sex and the Single Girl*, by Helen Gurley Brown. It's my new bible.'

Sherry found her voice. 'Are you saying you want to have *affairs*?'

'Sure. Why not?'

'Well . . . a man won't buy the cow if the milk is free.'

Pamela rolled her eyes and Allison started laughing again. Then Sherry had to laugh too. Thinking about it, it sounded pretty silly, comparing women and sex to cows and milk.

'It's what my mother says anyway.'

'My mother's always hitting me with her words of wisdom too,' Pamela offered. 'Her favourite is the one about how it's just as easy to love a rich man as a poor man. Actually, I can go along with that. But that business about free milk . . .' she shook her head. 'I mean, men have affairs before they're married. And sometimes *after*. Why can't women?'

Sherry had an answer for that. 'Because men can't get pregnant.'

'Women don't have to get pregnant either,' Allison pointed out. 'Have you heard of the pill?'

'Well, sure, but . . .' Sherry hesitated. She'd only just met these girls, and she felt very strange bringing up a topic she'd only discussed with her closest friends. Still, she was curious. 'Don't you want to be a virgin when you get married?'

Pamela responded with a mysterious smile. Sherry's eyebrows shot up and she leaned forward.

'You're not a virgin?' she asked in a whisper.

'Well, *technically* I am,' Pamela admitted. 'Only because I wasn't about to give myself to any of the jerks I went out with back home. But that doesn't mean I'm going to stay that way. I plan on meeting some very interesting men here in New York.'

'I'm a virgin,' Allison said. 'But I think I'd have sex before I get married, if I really loved the guy.' She turned to Sherry. 'You're really going to hold out until your wedding night?'

'Well, maybe after we're officially engaged, and we've set a date . . .'

Pamela grinned. 'And you've rented the hall and made a non-refundable deposit to the caterer? So it's too late for Johnny to back out?'

She was putting it rather crudely, but she made a good point. Sherry nodded. 'Yeah, that's about it.'

'Well, you can still have some fun here in New York without having an affair,' Pamela said, and then sighed. 'But I don't know how I'm going to get myself outfitted for New York nightlife.'

'There's still the samples closet,' Sherry reminded her. 'You'll just have to convince Miss Davison you've got a lot of "extraordinary events" to attend.'

'Speaking of extraordinary events,' Allison said, 'I'm going to go down to Greenwich Village tonight.

Anyone want to come with me?'

'What's in Greenwich Village?' Sherry asked.

'It's supposed to be a real scene. Clubs, music . . .'

Pamela brightened. 'I'm in.'

'Not me,' Sherry said. 'I have to write that review.'

'It's just two pages,' Allison pointed out. 'You could write it in the morning. It only took me an hour this afternoon.'

Sherry was torn. If only she'd done the assignment that afternoon instead of going to Times Square with Linda and Diane. She suspected an evening with these two would be much more interesting.

Reluctantly she shook her head. 'I hate to wait till the last minute to do an assignment. I won't be able to sleep tonight, thinking about it.'

'Good grief,' Pamela said. 'You really *are* a good girl. I'll bet you're the type who always turned in her homework on time.' The teasing smile on her face took any sting out of the words.

'Guilty as charged,' Sherry admitted.

'And you've got your future all mapped out,' Allison mused. 'Do you always stick to your plans?'

'Pretty much.' Sherry offered them both a rueful smile. 'Guess I sound like a real bore, huh?'

'It certainly wouldn't hurt to loosen up a bit,' said Pamela.

Would she ever get used to being around people who spoke their minds so freely? 'Anyway, I should

GL♥SS

spend some time with my roommate. We haven't talked much.'

'I don't think Donna said a word all day,' said Allison.

'She looks like a scared rabbit,' Pamela commented. 'A real wuss.'

For some reason Sherry felt compelled to defend the girl. 'She's probably just shy,' she said. 'I'll get her to open up. Have fun tonight, you two.'

She went upstairs to her room. Locked. She rapped on the door.

She could hear movement inside. And then a voice. 'Who is it?'

'It's just me. Sherry. Your roommate. I don't have my key.'

Donna opened the door, murmured a greeting that Sherry couldn't hear and then went over to her bed. She sat on the edge of it and eyed Sherry warily.

'What have you been up to?' Sherry asked casually.

'Nothing much. Just looking around.'

'Have you had dinner yet?'

Donna shook her head.

'Don't get the meat loaf,' Sherry advised. 'It's very dry.'

'Was it expensive?'

Sherry was puzzled. 'We don't pay for food here, Donna. Unless we eat out of course. We don't get any salary, but the room and the meals are free. That was all in the introductory packet. Didn't you get one?'

'I guess I didn't read it very closely,' she said. She got up and swung the backpack over her shoulder.

'I don't think you'll need to lug that to the dining hall,' Sherry pointed out.

'I like to keep it with me,' Donna murmured as she walked out. 'See you later.'

Maybe she believed the place was full of thieves, Sherry thought. That would explain why she wanted to keep the door locked and carry her things with her all the time. She couldn't think of any other explanation.

Sherry turned to the typewriter and examined the one line she'd typed so far.

BEACH BLANKET KISSES
A REVIEW BY SHERRY FORRESTER

Now that she thought about it, she realized Allison had made a good point. The movie was pretty much like every other musical beach movie she'd seen. Boy meets girl on the beach, he sings a song about her, she sings a song about him. They fall in love, sing a song together, then something happens to break them up. Then it all turns out to be a misunderstanding, and in the end they get back together. And sing another song.

But the songs were cute, and when the girl thought the boy had stood her up on a date, her heartbreak was pretty convincing. Sherry's fingers hovered over the keys, and then dropped. She needed inspiration.

She reached over and turned on the clock radio she'd put at the other end of the desk. Fiddling with the dials, she finally located a rock 'n' roll station, and a tune she recognized filled the room. She sank back in her chair and smiled.

It was the song about the 'itsy bitsy teenie weenie yellow polka dot bikini', and immediately an image of the lake back home appeared in her mind. Just a few weeks ago, the first week of summer vacation, there'd been a heatwave and the gang had spent just about every day there. There was a little snack bar on the shore that had a jukebox, and that song seemed to be playing constantly. Friends were always teasing her, because by pure coincidence she just happened to have bought a yellow polka-dot bathing suit this summer. It wasn't really an itsy-bitsy bikini, more like a modest two-piece, but still, every time the song came on, people looked in her direction. Johnny hadn't left for Washington yet so he was there, and he couldn't take his eyes off her . . .

The minute the song finished, her hands went back to the keys. Once she'd decided on the point of her review, the sentences began to take shape. As always happened when she was writing, time and place faded away and she went into some sort of inner world where nothing but ideas, words and phrases existed. She'd just put her third sheet of paper into the typewriter when another popular tune came on the radio, and made her pause.

Johnny Angel, how I love him . . .

She looked at the framed photo on the desk, the first thing she'd unpacked the day before. He really was special – so handsome, with soft wavy brown hair and a square jaw with the cutest little cleft in his chin, just like Cary Grant. When they met, they'd been sophomores, the same age and perfectly matched. They liked the same music, the same movies, the same TV shows. He was the quarterback on the football team; she was a cheerleader.

Everyone thought they made the ideal couple. Some day they'd make beautiful brown-haired blue-eyed babies – that's what all her friends said. He was a nice boy from a good family, and her parents had approved of him from the start. And even though a marriage wouldn't happen for at least another four or five years, she'd spent hours with her mother poring over *Gloss* or another magazine, looking at silverware patterns, china patterns, bridal gowns, debating whether her wedding colours should be pink and white or something else. How many bridesmaids? Which one would be maid of honour? What kind of flowers would she carry? Would they hold the reception at the country club or the new Hilton hotel? And where would they go on their honeymoon?

And why was she now experiencing the twinge of an incipient headache?

She finished the first draft of her review, and then read the sheets carefully. Seeing several places that she thought could use improvement, she went back to work on a second draft. When she was finished, she was surprised to see that it was only nine o'clock. But a wave of tiredness came over her, and she had yet to roll her hair.

Sitting on the bed after her shower, with the bag of rollers in front of her, she sectioned her hair with a rat-tail comb, wound the locks around the bristle-filled tubes. She imagined Linda and Diane sitting on their beds doing the same thing and wondered what Donna was doing. Pamela and Allison were probably still in Greenwich Village. And her thoughts went back to that strange discussion at the dinner table.

Had she really come across as boring, with her talk of future plans? And why did she care what they thought of her, those two girls who were so clearly not her kind of people?

There was nothing wrong with being a good girl and following the rules, she told herself as she climbed into bed and shut off the light. It was perfectly OK to plan for your future. And Daddy always said, 'When you have a plan, you stick to it.' She'd heard that a million times.

Only tonight as she drifted off to sleep, for the first time ever, she heard her own voice in her head, talking back to her father.

'But what if I didn't write the plan?'♥

Chapter Three

Sitting side by side on the subway, Allison examined her companion with interest. Pamela's style certainly wasn't anything like her own, but the fact that the platinum blonde didn't look like all the other interns made her appealing in Allison's eyes.

'I can't believe you've never been to New York before,' Allison said as the subway headed downtown. 'You're from Pennsylvania, right? That's not so far.'

'We're not much of a travelling family,' Pamela told her. 'Maybe a week at the shore in the summer, but that's about it. My parents made their very first trip to New York just last year, for their fortieth wedding anniversary.'

'Oh.' Then a certain word registered. 'Did you say *fortieth*? And you're what – seventeen?'

'My mother was sixteen when she got married. And I'm the youngest of six. My oldest brother, Ralph, is forty-one. That's why Mom got married so young. Get it?'

'Got it,' Allison replied. 'Wow, you've got a brother who's the same age as my father.'

Pamela nodded. 'Poor Mom, she thought she was

finished when I came along.' She grinned. 'I was an accident, just like Ralph.'

Allison was fascinated. People didn't talk like this back home, not in her family's Boston aristocratic world. And as far as children were concerned, there were no accidents – or maybe there were, but they were completely covered up.

Pamela misread her expression. 'Oh, they love me like crazy,' she assured her. 'And I was lucky. By the time I came around, they were wiped out when it came to discipline. I could get away with anything.'

Allison gazed at her in admiration. 'Wow. I was always watched like a hawk. I even had a nanny.'

'So you're rich, huh?'

Once again Allison was amazed. Back home, people never talked like this. Money – like religion and politics – just wasn't a subject of polite conversation. She really liked this girl.

When she'd first met Pamela, in the room they shared, she'd been startled but pleased. Her style was outlandish – Allison could imagine her mother calling the platinum blonde a 'floozy', and knowing that her mother would disapprove of the girl made her immediately attractive. And while Allison didn't care for her flashy, provocative clothes, at least she didn't look like the others Allison met at the dinner, all prim and proper in their nauseatingly sweet little pastel dresses and princess heels.

Maybe they weren't all awful though. That girl Sherry, she seemed to have a little spark to her . . .

Pamela was looking at her now, and Allison realized she hadn't answered her question.

'Rich? Not me personally. I'm on a strict allowance. But yeah, my family's got money. My great-grandfather had railroads.' She eyed Pamela anxiously, hoping she wasn't coming across as an old-family-type upper-class snob. But she needn't have worried.

'Neat,' Pamela said cheerfully. 'Dad's a mechanic, and he does OK. But with six kids, there was never much to go around.'

From the subway's barely audible system came an announcement, and Allison caught the last muffled words.

'This is us,' she said as the train rumbled into the West Fourth Street station. 'Now, don't forget, nobody says "Greenwich Village". It's just "the Village". And don't expect little cottages with thatched roofs.'

Pamela laughed. 'Hey, I might come from the sticks, but we've got movies and TV. I've got a pretty good idea what it's going to look like.'

So did Allison, and like Pamela, only from movies and TV. She'd been to New York before, with her family, many times. But they'd never ventured this far downtown. And as they climbed the stairs to the exit, her heartbeat quickened with anticipation.

What hit her first was the variety of people on the street – all ages, all colours, just like in midtown. But here they looked different. Maybe it was the clothes. If there was a uniform in the Village, it was rolled-up blue jeans, sandals, a lot of black – and not a briefcase in sight.

Walking down Sixth Avenue, looking to the right, she could see narrow streets jutting off the avenue at odd angles. Some were tree-lined, and they certainly weren't on a grid like most of the streets in the city. They zigzagged and twisted and new ones seemed to sprout up out of nowhere. There wasn't the bumper-to-bumper traffic of midtown, and there were no skyscrapers. Allison couldn't believe they were still on Manhattan Island.

'I wish we'd brought a map,' she murmured. 'I've heard Bleecker Street is supposed to be neat, but I have no idea how to get there.'

Pamela seemed to know how to deal with this. In her forthright manner she marched up to a good-looking young man who was coming out of a shop.

'Excuse me, can you direct us to Bleecker Street?'

The guy pointed. 'Two blocks that way, then make a left. You chicks out-of-towners?'

'Yep, we're tourists.' She cocked her head to one side and smiled flirtatiously. 'You have any advice for us?'

He didn't smile back, but gazed intensely at them

both. 'Yes, I have something very important to say to you. Keep in mind: the Village is not a place. It's a state of mind.'

Pamela stared right back, but her expression was blank. 'Huh?'

Allison quickly stepped in. 'I guess you know the area pretty well. Do you live here?'

'Yes. And I work here.'

'Yeah? What do you do?' Pamela asked.

'I am a philosopher. So you must take my words very seriously.' With that, he gave a slight bow and walked away.

Allison gazed after him in wonderment. 'A philosopher . . .'

Pamela wrinkled her nose. 'I don't think there's much money in that. Let's go.'

Bleecker Street was enthralling – Allison thought she'd never before seen a street that was so alive with interesting-looking people and places. They passed coffee shops advertising poetry readings, jazz clubs, folk-music clubs, signs and posters that proclaimed everything from 'The End Is Near' to 'Ban the Bomb'. In front of one doorway, a woman with heavy dark bangs that practically covered her eyes was handing out leaflets.

Allison took one. It was for a new play that was opening that week. Pamela looked over her shoulder to read it.

'*The Curse of the Ruling Class.* Is it a musical?'

'You're kidding, right?' asked the girl with the fringe.

'I thought all the plays were up around 42nd Street,' Pamela said.

'This is Off-Broadway,' Allison explained.

'Off-Off-Off-Broadway,' the girl corrected her. 'We're theatre for the real people. We reject the commercial garbage they show uptown.'

Pamela looked at her quizzically. 'Real people go to shows on Broadway. And it's not all garbage. My parents saw *Camelot* on Broadway, and they said it was the best play they ever saw.'

Allison couldn't see the girl's eyes, but she could imagine the disdain that filled them. 'Thanks,' she said quickly, and tugged on Pamela's arm. She was beginning to think that maybe the Village wasn't her roommate's cup of tea.

But Pamela's expression brightened as they moved down the street. 'Hey, there are nightclubs here.'

'Absolutely,' Allison exclaimed. 'Folk, jazz . . . look, this one is having an open-mic evening, and it's only a dollar to get in.'

Inside, they paid their dollar fees to a man with a scraggly beard behind a booth. He then directed them to go down some stairs.

A *lot* of stairs. And when they finally reached the bottom and passed through another door, Pamela's face registered serious disappointment. And as usual, she had no problem expressing her reaction verbally.

'This looks icky.'

Allison didn't think so. The small, dark, smoky room contained about a dozen little wooden tables, each one holding a fat, half-melted candle, and more than half were occupied by beatnik-types. The walls were black, but brightened slightly by a string of tiny coloured lights that hung just below the ceiling. There was a small raised platform at one end, with a microphone stand. And behind the microphone were two bearded men with guitars, and a woman with long, straight blonde hair singing one of Allison's favourite songs, 'Where Have All the Flowers Gone?'

They weren't the famous folk trio, Peter, Paul and Mary, but they looked like them and sang like them and that was enough to make Allison very happy. She and Pamela took seats at an empty table.

When they finished the song, Allison joined the applause enthusiastically. A waitress appeared at their table.

'What can I get you?'

Pamela spoke first. 'A martini, extra dry, with a twist, please.'

Her order was greeted with the same expression that Allison had imagined on the face of the Off-Off-Off-Broadway theatre girl.

'We don't serve cocktails,' the woman said. 'We got coffee and tea.'

Allison spoke quickly, before Pamela could complain. 'Two coffees, please.'

By now the singers had started another tune. Allison knew this song too, it was the one about the lemon tree that was very pretty but you couldn't eat the fruit. She loved the symbolism . . .

Clearly Pamela did not. When the song was over, she turned to Allison and made a face. 'I hate this kind of music. You can't even dance to it.'

'Just keep listening,' Allison urged. 'It'll start getting to you.'

But the next act wasn't a folk singer. A gaunt, sad-looking woman in grey took to the stage and recited poetry, accompanied by a man playing bongo drums. Allison couldn't understand it all, but she appreciated the fact that the audience was paying attention. But by the time that performer left the stage, Pamela looked positively sick.

The waitress reappeared with their coffees, and Pamela eyed hers balefully.

'I'll ask if they have something else,' Allison offered, half rising from the table to go after the waitress.

'No, never mind,' Pamela said. 'Actually, would you mind if I split? I need to wash my hair.'

Allison sighed. 'OK, I'll go with you.'

Pamela shook her head. 'Don't be silly. I can find

my way back on my own.' She patted Allison's hand. 'No hard feelings, OK?'

'You're sure you don't mind going alone?' Allison asked.

But Pamela was already halfway to the door.

Clearly her roommate was not going to be her regular companion on what Allison hoped would be frequent jaunts to the Village. It didn't really matter; she didn't mind at all being alone in a place like this. In fact, even though she didn't know a soul in the place, she felt like she belonged. Which she'd never felt back home.

She'd always been different, as her parents and older brother often reminded her. Actually, the word her mother more frequently used was 'difficult'. Even as a child, her mother said, she had constantly questioned everything – why does the fork *have* to go on that side of the plate? Why can't I eat dessert first?

Once she got into her teens, she found real things to rebel against – mainly at the private school she attended. The awful uniform, which denied students any means of expressing themselves with originality. The prayer they were forced to say before lunch. The lessons in etiquette and gracious living – too ridiculous. Allison complained incessantly, and she was almost suspended a couple of times for breaking rules.

Her parents shouldn't have been surprised when she turned seventeen and refused to be a debutante.

For generations, the women in her family had been presented at the same ritzy, exclusive club, where all the members could claim an ancestor who had come to America on the *Mayflower*. Allison wouldn't even go to the 'coming-out' parties thrown by her classmates. Instead she went alone to small cinemas where she could find foreign movies. Like *Breathless* – the French film that was dark and tragic and not entirely logical. She could totally relate to it. And the very next day after seeing it, she went out and had her long hair cropped in the style of Jean Seberg, the actress.

She'd always been a believer in fate and destiny. And that belief was affirmed when, while waiting her turn at the beauty parlour, she picked up an issue of *Gloss*. She knew about the magazine of course – she'd seen classmates reading it. It was a standard conventional rah-rah teen rag for girls who were more interested in prom dresses than in civil rights or the atomic bomb. It must have been sheer boredom at the beauty parlour that made her open the magazine that day.

But it turned out to be fateful, because she just happened to open it to the double-page description of the internship programme.

She'd always been a writer – mainly of poetry and short stories and her own opinions, which she'd submitted to her school's 'literary' magazine, but which had been rejected for being too weird. She picked out the one she thought *Gloss* would consider the least weird – a diatribe about school conformity and peer pressure – and sent it in with her application.

Her parents, strangely enough, didn't make a huge fuss when she showed them her acceptance to the *Gloss* programme. Maybe they hoped a traditional, popular magazine would influence her. Or maybe they were just pleased to get rid of her for the summer, before shipping her off to college.

In any case, here she was, in New York City's Greenwich Village, *the* Village, surrounded by people who looked just as unusual and unconventional as *she* did. And where she felt more comfortable than she'd ever felt in her life.

While she'd been daydreaming, the poet accompanied by the bongo guy recited another poem. When they finished, there was more applause, and they left the stage. Almost immediately, they were replaced by a guy with a guitar slung over his shoulder.

Someone introduced him, but since she was sitting way in the back, she couldn't hear the new singer's name. She could see him very well, however, and what she saw almost made her heart stop. This guy bore a close resemblance to a certain young folk singer who had just produced an album, an album Allison absolutely adored. His wild curly hair, his moody demeanour, and eyes that even from a distance she could tell were brown and soft. He hadn't shaved recently, and the shadow on his face made him look dark and mysterious. He was the antithesis of every ordinary baby-faced pop singer who made ordinary girls scream. Allison couldn't take her eyes off him.

He strummed his guitar, and began to sing. And although his singing more closely resembled mumbling, she could pick up enough of the lyrics to realize that this was an angry protest song, like the kind her idol sang. It was something about the working man who had to fight the establishment, and how all working men should unite and make a revolution.

When he finished, there was the usual smattering of applause. Then, to her surprise, he took off the guitar and left the stage. Was that all he was going to sing?

She checked her watch, and saw that she'd have to leave very soon if she was going to make it back to the residence before curfew. But how could she leave when she didn't even know his name? She waved to the waitress. 'Could I have the cheque, please?' she asked. And as the waitress jotted something on her pad, she asked, 'And could you tell me the name of one of the singers? The guy who looks like Bob Dylan.'

The waitress slapped the check on the table. 'No idea.'

'Could you find out for me?'

But the woman just shrugged and walked away.

Allison fished out some money, put it on the table and hurried out the door. Outside, she scanned the dark but still lively street. There was no sign of him. Maybe he was in one of the other clubs, or sitting in a coffee house.

She checked her watch again. There was no time to look for him now. But he was a folk singer, and this was the folk singers' scene. And she'd be back to hunt him down.

She was still thinking about him the next day, and dying to tell Pamela. Her roommate had been sleeping when she got back, and in the morning they both overslept and had no time to talk. The *Gloss* interns had been kept occupied with lectures and presentations all morning.

Pamela and Sherry were discussing this in the Hartnell cafeteria when Allison arrived at the table.

'I haven't been this bored since sophomore algebra,' Pamela was saying. 'I mean, really. Circulation management. Who cares?'

'Some of it was kind of interesting,' Sherry pointed out. 'For example, I didn't know that advertising revenues kept the subscription rates low. Did you know that, Donna?'

The dark-haired girl had been perusing an old issue of *Gloss* that she'd laid alongside her tray. She looked up and pushed away the long hair that had fallen across her face. 'What?'

Sherry repeated the question, and Donna nodded.

'Yes, that's interesting,' she said, without actually sounding very interested. Then she went back to her magazine and her food.

There was a *lot* of the latter, Allison noticed. Soup, Salisbury steak with gravy, mashed potatoes, creamed spinach, two rolls . . . and what looked like double portions of practically everything. She was eating steadily, as if this was going to be her last meal for a long time, and she turned the pages of the magazine as she ate.

'Well, I'd rather hear about fashion and beauty,' Pamela declared. 'That's what *Gloss* is supposed to be about, right?'

Allison disagreed. 'No, not really. It's supposed to be covering all things that teenage girls are interested in. And after what I saw last night, I can tell you for sure they're missing a lot.'

'I'm guessing you liked Greenwich Village,' Sherry commented.

'Liked it? It was a whole different world! Philosophers, poets, folk singers!'

Pamela wrinkled her nose, but Allison ignored her. 'And one folk singer in particular . . .' She let out a long, meaningful sigh.

Pamela perked up. 'A guy?'

'Mm. He reminded me of Bob Dylan.' Her eyes narrowed. 'You *do* know who Bob Dylan is, don't you?'

'I heard him once, on a TV show,' Sherry said.

'He's kind of hard to understand. He sounds more like he's mumbling than singing.'

'And from the pictures I've seen, he looks pretty grubby,' Pamela declared. 'Is that how this boy looked?'

Allison shook her head vigorously. 'Not grubby. Earthy, masculine. Like a real man, not a pretty boy. I really like that natural look.'

'Yeah, I can see that,' Pamela said, looking at her hard. 'You know, your eyes would look a lot bigger if they were a little less natural. Have you ever considered mascara?'

Allison turned to Sherry. 'How am I going to live with her all summer?'

'Opposites attract,' Sherry said. She turned to Pamela. 'You didn't see this Bob Dylan lookalike?'

'She walked out while the poet was reading,' Allison told her.

Pamela shook her head. 'Sorry, Allison, that just wasn't my scene. I didn't see one person who'd fit in at the Stork Club.'

'The Stork Club,' Allison repeated. 'Do you have any idea how pretentious places like that are?'

'How do you know?' Pamela asked. 'You ever been there?'

> 'Liked it? It was a whole different world!'

GL♥SS

Allison didn't answer. 'Well, I'm planning to spend my free time in the Village. You want to come with me, Sherry?' she asked.

'Maybe some time,' Sherry said vaguely.

'How about you, Donna?'

The girl looked up. 'Excuse me?'

'Do you want to go to Greenwich Village with me?'

'I'm busy,' Donna said, and went back to the magazine.

Allison blinked. Busy the whole summer? And why was she being so rude? She looked at Sherry, who just gave an 'I don't understand either' shrug.

'Does anyone know what's on the schedule for this afternoon?' Sherry asked.

'Not more lectures, I hope,' Pamela said. 'No, wait, I take that back. I wouldn't mind a little more sales-and-distribution talk.'

Allison was surprised. 'Are you serious? That was the worst. I couldn't understand half of what the advertising manager was talking about.'

'Oh, I wasn't *listening* to him,' Pamela said. 'Just looking. Anyone remember his name?'

'Alex Parker,' Sherry told her. 'He *is* handsome. But I don't think he's eligible for sugar-daddy duty, Pamela. He was wearing a wedding ring.'

Pamela shrugged. 'Helen Gurley Brown says it's OK to have affairs with married men, as long as you just think of them as pets, and don't take it too seriously.

And I've heard that a lot of these married men send their families off to the country or the beach in the summer. Did you ever see that old Marilyn Monroe movie?'

'*The Seven Year Itch*,' Allison said. 'They showed all her old movies on TV last August, just after she died.'

Pamela nodded. 'That's the one. The man's wife and kid are away, and he thinks he's going to have an affair with Marilyn Monroe while they're gone.'

Sherry shook her head firmly. 'I don't want to sound like a prude, but honestly, Pamela. Going out with a married man? That's just plain wrong.'

'I just want to go to a nightclub,' Pamela sighed.

'Well, there's always Mr Duncan, the accountant,' Allison suggested. 'The fashion editor's secretary warned me about him. He's famous for making passes at interns.'

'Which one's Mr Duncan?' Pamela wanted to know.

Allison looked around and lowered her voice. 'He's over there at the table in the corner, by the water fountain. In the grey suit.'

Pamela looked. 'Kind of short and balding, with a beer belly?' She shook her head. 'I'm not *that* desperate.'

As Sherry and Pamela went into a debate over the ethics of dating married men, Allison's thoughts went back to the singer of the night before. She had a sudden image of bringing him home to the stately townhouse of the Sanderson family, and introducing him to her parents. They would *die*. Of course, they wouldn't demonstrate their dismay. They'd greet him with their usual impeccably patrician manners, offer him tea and express their strong disapproval privately. 'N.O.K.D.,' her mother would say. Not our kind, dear.

Or maybe they wouldn't be so surprised. By now they had to realize she wouldn't be introducing them to a clean-cut Ivy League-educated, socially acceptable Episcopalian in a Brooks Brothers suit. They had to know by now that she was not going to live up to their standards. She'd made it very clear that she rejected everything about their privileged class and their expectations of her – their materialism, their concern with the family name and status and gracious living, the rules that had been drilled into her at home and at the snotty private school she'd attended for twelve years.

Pamela had fantasies about going to the Stork Club. Allison had gone to the Stork Club with her parents, her older brother and his snobbish fiancé, back when he graduated from Columbia University. All she remembered was a pretentious restaurant filled with overdressed people eating overpriced food. Her parents, her brother and his girlfriend fitted in perfectly. The place was totally artificial, just like they were.

'I'm not *that* desperate.'

She hadn't yet informed them that she wouldn't be attending the exclusive women's college they'd picked out for her in September. She hadn't told them she might not be coming home at all.

'We need to get back,' Sherry announced, and all the girls rose. From the corner of her eye Allison saw Donna stuff the rolls and the little plastic-wrapped crackers that had come with the soup into her backpack. How odd, she thought.

Donna must have caught her looking, because she averted her eyes. Allison tried to come up with a conversational subject.

'I wonder when we'll find out who had the best review,' she said.

Donna didn't respond. She flung the backpack over her shoulder and walked away.

'Strange,' Allison murmured.

'Very,' Pamela agreed. 'Sherry, have you two talked at all?'

Sherry shook her head. 'I can't get a word out of her.'

Back at *Gloss*, along with the other interns, they congregated in the conference room to get their afternoon schedule from Caroline.

'I'm assigning each of you to work with specific people today,' Caroline told them, and began calling out the interns' names. Each was sent to a particular editor or to the director of a department. Pamela got beauty, Donna would be working in entertainment, Diane was sent to home and food, Linda would be working with the publicity manager and Ellen was assigned to fiction. Vicky was ecstatic to find she'd be going to fashion, while poor Sherry was assigned to that grim-looking Mr Simpson in features.

'Allison, you'll be with Dear Deedee.'

'Dear Deedee?'

'The advice columnist,' Caroline said.

Allison was directed to an office, where she tapped on the door.

'Come in,' a voice called out.

She opened the door, and the pleasant-faced woman behind the desk looked up. 'Yes? Oh, you're one of the interns, aren't you?'

'I'm Allison Sanderson. I guess you must be Deedee.'

'Actually, it's Barbara, but we thought Dear Deedee sounded snappier. Have a seat, Allison. Now, you may not know anything about this column . . .'

'It's advice, right? Like, what purse to carry with what shoes?' She tried not to sound too disappointed with the assignment.

'No, that's "Help Me, Helen", the fashion advice column.'

'So it's what lipstick goes with what nail polish?'

The woman shook her head. 'No, that's "Beauty by Betty". We get so many questions from readers, we've decided to have three advice columns in every issue.

We'll be working on the social advice column.'

Allison brightened. 'Oh, I like that much more!'

'Good. And I'm looking forward to your assistance. I think it's important to get a young perspective on the problems our readers have. For example . . .' She ruffled through some papers on her desk, and picked up a sheet.

'This question comes from a fourteen-year-old reader. She writes, "Dear Deedee, I think I'm old enough to buy clothes on my own, but my mother doesn't agree. She insists on going shopping with me. How can I convince her I'm mature enough to choose my own clothes? Sincerely, Patti." Now, Allison, how would you respond to this?'

Allison considered the situation. 'She should just say something like, "Mom, please leave me alone, I don't need your advice, I know what I like."'

Barbara's eyebrows went up. 'Really?'

Allison nodded fervently. 'I think she should be honest and say what she thinks. Why beat around the bush?'

'You don't think she should try to compromise a bit?'

'No – you can't argue with overbearing mothers, they'll never understand. This girl's got to stand up for herself or she'll never get to do what she wants.'

'I see,' Barbara said. She put the letter aside. 'Let's try another one. "Dear Deedee, I'm thirteen years old.

There's a boy I like at school. He keeps asking me out to go to the movies, but my parents won't let me date yet. What can I do?"'

'Oh, that's easy,' Allison said. 'My parents wouldn't let me go out on dates either when I was thirteen. So I'd tell them I was going to a movie with a girlfriend and meet the boy there.'

'You'd tell her to lie to her parents? Do you really think that's good advice?'

'It always worked for me. But I'd tell her she has to be careful of course. It's important to inform the girlfriend, so she doesn't call you at home while you're supposed to be with her.'

Barbara was silent for a minute. 'Allison . . . here at *Gloss*, we stress getting along with parents. We tell readers to be honest with them.'

'I think we should be honest with the readers,' Allison declared. 'Parents have no idea what's going on in their lives, and they'll never understand.'

Barbara got up. 'Excuse me for a moment, dear.' She left the room.

Pleased with herself, Allison leaned back in her chair. She was determined to shake things up a little here, and she felt like she'd made a good start.

A moment later, Barbara returned, with one of the other interns. 'Allison, we're making a few changes. Linda's going to work with me. You're going to be with Lydia.'

GL♥SS

Linda gave Allison a patronizing smile, which Allison ignored.

'Doing what?' she asked Barbara.

But Barbara just ushered her from the office and pointed to a desk at the far end of the bullpen. 'She's the grey-haired woman over there. It's been a pleasure meeting you, Allison.' She practically pushed her out and closed the door behind her.

Allison crossed the space and approached the stern-faced woman with the eyeglasses dangling from a chain around her neck.

'Hi, I'm Allison.'

The woman didn't make eye contact. She shoved a stack of papers across her desk in Allison's direction.

'File these.' She pointed to a cabinet against the wall. 'And when you're finished with those, I've got more.'

She looked at the first letter on the top of the pile. 'Dear *Gloss*, I just loved your interview with Ricky Nelson, he's my favourite singer –'

'I said file them, not read them,' the woman snapped. 'By state. See the return address? That letter's from a reader in Kansas. So it goes under K.'

So this was her punishment for speaking her mind, she thought as she shoved the letters into folders. Well, she was just going to have to have a little talk with Caroline Davison.

She filed a few letters while she waited for the grey-haired woman to leave her desk, and then headed over to Caroline's office. The editor's door was open, but she had David, the photographer, and Belinda the fashion editor, in there with her. Allison hesitated outside.

'I like the idea of focusing on the trench coat in that layout,' Belinda was saying.

'What about shoes?' the photographer asked.

'I'm not sure. What do you think, Caroline?'

'How about red patent-leather pumps? There's a pair in the samples closet.'

Then Donna, Sherry's roommate, approached Allison. 'Are you waiting to see Caroline?' she asked.

'Yeah, I want to talk to her about my assignment.'

'What kind of job are you doing?' Donna asked.

Allison made a face. 'Putting old letters-to-the-editor into folders. It's absolutely deadly. You're with the entertainment editor, right?'

Donna nodded. 'Do you want to switch?'

Allison was nonplussed. 'You want to file?'

Donna nodded again.

'Sure!' Allison turned to see Lydia returning to her desk. 'See that lady? Just tell her you're taking my place.'

Donna went off in that direction, and Allison went in search of the entertainment editor. He turned out to be a harried-looking man sitting behind a desk on which a dozen record albums were stacked.

'Who are you?' he asked.

'I'm Allison. I'm one of the interns.'

He didn't introduce himself, but the nameplate on his desk told her he was Peter Connelly. 'What happened to the other one?'

'We switched jobs.'

'Yeah, OK. Look, I need a list of these new recordings with descriptions for a new music round-up, OK? No reviews, just the names of the artists and the albums and a couple of lines about each one. Is it romantic music, dance music, easy listening, that sort of thing. Just get the info off the liner notes and rewrite them a little, got it?'

'Got it,' Allison said. She happily picked up the stack of albums and went back out into the bullpen. Now, *this* was good. If she could make the editor happy with her work, maybe he'd want her to keep working for him. And maybe she could talk him into letting her write an article about folk music, and maybe she could interview that guy who reminded her of Bob Dylan . . .

Sitting down at her desk, Allison turned to see Donna doing the filing. Once again, she marvelled at the strangeness of the intern. Why would anyone prefer filing to writing about music?

She picked up an album and looked it over. Recognizing the singer's name, she could guess at the album's content – treacle, pure and simple. Teeny-bopper love songs, 'Oh baby, how can I go on without you?' as sung by a sweetly clean-cut and classically handsome non-threatening heart-throb. The words on the back cover – 'He sings his heart out' and 'Dedicated to all his wonderful fans' – pretty much confirmed this, and she was glad she wouldn't have to actually listen to it.

Who *did* listen to this garbage? The world was changing, the times were changing – teenagers were changing. *Gloss* needed to change too, to keep up with the younger generation.

But this time she wouldn't express herself honestly, like she had with Barbara. She needed to do everything she could to stay in Peter Connelly's good books if she was going to be able to actually do anything significant at *Gloss*.

Rereading the liner notes, she overheard Caroline and David returning from the samples closet.

'I don't know, maybe someone borrowed them,' the editor was saying. 'Check with Belinda and see if she gave permission.' She disappeared into her office and came back out a few minutes later.

'Could I see all the apprentices in the conference room, please?' she called out loudly.

She must have made calls to the other floors too, because within minutes all eight of the interns were there.

'I've read and critiqued all your film reviews and made some notes in the margins. I hope you'll find my comments useful in your future assignments. I'm afraid I can't give you back your review, Sherry.' She smiled. 'It has to be copy-edited. Your review has been selected for publication.'

Sherry gasped, and there was a polite round of applause from the other girls. A few looked disappointed, and one or two even jealous, but they all congratulated her. Allison wasn't surprised at all about not having *her* review chosen. Given the fact that she'd written a scathing attack on teen films in general, she knew it wouldn't be in line with the prevailing style at *Gloss*.

'Congratulations, Sherry,' Caroline said. 'You can all go back to work now. Except for you, Donna. I'd like to speak to you privately.'

As Allison turned to close the door, she caught a glimpse of Donna's face. She'd gone completely white. And Allison could have sworn the girl was shaking. The image of a small animal caught in a trap flashed through her mind.

What was Donna so afraid of?

Curiouser and curiouser. True, Caroline could be a little intimidating, but not so fearful as to give rise to a reaction like that. What was Donna so afraid of?♥

Chapter Four

16 May, 1962

Mrs Forbes had a habit that Donna didn't like. Whenever there was something to be handed back to the students, she would ask one of them to do the distribution. Donna was never sure if this was because the fat teacher didn't want to get up from her desk, or if she wanted to show favouritism, or if she simply wanted to humiliate the students who hadn't done well by letting another student see the poor grades. Probably the last reason.

Donna wasn't wild about any of her teachers, but Forbes was the worst. She had her 'pets' and she made no attempt to hide her preferences. She also made it very clear whom she held in contempt, and Donna was one of those. It didn't help that Forbes taught the subject that came hardest to her.

This particular assignment had been an essay on *David Copperfield*, a book that was almost a thousand pages of long, old-fashioned words. Reading was a slow and painful process for Donna, and it had taken hours and hours just to get through the first chapter. Writing was just as hard, and it was made worse in this case by the fact that she could barely understand what she was reading.

She knew that some students went to a bookstore that sold Cliff's Notes, little pamphlets that gave summaries of classic books and told you what you needed to know for writing a paper or taking a test. But Cliff's Notes cost money. And even they weren't all that easy to read. At least, not for Donna.

The essay was placed on her desk by one of Forbes's favourites, Sandy Clement, and it held no surprises. The great big red letter F was circled, and there was another circle around her name, with a scribbled note in the margin from the teacher: 'At least you spelled your name correctly.'

She kept her eyes on her desk so she wouldn't have to see the expression on Sandy's face, but she couldn't avoid hearing the snicker, which was just loud enough for Donna and everyone around her to hear. It didn't upset her. She was used to it.

This was the last class of the day, so when the bell rang everyone raced to the door. Donna moved in that direction too, but she wasn't able to make an easy escape.

'Donna!'

She stopped, turned and went to the teacher's desk. 'Yes, Mrs Forbes?'

'That essay was particularly bad, even for you,' the woman said.

Donna clutched her books tightly to her chest, as if

they could protect her from the words.

'Do you have anything to say for yourself?'

Donna shook her head.

'Well, there's not enough time left in the semester for you to pull up your grade. You won't be passing English.' There wasn't the slightest trace of sympathy in her tone. She actually sounded triumphant.

And she continued. 'I've informed the guidance counsellor about this. Mr Breed wants to see you. Now. You're excused.'

Donna fled the classroom. In the hallway she looked up at the big clock on the wall. She had twenty minutes before she had to pick up her little sister.

When she reached it, the door to the guidance counsellor's office was slightly ajar, but she tapped anyway.

'Come in.' As she did, Mr Breed looked up. 'Hello, Donna. Have a seat.'

She did, but she made a point of looking at the clock.

'This won't take long,' he assured her. 'We're concerned about you, Donna.'

She nodded.

'What can you do about your grades?' he asked.

'Work harder,' she muttered.

He looked over some papers. 'You've been absent quite a bit.'

'I get a lot of colds,' she lied.

'I don't see any doctors' notes in your file.' He peered at her intently. 'Are there problems at home, Donna?'

'No, sir.'

'Do you realize that this means you'll need to attend summer school?'

She nodded, and again looked at the clock.

'That will be all,' the counsellor said.

Once outside the building, she had her first bit of luck for the day. Sticking out at the top of a trashcan was a discarded copy of the magazine *Gloss*. She snatched it up and stuffed it in her backpack.

Summer school – *that* had been a blow. She was sixteen now, and she'd planned to get a summer job. They were hiring at Dairy Queen – minimum wage of course, but that was better than nothing.

What would happen if she refused to go to summer school? What if she just dropped out? But then again – did she really want to operate soft-serve ice-cream machines for the rest of her life?

In any case, she wasn't even sure if she could get a summer job at DQ – plenty of classmates would probably apply. In a factory town like this, where the majority of parents didn't have huge incomes, teenagers were always looking for ways to make money. And there was another problem. If she did get a job there, would she be able to count on her mother to watch the kids?

Too many questions, too many problems . . . Her

worries were slowing her down. She quickened her pace, but she was still late. By the time she arrived at the nursery school, her little sister was the only child still waiting. The teacher glared at Donna.

'Sorry,' Donna muttered, refusing to meet the woman's eyes. She'd had just about all the dirty looks she could handle in one day. Four-year-old Kathy took her sister's hand, and Donna hurried her away.

'Look what I made,' Kathy said, handing Donna the paper she'd been clutching in her other hand.

Donna took the drawing. 'That's a beautiful rainbow!'

'I used all the crayons in the box,' Kathy said proudly.

'It's going right up on the wall,' Donna told her. 'And I think you deserve a prize. How about some new paper dolls?'

'Yes!' Kathy exclaimed. She began to skip, which pretty much forced Donna to skip too.

She looked down fondly at her. Kathy was like a little doll herself. She had their mother's pink cheeks, blue eyes, blonde hair. Donna had been less favoured, with the mousy brown hair and sallow complexion of their father, Martin Peake, assuming he still had any hair at all. She hadn't seen him for two years; he'd left before Billy was born. Kathy had been two.

It was almost two miles to Eastside Trailer Park. By the time they arrived, Kathy had long since stopped skipping, and Donna was practically dragging her. As they approached their lot, she was alarmed to see their neighbour coming out of the Peakes' mobile home.

'What's the matter?' she asked.

'I could hear your little brother screaming,' the woman told her. 'Poor thing was hungry.'

Donna's heart sank. 'Where's my mother?'

The neighbour cocked her head back towards the trailer and walked away. Donna held tightly to Kathy's hand as they went up the steps to the door. Inside they were greeted with the pungent odour of spilled beer.

'Go watch TV,' Donna ordered, and pushed Kathy towards the bedroom. Once she had her settled in front of a cartoon, she went back into the so-called living room to assess the damage.

Billy was in the little swinging contraption that Donna had found in a second-hand store a year earlier. At almost two years old, he was too big for the swing, but he could still be squeezed in and it made him sleep. Shirley Peake lay on the sofa, snoring softly. So at least she was alive.

Donna moved into the kitchenette area, opened the refrigerator and checked the contents. There were still a couple of jars of baby food. Billy was really too old for baby food, but he liked it and it was cheap. There were some eggs she could scramble for the rest of them. Her mother never ate much when she woke up after one of her binges.

Back in the bedroom, Kathy was still mesmerized by Mighty Mouse. Donna settled down on the bed with her precious copy of *Gloss*. First off, she examined the girl on the cover. The shiny-haired model with the wide rosy-red smile wore a soft yellow scoop-neck dress with a gathered skirt and a coral-coloured belt. A matching coral band was in her hair. Nice colour combination, Donna thought. But the white pumps were all wrong – too white, they distracted from the delicate shade of the dress. Beige shoes would have been better.

Leafing through the magazine, she continued her critique of the fashions. There was a gorgeous pink gown with an overlay of lace, perfect for a senior prom, though a squared neckline would be more becoming than the V. A simple pale blue sheath was nice, but too plain. Donna would have added a little something – maybe a scarf at the neck, to give it more punch.

There was a full-page ad for a deodorant that caught her attention. The effectiveness of the deodorant was demonstrated by a photograph of two pretty girls and two handsome boys, all in swimwear, playing volleyball on the beach.

She knew it was posed, that this wasn't some kind of real-life snapshot, but even so, it made her feel something. The people all looked so happy, so carefree. Were there real teenagers out there who could relate to this, who could look at this picture and see their own lives?

In the table of contents she saw the name of an article that looked interesting: 'Is There a Place for You in the Peace Corps?' Maybe later, if she wasn't too tired, she'd try to read it.

A teacher the year before had practically accused her of being illiterate. That wasn't true. She *could* read, and write too – just not very well. It had been a problem for as long as she could remember. She would look at a word, but the letters seemed mixed up – sometimes she'd have to spell it out in her head before she could recognize it. And writing – she'd know the word she wanted to write, she even knew how to spell it, but somehow it always came out wrong. Way back when she was in elementary school, a teacher had told her mother to take Donna to some specialist for testing. Shirley Peake never got around to it.

GL♥SS

'Donna, look!' Kathy cried out.

She raised her eyes from the magazine. The TV was showing a commercial for some sort of toy, a battery-powered robotic creature that moved on its own. A chorus of voices sang the jingle.

'Here he comes, here he comes, greatest toy you've ever seen, and his name is – Mister Machine!'

'I want a Mister Machine!' Kathy declared.

In your dreams, kid, Donna thought sadly. 'Maybe for Christmas,' she said out loud. That was more than half a year away, and hopefully Kathy would have forgotten all about Mister Machine by then.

But she remembered her earlier promise, and leaned over to open a drawer in the rickety nightstand. She took out a scissors, some glue, and her special stash of cardboard scraps. She found an ad for lingerie, and very carefully, she began cutting out some of the models who wore nothing but underclothes. These would then be glued to pieces of cardboard. Later she'd cut out clothes, adding tabs so the clothes could be attached to the models. And presto – brand-new paper dolls for her little sister.

It was fun for *her* too. She could adjust the outfits to suit her own ideas of what would look nice. Add a belt, a scarf, a necklace . . .

There was a rapping sound. She leaped off the bed, in a rush to get to the door before the noise woke Billy. Through the small glass window on the door she saw a young man, holding a toolbox and wearing a jacket with the emblem Ransome's Repair over a pocket.

She opened the door a crack. 'Yes?'

'I'm here to fix the toilet,' he said.

'There's nothing wrong with our toilet.'

He pulled a pad from his pocket and looked at it. 'Henderson?'

She shook her head.

'Isn't this number 71?'

She pointed to the markers painted on the pavement in front of the mobile home. 'No, it's 17.'

A flush came over his face.

He's embarrassed, she thought. 'I do that too, sometimes,' she said quickly. 'See things in reverse.'

'Yeah?'

She nodded. 'Only for me it happens more with letters than numbers.'

His lips twitched into something that faintly resembled a smile, and his eyes swept over her. 'What's your name?'

She noted his strong jaw and his hooded eyes. 'Donna. Donna Peake. What's yours?'

He pointed to the label above the pocket on his jacket.

'Ron Feerman,' she read.

He corrected her. 'Freeman.'

She smiled. 'See? It's like I told you. Letters get switched around in my head.'

GL♥SS

'Yeah.' He gave her an appraising look. 'You live here?'

'With my mother,' she said. 'And my brother and sister. Are you living here in the park?'

He shook his head. 'Riviera Apartments, on the highway.'

She was impressed. The apartment complex wasn't luxurious, but it wasn't a slum either.

He glanced at his notepad again. 'Look, I gotta get to this job.' But he didn't dash off. He shifted his weight from one leg to the other, looked up at the sky, and finally back at her. 'Maybe, I don't know . . . you want to hang out?'

'Hang out?' she repeated.

'Grab a burger or something.'

She shrugged. 'I guess . . .'

'What about tonight?'

'Tonight?' She wanted to kick herself for repeating everything he said.

'Yeah. Around seven?'

She wouldn't be able to get Kathy down by then. 'How about eight?'

'Eight's OK. I'll come by here and pick you up.'

'No, not here.' Her mother would be up by then, and heaven knew what kind of condition she'd be in. It was highly unlikely that she'd make a good impression. 'Meet me at the entrance to the park, OK?'

He nodded. 'Right. See ya.'

'See ya,' she echoed, and watched as he ambled down the road, checking the pavement numbers as he walked.

She went back inside and shut the door. This was the noise that woke Billy.

As he whimpered, she lifted him up and carried him into the kitchen area and put him in his high chair. It was just as well that he was awake now, she thought as she poked around in the refrigerator for baby food. Otherwise he'd never be asleep again by eight.

She hummed under her breath as she struggled to get the lid off the jar. Ron Freeman. He seemed nice. And he was taking her out for a burger.

There wouldn't be any sand or volleyball. But maybe, just maybe, she could be happy for a couple of hours.♥

Chapter Five

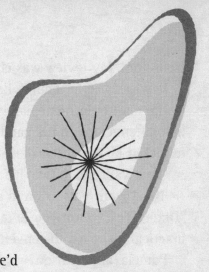

There had been times in her life when Sherry had experienced an exhilaration so strong she'd floated on air, like when she was seven years old and discovered she could ride her bike without training wheels. And there was the moment at the Miss Teen Georgia pageant, when her name had been called as one of the ten finalists. And of course, when Johnny had slipped his senior-class ring off his finger and handed it to her – that was special.

This was different. Not necessarily better, but different. Maybe because it wasn't something she'd even fantasized about, or maybe because it wasn't anything she'd ever thought she'd want. She was going to be published. Millions of girls were going to read her words, see her name, in a famous magazine.

But she came back down to earth with a thud when Mr Simpson spoke.

'Where have you been?' he demanded to know.

'Miss Davison wanted to see all the apprentices.' Maybe this was an opportunity to get a little approval from him. 'My review was chosen to be published.'

It was as if he hadn't heard her. 'This has to go to the mailroom immediately,' he said, indicating the manila envelope in his hand. 'I can't wait for the boy to pick it up this afternoon.'

'You want me to take it?'

'No, I want you to stand on your head and whistle "Dixie". Yes, I want you to take it to the mailroom.' He practically shoved the envelope into her hand.

Pamela and Allison were nearby, and they must have overheard. As soon as the man took off they gathered around her.

'What a jerk,' Pamela murmured. 'You know what he had me doing this morning? Straightening up his desk. And then he criticized me for putting his red pencils in the regular pencil holder.'

'This isn't what we're supposed to be doing,' Allison declared. 'We're apprentices, not slave labour. We're supposed to be learning – we're supposed to get experience working on a magazine.'

'It's just Mr Simpson, I think,' Sherry said. 'No one else is acting like that.'

'You haven't met Lydia,' Allison said.

While Sherry was waiting for the elevator, Donna came out of the office. She looked even paler than usual, her eyes were red and she went directly into the ladies room. Sherry remembered that Caroline had asked to see her alone, and she wondered what had happened. She was half tempted to go after her, but then the elevator doors finally opened. And she had her orders.

The mailroom was in the basement of the building. She got off the elevator, went through the swing doors and found herself in a huge space where boxes were stacked on the floor and men in grey jackets pushed carts packed with envelopes and packages. She had no idea where to go, and nobody asked her if she needed any help.

Then she spotted a familiar face – the boy who'd delivered the mail to her floor yesterday. Michael. He was standing behind a table, taking envelopes out of a sack, giving each one a quick look and then putting them into various cubbyholes on the wall. It was always interesting to watch other people working alone when they didn't know they were being observed, she thought.

He didn't have the athletic, clean-cut looks of the kind of guys she went out with, like Johnny and the ones she'd dated before him. Yet there was something about him that was oddly attractive. His hair was a little too long, covering his ears, and his thin body was swallowed by the jacket that was way too big for him. He was clearly no athlete.

But his eyes . . . they were so deep and dark, almost mysterious. And he had pouty lips. Mentally she replaced the Hartnell jacket with a leather motorcycle one, and an image of Elvis Presley crossed her mind.

Oh, if her friends back home could read her mind right now! They were so hooked on those squeaky-clean TV heroes. None of them knew that she'd always felt a little something for the bad-boy types, that watching Elvis in a movie always gave her a funny, secret shiver.

She tried to block the Elvis image and focused on the real person, Michael. Whatever he was doing, it had to be boring, but his face was serious, intense even. Was it taking him that much effort to read addresses?

He looked up and caught her eye. He didn't smile exactly, but she thought she saw a flash of recognition in his expression, and she approached.

'Hi, I'm Sherry. From *Gloss*.'

He put a hand to an ear and took out an earphone that had been hidden under his hair. 'Sorry.'

She saw that the cord from the earphone went into a pocket. 'Transistor radio?'

He nodded. 'I couldn't do this all day without something to distract me.'

Automatically she recalled rule number one for talking to boys – show an interest in what he's doing. 'What are you listening to?'

He handed the earphone to her and she put it close to her ear.

'Classical music!'

'You don't like classical music?'

'Oh, I do! I was just surprised—'

'That a mailroom boy listens to it?'

She wasn't used to boys interrupting like that.

'No! It's just that, well, people our age—'

Again he tried to finish the sentence for her. 'Are only listening to crap.'

She wasn't used to that kind of language either. Was he trying to shock her?

'I remember seeing you yesterday,' he said. 'You're one of those apprentices.'

Oh, if her friends back home could read her mind right now!

'Yes, they call us interns.' Standing closer now, she was struck by his eyes. They were more like black than brown. And that Elvis image returned in full force.

She was in no rush to get back upstairs, so she looked around and tried to look interested in the activity around her. 'Do you like working in the mailroom?'

He raised his eyebrows, and this time her face got so warm she knew she was going red. What a stupid question.

A smile came and went so quickly she might have imagined it. 'It's just a summer job. I'm saving money for university in the fall.'

'Where are you planning to go?'

'NYU.'

'Are you a native New Yorker?'

'Born and bred. I was raised in Brooklyn.'

'That's nice,' she said politely.

'You've been there?'

'No.'

'Then how do you know it's nice?'

'It's *not* nice?' she countered, feeling flustered.

Now she actually got something she could call a real smile. 'It's OK. Where are you from?'

'Georgia. A small city, north of Atlanta.' She steeled herself for the Scarlett O'Hara joke. To her surprise, it didn't come.

'So you want to go into the magazine business?' he asked.

'Not really,' she said.

'Then what are you doing here?'

'I just thought it would be interesting.'

'Is it?'

The questions were coming so fast. She felt like she was being interrogated, and she had a sudden desire to impress him. 'Sometimes. I wrote a review of a film, and it's going to be published in the magazine.'

'You're a writer?'

'Well . . .' She was about to say, 'not really,' but he kept talking.

'I'm a writer too,' he said. 'That's why I took this job. I thought working at Hartnell would mean I'd be around literary types.' He looked around and uttered a short laugh. 'But they don't come down to the mailroom.'

'What do you write?' she asked.

'I'm kind of working on a novel right now.'

She grasped at the chance to turn the tables and become the interrogator. 'What do you mean, "kind of"? Either you're writing a novel or you're not.'

He actually laughed. 'I was afraid I'd sound pretentious if I said that without the "kind of".'

So the dark, brooding, intense guy had a sense of humour. She smiled.

'Um, do you need something?' he asked.

She realized she was staring, and she felt her face go warm again. 'Oh, right. Yes. One of the editors asked me to drop this off.'

He took the envelope from her, glanced at the address and then put it in a box. 'Mission accomplished,' he said.

'Hey, Dillon,' an older man yelled. 'Give me a hand with these sacks.'

'Coming,' Michael called back.

'Nice talking to you,' Sherry said.

'Same here,' he said. 'I'll see you later.'

'You will?'

'Four thirty. That's when I drop the afternoon mail off at *Gloss*.'

'Right, of course,' she said, turning away before the flush could creep up her face again. 'Bye.'

What an unusual boy, she thought. He was so . . . so *direct*. The way he'd stared at her . . . She wasn't used to boys making that kind of eye contact.

When she returned to the *Gloss* offices she learned that Mr Simpson was off at a meeting. He'd left a stack of letters for her to type, but at least he wouldn't be looking over her shoulder.

Caroline came out of her office. 'Sherry, I was just looking for you. I meant to tell you earlier, there's a little perk that comes along with your review.'

'A perk?'

'A perquisite. A fringe benefit.' She handed Sherry an envelope. 'Tickets to the premiere Friday night at Radio City Music Hall.' From her office, the phone began to ring and she disappeared back inside.

Sherry had to tell someone. She spotted Diane coming out of an office, and they exchanged little finger-wiggling waves. She was just about ready to head over to her, when she saw Pamela cross the room. She hurried towards her, and told her the news.

'Oh, Sherry, you are so lucky!'

Sherry stared at the envelope in her hand. 'I know, I can't believe it.'

'What are you going to wear?'

Sherry's head was spinning. 'I don't know! What do people wear to a movie premiere?'

Pamela rolled her eyes. 'Don't you ever read movie magazines? They wear gowns!'

'But I don't have any gowns here,' Sherry wailed. She could have kicked herself. Back home, in her closet, there were two gowns – the one she'd worn to her senior prom and a bridesmaid gown from a cousin's wedding, two dresses she thought she'd never wear again. It hadn't even occurred to her that she would need a gown in New York. And there wouldn't be enough time for her mother to ship one of them here.

'Then you'll have to buy one,' Pamela declared.

'Buy . . . a gown?' She considered the sum of money her parents had given her for the summer. A gown would make a big dent in it.

Allison joined them. 'What's going on?'

'I'm going to the premiere of *Beach Blanket Kisses*,' Sherry told her.

Allison made a face. 'You mean, you have to watch it *again*?'

Pamela glared at her. 'Allison, this is a big deal! And she doesn't have anything to wear!'

'You don't happen to have a gown I could borrow, do you?' Sherry asked without much hope. Allison was a good four inches shorter and at least a size smaller. Nothing she owned would fit her. And Pamela's taste wouldn't suit her at all.

'Maybe this is the kind of special occasion Caroline was talking about when we saw the samples closet,' Pamela suggested. 'You could borrow something from there.'

'You've got something else to think about too,' Allison said. 'I'm assuming there are two tickets in that envelope.'

Sherry looked. Allison was right. 'Great! I could take one of y'all. You could flip a coin or something.'

'It's all yours,' Allison told Pamela. 'I'm not sitting through that garbage again.'

Pamela shook her head firmly. 'No, she needs a date, an escort.'

Sherry drew in her breath. 'Mr Simpson!'

'You want to take *him*?'

It was Sherry's turn to roll eyes at Pamela before dashing back to her desk. By the time Mr Simpson passed, she was busily typing away.

For one fleeting moment she considered calling Johnny and summoning him to New York. But she knew this was out of the question. They'd discussed the possibility of visiting over the summer, and he'd informed her, sadly of course, that it was impossible. The congressman he was working for was up for re-election, and Johnny was expected to work all the time, even to be on call at weekends.

Michael Dillon . . . no, that was crazy. She knew nothing about him. Except for the fact that he was writing a novel and that he thought popular music was a four-letter word. Which meant he'd probably turn up his nose at the mere idea of watching a movie like *Beach Blanket Kisses*. Would he even own a suit to wear to the premiere?

But on the other hand . . . hadn't she seen a tiny flash of something in his dark eyes when they were talking? In her experience, if a boy was interested, he'd be willing to do what a girl wanted to do just to be with her. She thought back to all those times she'd easily coaxed Johnny into going to the roller rink, when he wasn't crazy about skating at all.

Pamela had said she thought Michael looked a little like a hood. That was such an exaggeration. True, he wasn't a 'pretty boy' in the fashion of Troy Donahue or Richard Chamberlain as Doctor Kildare. And so what if he did look a little like a hood? Elvis looked like a hood, but he always turned out to be a good guy in his movies. And Michael had those smouldering eyes . . .

Oh, this was terrible! How could she be thinking about a boy in this way when she was in a completely committed relationship with Johnny? Guilt drove the picture of Michael out of her mind. But even so, at quarter after four, she ducked out of the offices and went to the ladies' room. There, she teased up her hair a bit with a comb, reapplied some lipstick and dabbed some of her precious Shalimar on her wrists and behind her ears. Back at her desk, she kept an eye on the entrance.

At four thirty on the dot, the doors opened, and Michael wheeled in his cart. She was encouraged by the half-smile and nod that he aimed in her direction. As he was passing her desk, she rose and spoke in a low voice.

'Michael, could you stop by before you leave? There's something I want to ask you.'

'Sure,' he said, and moved on.

She went back to typing Mr Simpson's correspondence, but she found herself dipping into the little bottle of liquid paper more frequently than usual to correct errors. Very silly to be so nervous, she told herself. It wasn't as if she had a crush on the guy or anything like that. She had a boyfriend, for crying out loud.

Mr Simpson came by and dropped a file folder on her desk. 'Give this to Miss Davison,' he ordered.

She picked up the folder and hurried towards Caroline's office. She guessed it would take Michael about ten minutes to make the rounds of the *Gloss* offices, and she wanted to be sure she was at her desk when he was on his way out.

'Hey, where's the fire?'

She'd practically collided with Ricky Hartnell.

'Oh, excuse me, I'm sorry.'

He flashed his I'm-so-sexy smile. 'I'm not. No, I take that back, I *am* sorry. If you hadn't stopped, we'd be cheek to cheek by now.'

He certainly had lines. She smiled politely, and moved to walk around him. He stepped to the side.

'Excuse me,' she said again.

'Hold on, honey child, I'm about to do you a favour.'

'A favour?'

'A little birdie told me you need a date for a film premiere Friday.'

Her stomach dropped. 'A little birdie with platinum hair?'

'So I am offering you the pleasure of my company,' he said, with a small bow.

Sherry Ann Forrester had never uttered a four-letter word out loud in her life, but she mentally ran through a few of them. Now what? Did she dare turn down an invitation from the boy whose name was on the building she worked in?

'Thank you,' she said politely, and managed a smile.

Ricky acknowledged this with a wink, and sauntered away.

Immediately Pamela came tearing over. 'Well?'

Sherry nodded.

'So don't I get a "thank you, Pamela"?'

'Thank you, Pamela.'

The girl frowned. 'You could sound a little more enthusiastic. You've got a date with Ricky Hartnell!'

'Yes, and I'm glad I've got an escort. But don't get excited, Pamela. I've got a boyfriend, remember? And Ricky's really not my type.'

'Rich and handsome isn't your type?' Pamela did her eye-roll thing, shook her head in bewilderment and moved on. Sherry went into Caroline's empty office and placed the folder on her desk.

Back at her own desk, she resumed typing. A moment later Michael came back with his cart.

'Did you want to ask me something?'

Sherry looked up. 'Um . . . I was just going to ask, I mean, *say*, that if you'd like to talk about your novel sometime, I'd like to hear about it.'

He cocked his head to one side and looked at her.

'Maybe we can take a coffee break together.'

'Yes, that would be nice,' she said.

She gazed after his departing figure. It would be interesting to talk to him, she thought. She'd never known anyone who called himself a writer.

And suddenly she recalled one of her favourite Elvis movies – *Wild in the Country*. Bad-boy Elvis wanted to be a writer in that one.

A coffee break . . . not something she imagined Elvis suggesting, but it was better than nothing. But oh, what would Johnny say if he knew she was having Elvis fantasies about another boy?

With a sigh, she went back to the keyboard.♥

Pamela gazed across the bullpen at Sherry, typing away furiously with an expression that didn't express jubilation, excitement or any of the feelings Pamela would have if *she* was in her situation. Sherry was going to a film premiere with the only eligible young guy at *Gloss*. Pamela would be over the moon!

Her eyes moved to the office entrance, where Doreen, the beauty editor, and Darlene, her assistant had just returned from wherever they'd been all afternoon. They were both swinging identical tote bags labelled Lovely Lady Cosmetics. That wouldn't help Pamela with her endless attempts to tell them apart. Not only did they have similar names, they were almost the same height and shape, and they both wore their light brown hair in the same bubble shape, with the only distinction being the fact that one of them had fluffy bangs and the other had little spit curls at her ears. Today even their dresses were similar – sleeveless sheaths, one in blue, the other in green.

At least they didn't seem to have a huge wardrobe of pocketbooks. One of them carried a yellow patent-leather bag over her arm, the other held a smaller beige woven pocketbook that she carried in her hand, the same ones they'd held the day before.

Ever since being assigned to the beauty department yesterday, Pamela had been mentally chanting, 'Doreen, bangs, yellow,' and, 'Darlene, spit curls, beige.' Or was it Doreen, bangs, beige?

They both smiled brightly and wiggled their fingers as they passed Pamela and she wiggled her fingers in response. Then she went back to work.

The beauty editors had given her a simple assignment – to go through a stack of rival magazines – *Seventeen*, *Ingenue*, *Calling All Girls* – and make a list of all the beauty products they'd recommended in recent months. It had sounded like a fun way to pass a couple of hours, but she was starting to get bored. It was as if every magazine was recommending the exact same looks to their readers. Eyeshadows so pale she could hardly tell what colour they were. Lipsticks so light they were barely visible. And the hairdos! Page after page of the same feathered layers, the same bubble cuts, the same little flips.

Where were the Cleopatra eyes, the slash of dark red on the lips, the rouge applied so high it created cheekbones? Where were the beehive hairdos and enormous bouffants? Where were the directions on how to properly tease hair or put on false eyelashes?

It wasn't to *Gloss*, or any of the others now resting on her desk, that Pamela had ever turned for beauty ideas. Movie magazines – *Photoplay, Modern Screen, Movie Life* – that was where her style came from. Liz Taylor – now *that* was a woman who knew how to wear make-up. Of course, Liz Taylor was a lot older, but Pamela could certainly take cues from Natalie Wood, who was younger. Kim Novak! She was the best, and Pamela secretly thought she looked a bit like her.

Armed with the carefully cut-out photos from the magazines, Pamela liked to go to a five-and-dime and try to replicate the looks by purchasing cheap versions of the cosmetics. Or occasionally by lifting them.

She smiled as she recalled how Sherry had looked when Pamela told her she'd swiped that lipstick at Woolworth's. Now Sherry probably thought she was some kind of serious criminal. Back home she'd never been a major shoplifter, not like some of her friends. But every now and then, just to go along with the others – and for the little thrill of course – she would slip something very small into a pocket or a handbag. She really shouldn't do it here in New York though, she decided. If *Gloss* thought she was a crook, she could get sent home – and she had too many plans for the summer to risk it all for the sake of a lipstick.

And it was going well. So far, so good. Well, maybe not *good,* but this was only her third day at *Gloss*. The work didn't seem like it was going to be too hard. The room at the residence was OK, and she was used to sharing. Growing up with five siblings, none of them had rooms of their own in the little three-bedroom cottage outside Pittsburgh where she'd lived all her life.

'Pamela!'

She turned to see Doreen – or maybe Darlene – waving her into the big office the two women shared. She picked up the list she'd created from her review of the magazines, and left her desk.

They both smiled identical bright smiles at her, and one of them pointed to the tote bags they'd carried in, which now rested on one of the desks.

'We got oodles of free samples at the launch of this new cosmetics brand,' one of them told her. 'Help yourself!'

'Thanks,' Pamela said, and began rummaging through the bags. 'Ooh, turquoise eyeshadow! I've never seen that before. Are you sure you don't want it?'

The two women exchanged looks. 'No, dear, it's all yours,' Darlene said.

'This would suit you,' Doreen said, and took another eyeshadow from the bag. It was a very pale tan, almost flesh-coloured. Totally unappealing, but Pamela accepted it politely.

Doreen then announced that it was five o'clock and she was dismissed for the day. With her sack of samples, Pamela trotted back out into the bullpen and headed over to where Allison was standing by Sherry's desk.

'You guys want to go out for something to drink?' she asked.

'You could come with me to a coffee shop in Greenwich Village,' suggested Allison. 'That's where I'm headed.'

Pamela wrinkled her nose. 'Actually, I was thinking about that cocktail lounge just across the street.'

'I think you have to be twenty-one to go in a cocktail lounge,' Sherry said.

Pamela's eyebrows went up. 'Don't you have a fake ID?'

From Sherry's expression, Pamela could have been asking her if she had a gun. 'Actually, I don't.'

Pamela glanced at the desk where Donna was sitting, staring into space. She seriously doubted that Donna would be interested in a visit to a cocktail lounge. Besides, she wouldn't be any fun.

But there were other interns, and she overheard two who might be candidates for companionship. They were both talking about their day, and not happily.

'I can't believe I'm stuck in food,' Diane complained. 'So boring.'

'I thought fashion would be a great place to work,' Vicky said, 'but all I did today was address envelopes. I need something to cheer me up.'

Pamela boldly entered the conversation. 'How about a drink?'

Vicky brightened. 'Ooh, a hot-fudge sundae! We could go to the diner down the street.'

'That wasn't what I had in mind,' Pamela murmured, and backed away.

She went back to Sherry.

'Listen, I'll bet they don't check for IDs. Come with me?'

Sherry shook her head. 'Not this time, thanks anyway. I need to plan my outfit for the premiere.'

'Lucky you,' Pamela said. 'And think about what you're going to do *after* the premiere. Maybe Ricky's a member of Le Club.'

'What's Le Club?' Sherry asked.

The poor girl really must be from the boondocks, Pamela thought. 'It's this private members-only place where all the society people go,' she told her. 'Or maybe you should ask him to take you to the Peppermint Lounge. That's the dance place where the Twist was invented. You do know how to Twist, don't you?'

Sherry smiled. 'Yes, Pamela, even in Georgia we do the Twist.' She got up from her desk. 'Well, I guess I'll go ask Caroline if she'll let me into the samples closet.'

Donna suddenly looked up. 'You're going into the samples closet?' she asked Sherry.

'If I'm allowed. Would you like to help me pick something out to wear?'

Unbelievable, Pamela thought. Well, Donna was her roommate; she had to be nice to her.

So she was on her own. But maybe that wasn't such a bad thing. She might have better luck that way.

The lounge across the street was called 'Charlie's'.

It wasn't one of the famous places she'd read about, but it looked like it *could* be. There were plush velvety-looking purple banquettes, a gleaming bar, and a handsome bartender standing behind it. The banquettes were already filled, but there were a couple of empty places at the bar, so she made her way over there.

Perched on a stool, she smiled brightly at the bartender. 'A martini, please. Extra dry, with a twist.'

The bartender didn't smile back. 'Could I see some identification, please?'

Pamela uttered a little laugh, as if the question was absurd, but she nodded. 'I know, I look young for my age. That will be an advantage in a few years, won't it?'

The bartender said nothing. Pamela pulled out her wallet and extracted the card she'd paid twenty-five dollars for just last month. It was an exact replica of her driver's licence, with a slight change in the year of her birth date.

The bartender examined it and shrugged. 'Dry martini, with a twist.'

'*Extra* dry,' Pamela corrected him. Twenty-five dollars had seemed exorbitant for a little square of laminated paper, but she realized now it had been well worth the price. Realizing that the bar stool had a seat that twirled, she gave a little spin of exhilaration. This was a good way to check out the scene too.

Charlie's had a nice-looking clientele, she thought. Lots of prosperous-looking businessmen, in suits and carrying briefcases. Well-groomed women in nice dresses and moderately high heels. Not particularly glamorous, but that made sense, since it was only just after five o'clock and they'd probably come straight from work. For the first time since she'd arrived in the city, she was at the kind of place she'd planned on frequenting. And any doubts she'd had about applying for this internship vanished.

Months ago, when she saw the double-page ad in *Gloss* inviting girls to work there for the summer, she'd barely noticed it. She didn't have any particular interest in magazines, and besides, she'd already made her post-graduation plans – a one-week vacation at the shore with a bunch of girlfriends who would pitch in for a hotel room where they'd sleep four to a bed. After that, she'd enrol in the local secretarial school for a twelve-week course to learn shorthand and improve her typing skills. Then, in the fall, she'd start looking for a job, maybe in Pittsburgh.

But the ad came at around the same time Pamela discovered *Sex and the Single Girl*. If Helen Gurley Brown, this woman who wasn't beautiful, who didn't go to a university, who had been actually poor rather than just working class, could make a fabulous life for herself in New York City, then why couldn't she?

At school, she hated writing book reports. But this time she had a book that actually inspired her. She wasn't stupid – she knew that all the author's advice

GL♥SS

on having affairs wouldn't impress her teachers. So she concentrated on the chapters where Miss Brown wrote about single women taking care of themselves – finding jobs they enjoyed, making their own money and spending it carefully, getting an apartment and fixing it up, and not seeing marriage as the only option for the future.

She'd gotten a B-plus from her English teacher. But more importantly, she was accepted as an intern at *Gloss* on the strength of that same essay.

Out of the corner of her eye she thought she recognized someone sitting alone at the other end of the bar. Yes – it was that good-looking advertising-sales manager from *Gloss*, Alex Parker. She stared at him, willing him to look in her direction. Finally he did – but his eyes passed right over her.

'Another martini, miss?'

She hadn't even realized that she'd finished the first one.

'Um . . . how much does a martini cost?'

When he told her, she winced. She barely had enough to pay for *one*. As she fumbled in her wallet to count out the money, she realized she was feeling a little dizzy. She needed to learn the name of a cocktail that wasn't quite as strong to order next time.

And as she walked very carefully to the door, she hoped that maybe next time she wouldn't be buying her own.♥

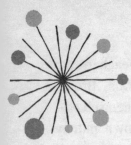

Chapter Seven

Early Friday evening, Pamela emptied her huge cosmetics bag on Sherry's bedroom desk. Then she opened the magazine she'd brought in with her and pointed to a photo. 'How about *this*?'

Sherry wrinkled her nose. 'It's a little too much, I think. She looks kind of slutty.'

'Slutty?! That's Connie Stevens – she's beautiful! She's dating Troy Donahue!'

Sherry stifled a groan. Oh why, why, why had she accepted Pamela's offer to do her make-up for the premiere? Sometimes being nice had its consequences. What was it Mama often said? *The road to hell is paved with good intentions.* Of course, Mama would never use the word 'hell' – she'd say 'aitch-ee-double-hockey-sticks'.

She flipped through the pages portraying celebrities on the town and found an illustrated article. 'I like this.'

'"The beauty routine of All-American TV star Shelley Fabares",' Pamela read out loud. Then she let out a world-weary sigh. 'Well, if you're sure that's what you want.'

GL♥SS

'I'm sure,' Sherry said, pleased that she wouldn't have to argue.

Pamela continued to read. '"Shelley starts with pressed powder – on the nose, chin, and forehead areas, where skin can get a little shiny." You know, Sherry, liquid foundation gives much better coverage.'

'I don't need that much coverage,' Sherry said firmly, and pushed her own pressed-powder compact across the desk in Pamela's direction.

Pamela went to work. 'Where's your roommate?'

'In the laundry room probably. She doesn't have many clothes, so she's always having to wash them.'

'Well, at least she's clean,' Pamela commented.

'True. And that's practically all I know about her.'

'That's so strange,' Pamela said. 'You've been sharing a room for almost a week now. I know absolutely everything about Allison. She comes from a very hoity-toity family. Real snobs, Allison says. Terribly proper.'

Sherry had guessed as much. It would explain why Allison was such a rebel.

'It's funny, I'd never know a girl like that back home,' Pamela continued. 'Someone from that kind of family. My folks are like the opposite. I mean, we're not *poor*, but my dad's a car mechanic and my mom sews a lot of our clothes. Not exactly upper-crust types, like Allison's family. Or yours.'

'We're not upper-crust,' Sherry objected. Would

she ever get used to Pamela's blunt way of speaking? Where *she* came from, people never talked about social class.

'We're not like Allison's people. I guess we're what you'd call middle-class. Daddy's a doctor, and Mama does volunteer work.' That was about all she was comfortable saying, so she changed the subject. 'You know, Donna really is a mystery. When I ask her about herself, she totally clams up.'

'What does she do here? Like, in the evenings, after supper.'

'She goes down to the lounge to watch TV shows. *My Three Sons*, *Ozzie and Harriet* . . . The only time she ever answered one of my questions was when I asked her what her favourite show was. She said it was *Father Knows Best*, and she told me she was really sad when it went off the air a few months ago.'

'All "happy family" shows,' Pamela mused. 'Maybe she's homesick and they remind her of home. OK, time to choose a lipstick. Where's your dress?'

'Hanging in the closet.'

Pamela took out the gown, laid it carefully on Sherry's bed and stepped back to examine it.

'Well, it's not what *I* would have picked, but it's pretty.'

Sherry thought so too. 'You know, Donna came with me to the samples closet. I spotted a pink gown right away – pink's my favourite colour – but Donna said the pink was too pale, that the light blue dress was much better for my complexion, and she was right.' She cocked her head thoughtfully. 'That was the longest conversation I've ever had with her.'

'Well, you can wear just about any colour lipstick with light blue,' Pamela declared. She returned to the desk and picked one up. 'This is a nice rosy pink, not too pale. Try it.'

Sherry took it uncertainly, wondering if the lipstick might be shoplifted.

'Do you know where you're going after the premiere?' asked Pamela.

Sherry shook her head. 'All Ricky told me was that he'd pick me up here at the residence at seven thirty. Maybe he doesn't have any plans to take me out after.'

'Then *you* make plans,' Pamela instructed her. 'He *has* to take you out to dinner, that's the rule.'

'I don't know if I'll want to eat anything,' Sherry murmured, looking at the dress on the bed. 'I'm so afraid of spilling something that will stain it.'

Pamela ignored that. 'And remember the names of places for dancing. If he's not a member of Le Club, tell him you'd like to go to the Peppermint Lounge.'

'I don't even know if I should dance in that dress,' Sherry said. 'What if I rip it?'

Pamela rolled her eyes. 'Oh, don't be such a worry wart,' she said, and began gathering up her cosmetics.

'I have to go and get ready myself. Did I tell you I have a date tonight?'

'No! Who with?'

'Well, I met this girl, Brenda, in the dining hall downstairs. She's a nurse at City Hospital, and her boyfriend's a doctor there. She's fixing me up with a friend of his and we're all going out together.'

Sherry was pleased for her. In her experience, doctors were very respectable. 'That's great, maybe he'll be Mr Right.'

Pamela shrugged. 'All I know is that doctors make a lot of money.' She grinned. 'Hey, maybe I'll see you at the Peppermint Lounge!'

The little intercom on the wall dinged, and this was followed by the voice of the receptionist. 'Sherry, you have a phone call.'

Sherry hit a button and said, 'Thank you.' Then she pulled on a bathrobe and the girls left the room together.

'Thanks for the make-up,' Sherry called after Pamela, and headed to the phone booth at the end of the corridor. It suddenly struck her that this could be Ricky, breaking their date, and it was with some trepidation that she took the receiver off the hook.

'Hello?'

It was a great relief to hear the voice of her father. 'Hey, sugar, how are you?'

'Daddy! I'm fine! Is anything wrong?'

'No, no, sugar, everything's just peachy. Your mama and I were just getting a little worried about you. We've had one letter and that's all.'

'I'm sorry, Daddy. I've just been so busy.'

There was a click, the sound of an extension phone being lifted, and another voice trilled, 'Honey, we just miss you so much!'

'I miss you too, Mama. But listen, y'all, I can't really talk now. I'm getting ready to go out.'

'Where are you going?' her father wanted to know.

She really should have written them her big news. 'To the premiere of a movie. I wrote a review of it for the magazine, and it's going to be published.'

'Well, isn't that just fine,' her father said, but her mother was clearly more interested in something else.

'And who are you going with? The other apprentice girls?'

'No, actually I'm going with a boy.' She continued in a rush, before the questions could start coming. 'He's a very nice boy from a good family, he's the son of the magazine's publisher, and he's only acting as my escort, it's nothing else.'

Her mother made a *humph* sound. 'Well, I don't know if you should write Johnny about this. He could get mighty jealous.'

'I won't,' Sherry said.

'But I do hope you're writing him more regularly than you're writing us,' she went on.

'Well, I *would*,' Sherry said, 'if he wrote *me*. I wrote him the second day I was here, and he still hasn't written back.'

'Now, honey, you know men don't like to write letters,' her mother said. 'It's up to you to keep the relationship moving along in the right direction, you know that.'

'Yes, Mama, I know. I'll write him tomorrow, I promise. Now, I really have to go, y'all, and I promise to write you too and tell you all about it.'

But her father wasn't ready to let her go. 'Sugar, you sure you're OK? You sound different.'

'Different how?'

'I don't know, just different. Now, don't you go be letting New York City change my sweet girl.'

'I won't, Daddy, and I really have to go now. Bye-bye. Bye, Mama!'

Having finally freed herself, she went running back to her room, where she turned on the radio and went into the bathroom. She still had to get her rollers out.

As she unwound the locks of hair from the tubes of wire filled with bristles, she thought about what her father had just said. How could she have changed in less than a week here? True, she was having experiences she'd never had before. She was meeting people unlike anyone she'd ever known too. The other interns of course. But also people like Caroline Davison. Women who worked real jobs.

Sherry wasn't sure how old Caroline was, but she would guess early thirties. By now she knew the editor lived alone, in an apartment on the Upper West Side. And her job seemed awfully important to her. She frequently stayed late at the *Gloss* office, and sometimes she even took work home.

Why wasn't she married? Sherry wondered. Surely a woman so pretty and charming could get a husband. Maybe the job took up so much of her time that she didn't have the opportunity to meet anyone. But then why work at a job like that? It was a puzzle to her.

She was just teasing up the crown of her hair with a rat-tail comb when she heard a rap on the door.

'It's me, Allison.'

'Come on in,' she called from the bathroom.

'I wanted to see you in your dress,' Allison said.

'I'm just about to put it on,' Sherry told her. She came out from the bathroom and took a girdle out of her dresser drawer. As she struggled to get into it, Allison winced.

'Why are you wearing that? You're not fat.'

'Mama says nice girls always wear girdles. So they won't, you know, jiggle.'

'I guess it also serves as a kind of chastity belt,' Allison said. 'A guy would have a hard time getting that off of you.'

Sherry laughed. 'I never thought of it that way. Don't you ever wear a girdle?'

'Oh, my mother has tried a zillion times to force me into one, but I absolutely refuse. And it's not like I have enough meat on my bones to jiggle.'

It was true – Allison was very slim. But – 'How do you keep your stockings up?' Sherry asked as she began attaching hosiery to the garter clips hanging from the girdle.

'Don't wear them,' Allison replied.

'Well, neither do I, during the day in the summer. But when you're wearing a party dress, don't you feel naked without stockings?'

'I never wear party dresses.'

Sherry shook her head in wonderment. The girl really was a rebel. Gingerly she lifted the dress and stepped into it. Allison zipped her up.

'You do look nice,' she admitted.

'Wait, I'm not finished.' Sherry fished through her jewellery box and extracted a string of pearls that she put around her neck.

'There. Now what do you think?'

'You could be going to one of those debutante balls I refused to attend in Boston,' Allison declared.

Sherry had a feeling this was as much of a compliment as she could expect from Miss Anti-fashion. She studied herself in the mirror.

It was a lovely gown, and it fit her perfectly – snug from the bosom to the waist, and then it flared out almost in a bell shape. The delicate white lace at the neckline stood out against her tan. She could have stepped right out of the pages of *Gloss*.

'I hope I'll be able to dance in this,' she murmured. At that very moment the radio was blasting Chubby Checker.

'*Let's do the twist . . .*'

'Try it,' Allison suggested.

Sherry went into some careful Twist moves, moving back and forth, turning her shoulders and her knees in opposite directions. Just then Donna walked in the door. For one very brief moment, Sherry actually got a glimpse of a smile.

'Hi, Donna,' Allison said. 'I gotta go.'

'I can leave if you want,' Donna said.

'Don't be silly,' Sherry said, trying not to sound impatient. Donna's antisocial behaviour was beginning to get on her nerves. 'This is your room too, Donna.'

'And I'm heading down to the Village,' Allison told them.

'Still looking for your Bob Dylan guy?' Sherry asked.

'Yep, and tonight I'm going to find him. See you guys.'

After she left, Donna sat down on her bed. 'You sure you don't mind me being here?'

'Donna!' Sherry exclaimed in exasperation, and then closed her eyes and counted to ten. Calmer, she smiled. 'I like having people around when I'm getting ready to go out. It reminds me of home. My little sister always came in my room and watched while I was getting ready for a date with Johnny.'

'That's nice,' Donna said.

'Do you have any brothers or sisters?' Sherry asked.

She thought there was a second of hesitation before Donna said, 'No.'

'Only child, huh?'

There was no reply. Sherry took another look at herself in the mirror and frowned. 'Do I look OK? Something seems wrong.'

'It's the necklace,' Donna blurted out.

'What?'

'Those pearls. They're too much with all that lace.'

Sherry gazed at her reflection thoughtfully. Then she reached around to the back of her neck and unclasped the string of pearls.

'You're right!' she said. 'Anything else?'

'Do you have any earrings?' Donna asked. 'You could use something to balance the decoration on the neckline.'

Sherry went back into the jewellery box, and took out some fake pearl drop clip-ons. She held them to her ears and looked at Donna questioningly. Donna nodded.

'And maybe something more,' Donna said. 'Wait a minute.' She went to the closet, took out a bag and emptied a pile of fabric scraps on to her bed.

'I found these in the lounge. Someone was sewing and she was going to throw these scraps away,' she murmured as she examined the pieces. Then, 'Here!' she cried in triumph. It was a scrap of a patterned piece, tiny blue dots on white. She picked up a pair of scissors and cut a strip. Then she took a needle and thread from the bag.

Moments later, she showed Sherry a neat, tiny formed bow. 'Do you have a bobby pin?'

'Here.'

Donna took it, and neatly inserted it into the fold on the back of the bow. Then she pushed back a lock of Sherry's hair on the right side and fixed the bow just above her ear. 'OK. Now look.'

Sherry went back to the mirror. The blue dots on the bow matched the blue of the dress. 'It's perfect! Donna, you have a great eye!'

Donna shrugged, but Sherry could have sworn she saw pleasure in her eyes. She took another lingering look at her reflection. If only Johnny could see her like this . . .

The intercom dinged. 'Sherry, you have a visitor.'

Sherry pressed a button. 'I'm coming!' Quickly she put on her freshly polished white low-heeled slippers and picked up the little white clutch bag, another loan from the closet. At the door, she turned back to Donna. 'Thanks for your help.'

An actual smile – brief, but real – crossed Donna's face. 'Have a nice time.'

When she got off the elevator she spotted Ricky right away, and despite her less-than-positive feelings about him, she was impressed. If he'd been handsome before, in ordinary clothes, he looked really smart now, in a black tuxedo with shiny lapels. As she approached him, he raised his eyebrows in approval.

'Nice.'

He could have expressed this more elegantly, but she accepted the praise. 'Thank you,' she said. 'And you look very nice too.'

At least he had the kind of manners she expected from a well-brought-up boy. He took her arm, escorted her to the door and opened it for her.

He didn't have to open the door of the car. A uniformed chauffeur stood at attention just by the side of the long white limousine, and practically bowed as he opened the door with a flourish.

Sherry had been in a limousine before. For the prom, Johnny had pitched in with three friends for a limo to take them to the senior prom, and it had been big enough for the four couples to ride comfortably. This limousine was just as big, and it was only for her and Ricky.

And it didn't appear to be rented. Ricky tapped on the glass window that separated them from the front of the limo, and it magically came down.

'We're going to Sixth Avenue and 51st, James. Radio City.'

'Yes, Mr Hartnell,' the man replied.

She shouldn't have been surprised to learn that the family had a private limousine. Pamela had secured information on the Hartnells from one of the secretaries at *Gloss*. They were fabulously rich, with a penthouse on Park Avenue, a summer house on Long Island and apartments in Paris and London. Ricky had gone to the best private schools in Manhattan – schools, plural, because he'd been thrown out of several, for poor grades and various acts of mischief. Despite all this, his father had been able to use his influence to get him into an Ivy League university, but Ricky had refused to go. So instead he was working at Hartnell Publications, the company he was destined to inherit some day.

'Working' was an exaggeration, Sherry thought. From what she'd observed, he came in late to the office (when he came in at all) and spent most of the day reading magazines or wandering around looking for girls to flirt with.

He was what her father would describe, in his old-fashioned way, as a 'ne'er-do-well', and he wouldn't be pleased at all to know his daughter was spending an evening with a type like this. 'Do you have the tickets?' he asked her.

'Yes.' She reached in her bag and handed him the little envelope. Of course a gentleman would carry the tickets and hand them to the usher.

He put the envelope in the pocket of his jacket. And pulled out something else – a silver flask. Unscrewing the cap, he offered it to her.

'What is it?' she asked.

'Scotch,' he said. 'Very good scotch. Single malt. From my father's private stock.'

She'd never drunk Scotch in her life, and she had no idea what single malt meant, but it didn't matter.

'No, thank you,' she said politely. He shrugged and took a swig.

She imagined he now probably thought she was a prude. Which was *not* true. It had never bothered her that Johnny liked a beer once in a while, and at parties she herself had indulged a few times in a Purple Passion – a little vodka mixed with a lot of Hawaiian Punch.

'I'm afraid of spilling something on my dress,' she offered by way of explaining her refusal.

He grinned and took another swig before putting the flask back in his pocket.

GL♥SS

'You like working at *Gloss*?' he asked.

'Very much,' she said.

'Let me know if anyone gives you a hard time,' he said. 'I'll get my father to fire them.'

For one fleeting moment she considered mentioning Mr Simpson. But she doubted that Ricky had that kind of influence with his father. Still, it was kind of cute that he'd offered . . .

It was a short ride to the theatre. 'Radio City Music Hall,' the driver said as they pulled up in front of it.

His announcement was totally unnecessary. The words were emblazoned in lights, not just across the entrance but vertically on both sides. On the strip of pavement leading to the doors, velvet ropes held back a crowd of onlookers and men holding television cameras. It took Sherry an enormous amount of self-restraint to keep from gasping.

'Why are all those people watching?' she asked Ricky.

'They're waiting for the stars to arrive,' he told her.

Of course! The actors, the actresses, the director – all the important people would be coming tonight. She couldn't remember exactly who had been featured in *Beach Blanket Kisses*, but that made no difference. This was unbelievable – she, Sherry Ann Forrester of North Georgia, would be sitting in a theatre with real movie stars. She almost wished she'd carried a pad and pen to take notes. Somehow she'd have to commit every second of this evening to memory.

Their limo inched forward, and now it was their turn. Ricky took another quick swig from his flask, and stuck it back in his pocket just as the guard opened their door. But she needn't have worried about his public behaviour – he got out of the car first, and extended his hand to help her out. Then he took her arm, walked her down the red carpet, and took out the tickets to give to the man who stood beside the entrance.

Ricky nodded. 'It's the biggest theatre in the world,' he told her.

And it wasn't just big, it was *grand*. As the usher led them in, she saw magnificent winding staircases on each side, leading up to the balconies. Sweeping arches formed the walls and the ceiling, and in front of the stage there was a shimmering golden curtain.

They were shown to very good seats – actually she couldn't imagine there was a bad seat in the place, since there were no columns to block the view. She recognized the distinct chords of an organ, but it was nothing like the one in her church back home. This sound was incredible, filling the gigantic space with melody.

'This is amazing,' she said to Ricky.

Ricky gave a nonchalant shrug. 'It's New York. Just stick with me, baby, and you'll see only the best.'

She glanced at him uncertainly. Was he just fooling

GL♥SS

around? Surely he didn't think this was the beginning of something between them.

Just then a murmur went up from the seats as the celebrities began to arrive. She caught a glimpse of the familiar figures as they passed their aisle. And then it was show time.

The golden curtain rose as the organ began playing a jazzier tune and about two dozen beautiful girls dressed in silver leotards danced out from the wings.

'Those are the Rockettes,' Ricky told her. After a moment he added, 'I've dated a couple of them.'

And he was telling her this – why? To impress her? She decided it wasn't necessary to reply; a smile and quick nod were enough to acknowledge his comment. Then she turned back to watch the show.

Now *this* was impressive. The girls danced in absolute unison, performing high kicks to exactly the same level, moving together as if they were attached to each other. She'd been told that New York audiences were blasé, that they weren't easy to impress, but this audience responded just like she did, with enthusiastic clapping and cheers.

Then it was time for the movie. She'd seen it the first time on a small screen that had been set up in a conference room at *Gloss*, with a noisy projector. Now, watching it on a huge screen with a fantastic sound system, she could appreciate it a lot more. It was still a corny story, and very predictable, but it was cute and lively, and a person could get caught up in the romance.

Throughout the film, out of the corner of her eye, she saw Ricky taking surreptitious gulps from his flask, and she wondered what kind of effect the alcohol would have on him. At least she didn't have to worry about him driving later. Even if he hadn't shown up with a chauffeur, she'd followed the hard-and-fast rule her parents had set forth when she started dating boys who could drive. She always carried enough money for a taxi.

A little more than halfway through the film, she felt Ricky's hand on her knee. It wasn't that big a deal, she supposed, since her dress covered her legs, but she wasn't about to let him get any ideas. Gently but firmly, she removed the hand.

He didn't resist – but now she couldn't allow herself to get lost in the film. She kept wondering if he'd try it again. But he made no more attempts, and finally the movie was finished. The stars and the director made appearances on the stage, two of the stars sang a duet from the film, and another one made a little speech. The show ended with an invitation from the director to the audience to join them in the grand foyer for a champagne reception.

'These things are deadly,' Ricky told her. 'I've got better plans for us.' She could smell the whisky on his breath, and his words were a little slurred.

She wouldn't have minded a glass of champagne – something she'd only had at weddings. And it would have been neat to get a closer look at some of the stars. But she didn't want to make a fuss, and she *was* hungry. Surely they'd get something to eat before hitting the nightclubs or whatever else he had in mind.

Back in the limousine, he said something to the driver that she couldn't hear and then the glass window went back up.

'Where are we going?' she asked brightly. 'Shall we have some dinner?'

'I thought we'd take a little ride first,' he mumbled, edging closer to her. And then he lunged.

It happened so fast she froze. He was practically on top of her, his mouth pressed against hers, and his hands were on her shoulders, pushing her down on to the seat. She was practically flat on her back before she could react.

With all the force she could muster, she pushed him away. 'Stop it!' she yelled. 'Get off me!'

Fortunately he was too drunk to put up much resistance. 'Hey, come on, baby,' he slurred.

'I am not your baby! I'm practically engaged, for crying out loud!'

He looked at her through glazed eyes. 'Then what are you doing out on a date with me?'

'This isn't a date,' she hissed. 'You're my escort, that's all.'

'Same difference,' he muttered.

'Not to me!'

His brow furrowed, as if he couldn't quite make out what she was saying. Then he shrugged, leaned back and closed his eyes.

Within seconds he started to snore. And suddenly she felt the urge to cry. Oh, how she missed her Johnny . . .

She waited another minute, and then she tapped on the glass. The window came down.

'Yes, miss?'

'Could you take me back to the Cavendish Residence for Women, please?'

'Certainly, miss.'

The driver didn't sound surprised. She even thought she could detect a hint of sympathy in his voice. This probably wasn't the first time he'd had a request like that from one of Ricky's companions.

He was still asleep when the limo arrived at the residence, which was just as well. She wouldn't have to worry about him throwing up on her borrowed dress.

And as the chauffeur opened the door, she tried to look on the bright side. At least she hadn't had to spend her taxi money.♥

Chapter Eight

Allison tapped her foot impatiently as she waited for the elevator, and cast an anxious glance at the clock on the wall. She didn't want to be late two days in a row. She really should get an alarm clock. Or maybe stop staying out so late.

She smiled. No, that really wasn't an option. Especially since she'd realized that a large brick, placed strategically in a back door of the residence, would keep the door open and she wouldn't have to wake anyone to let her back in after curfew.

A stocky, balding man arrived at the bank of elevators and stood close by her. He looked vaguely familiar. She gave him a tentative smile and a nod of her head.

He smiled back at her. 'You're one of the *Gloss* interns, aren't you?'

'Yes, I'm Allison.'

'Felix Duncan.'

Duncan . . . from accounts. She remembered how a secretary had warned her about him.

The elevator door opened and they both entered.

'How do you like working at *Gloss*?' he asked.

How did he manage to make a simple question sound like a come-on?

'Very much,' she replied politely, watching the lights above the door that showed the floor numbers, and wishing the car would move faster.

'We're happy to have you here,' he said. 'And speaking for myself, it's very nice having pretty young faces around.'

She kept her eyes on the numbers and said nothing.

'You staying at that ladies' hotel?'

She nodded.

'Must be kind of boring. All girls all the time.'

'It's OK,' she said.

'But I'll bet you'd like to get out occasionally and have a nice meal in a real restaurant.'

When she didn't reply, he pressed on. 'Wouldn't you enjoy that?'

'Depends on who I'm having the nice meal with,' she replied.

'Hmm, you're a little spitfire, aren't you? I like that in a girl.'

Silently she groaned. This was so wrong; she'd done nothing at all to elicit this attention. She could understand how men would hit on girls like Pamela, who had an hourglass figure and dressed to succeed with men. Allison, on the other hand, wore a triple-A-cup bra, and her outfit certainly offered nothing to attract a roving eye. Today she wore what she

GL♥SS

had adopted as her working-day uniform, ever since Caroline had taken her aside and gently told her that capri pants weren't appropriate for the office. Now Allison wore a straight black pencil skirt – which on her was totally shapeless since she had no hips to speak of – over a black leotard. A black beret was bobby-pinned to her hair, and there were black Mary Janes on her feet. It was a complete beatnik look, and not designed to appeal to middle-aged businessmen out for a good time.

On the other hand, men like Felix Duncan would probably try to make it with anything remotely female. And when you were trapped in an elevator, with someone who worked in your company, especially someone who was in an important position – then what? Finally the elevator stopped, the doors opened and she fled. Thank goodness the creep didn't work on her floor.

She said the usual 'good mornings' to everyone she passed on the way to her desk and sat down to resume the task she'd been given by the entertainment editor the day before.

She had to proofread articles for the next issue, which wasn't very exciting. Mainly she was supposed to be looking for errors in spelling, grammar and punctuation. Having always made top grades in English, this wasn't too demanding. But today she was pleased to have an assignment like this. She could get through it quickly, and then pretend she was still working while she enjoyed a little daydreaming.

Or maybe proofread later and daydream now. About Sam. He was everything she'd hoped he would be.

It had taken her long enough to find him. Friday night was a wipeout. She'd gone from cafe to club, spending practically all her money on the cover charges she had to pay just to get into some of the places. She'd heard some good music, some pretty bad comedy and a lot of poetry. But there was no sign of her folk singer.

She'd planned to spend all day Saturday in the Village, but poor Sherry was in a wretched mood after a disastrous evening with Ricky, and she was missing her boyfriend. So Allison had ended up spending the entire day with her, even joining her to hit a sale at Bloomingdale's in an effort to cheer her up. Once Sherry had recovered enough to go to a movie with Pamela that evening, Allison was free to go back to the Village, but it turned into another fruitless search.

It occurred to her then that the mysterious folk singer might not even be in the vicinity. Guys like him were probably free spirits, roaming from place to place, no real destination in mind, only stopping to play some music, sing a song. She pictured him by the side of a road, guitar in hand, with a thumb stuck out in an effort to hitch a ride to anywhere. He could be so far away by now that she'd never find him.

But she didn't give up. Somehow she knew that she and he were meant to meet up again. And the next day, Sunday, she took the subway back down to the Village.

For about an hour she strolled through the streets – Bleecker to Mercer, turning on West Third, then up MacDougal to Washington Square Park. As she entered the park, she realized she was hungry. She spotted a hot-dog vendor at the other end, and it was on her way there that she saw him.

He was standing under a tree and strumming his guitar, and for a moment she couldn't catch her breath. She took in the same wild, unkempt curly black hair, the same lean torso, the same red bandanna around his neck. The same faded blue work shirt over black jeans. The only addition was a pair of sunglasses.

There were three people standing around listening to his music. It was the same music he'd been playing in the coffee house, and once again she couldn't quite make out the words. One of them tossed a coin into the empty guitar case that lay at his feet and left. Allison moved closer, and joined the couple who were still listening. Just as she arrived, they ambled away.

He stopped singing, strummed a few more chords, and then took off the guitar. Before he could put it back in the case, Allison went into her bag, found a dollar, and quickly put it in.

He picked it up, along with the dime the other person had left.

'Thanks,' he muttered.

'No, thank *you*,' she said.

He stared at her. At least, she *thought* he was staring. With his sunglasses on, she couldn't really tell. But his head had turned in her direction.

'I really like that song,' she blurted out. 'I heard you sing it before. In a coffee house, last week.'

'Oh, right. I was trying out, for a gig.'

'Did you get it?'

He scowled. 'Nah. They went for some crummy trio singing Peter, Paul and Mary crap. Actually I'm glad I didn't get it. People who hang out there, they don't appreciate original stuff. They want to hear "Michael, Row the Boat Ashore". Bunch of yahoos.'

Allison flinched. Clearly, her personal taste in folk music needed development. 'What a shame,' she murmured.

He nodded. 'These squares, they listen to the New Christy Minstrels or the Kingston Trio, and they think they're listening to real folk music. It's all fake.'

She wished he would take off his sunglasses.

'What's your name?' she asked as he placed the guitar back in its case.

'Sam,' he said, without offering a last name.

'I'm Allison.'

There was no 'pleased to meet you' or 'nice to know

you'. He arranged the strap of the guitar case over his shoulder, and it seemed like he was about to take off. But after all she went through to find him, Allison was not going to let him get away so quickly.

'Would you like to get some coffee?'

He hesitated, and she remembered the meagre amount of money he'd collected.

'My treat,' she added.

He shrugged. 'Yeah, OK.'

They walked together across the park to the street. Allison tried desperately to think of something to say, a comment that would show him she wasn't like those jerks who couldn't appreciate his music.

'You know, people have the wrong idea about folk music,' she began. 'They think it's just old songs. But honest folk music, it's *about* something. Feelings, and struggles, and conflicts. Philosophy. Real folk music, it makes statements. And it asks real questions.'

'Yeah? Like what?'

Surely he knew. He was just testing her.

'Well, questions like, like, what's it all about? How do people connect to each other? What does life mean? The struggles of the common man, compassion, equality . . .' She trailed off, noticing that he had taken off the sunglasses and was actually looking at her. His eyes were definitely brown, and his lashes were spectacularly long.

'I dig Bob Dylan,' he said.

'Oh, me too!' she cried out. 'In fact, you remind me a little of him.'

He didn't smile, but she could tell he was pleased. 'What did you like about my song?'

'Well, the tune . . . and I could tell the words meant a lot to you, it was all over your face. It was pretty intense.'

'You liked the lyrics?'

She hesitated. Here was where she could be caught out. 'I couldn't understand all of them,' she admitted. Then quickly she added, 'Of course, I don't understand all of Bob Dylan's lyrics either.'

He smiled proudly. 'We try not to make the words too distinct. So people have to listen harder.'

'Oh! That makes sense. Look, here's a cafe with tables outside. Is this OK?'

He shrugged and took a seat. A girl came by and dropped two menus on the table. He picked his up, then threw it down with a look of disgust.

'These prices . . .'

'It's my treat,' Allison said again.

'That's not the point. It's this rotten capitalist society, it stinks. All anyone cares about is money. That's all they talk about – how much something costs, what they can afford, how they can make more money so they can buy it. Men in suits, running in circles, chasing the almighty buck. It's a rotten world, Allison.'

He remembered her name! She nodded fervently. 'I have a friend who shoplifts sometimes. And that doesn't shock me at all. Just because she doesn't have money, why shouldn't she have a lipstick?'

He raised his bushy eyebrows. 'A lipstick?'

She flushed. That had to sound pretty stupid. 'Well, it's just an example,' she murmured. What would he think if she told him she worked for a fashion magazine?

The girl came back by their table, and Allison ordered two coffees.

'Anything to eat?' she asked.

She looked at Sam. He shrugged again, but she saw him glance at the table next to theirs, where a couple were sharing a slice of cheesecake.

'And two pieces of cheesecake,' she added.

After the waitress left, she asked, 'Do you live around here?'

'I've got some friends who're squatting in an abandoned apartment. I'm crashing on their couch for a couple of days.'

'And then where will you go?'

'Dunno. Even if I could afford an apartment, I wouldn't give money to some fat-cat landlord.' He shook his head sadly. 'Artists don't stand a chance in this rotten world, Allison.'

She couldn't resist. She reached across the table and laid a gentle hand on his arm. 'I know.'

'I don't ask for much,' Sam said. 'Just freedom. You dig?'

'Yes,' Allison breathed. 'Yes, I dig.' I dig what you say, she said silently. And I dig what you do, and I dig how you look, and I dig . . .

'Allison? Allison!'

She blinked. The entertainment editor was standing by her desk.

'Oh, I'm sorry, Mr Connelly, I didn't hear you. I was concentrating on . . . on –' she looked at the paper on her desk – 'this article about new girl singers.'

'Come in my office for a minute. I want to talk to you about something.'

Mr Connelly was smiling as he offered her a seat across from his desk.

'How would you like to try your hand at an interview?'

'I'd love to do an interview!' she replied promptly. 'Who with?'

'Well, what would you say to . . . the one and only Bobby Dale?' He leaned back in his seat and beamed, as if he'd just offered her a fantastic gift.

'Bobby Dale,' she repeated. The name was vaguely familiar.

Mr Connelly picked up an album. 'As I'm sure you know, this is coming out next month, so his people are making him available.'

The album cover showed a typically boyish, clean-

GLØSS

cut young singer who looked like a cross between Bobby Rydell and Bobby Vee. Why were all these young singers named Bobby? she wondered. And then she recalled a huge hit a few months ago, something called 'You're My Girl'. She was pretty sure Bobby Dale sang that one.

Mr Connelly was watching her expectantly.

She smiled. 'Great!' she said, trying to sound appropriately enthusiastic.

'I'll let you know when we've got a date set up,' the editor continued. 'Meanwhile, you might want to go to the library and get some background on him.'

'OK,' she said, and got up. But when she reached the door she turned back to him. 'Mr Connelly . . . have you ever thought about an article on the new folk-music scene? You know – Bob Dylan, Joan Baez . . . or maybe an interview with some young up-and-coming folk singer.'

He frowned and shook his head. 'That's more for college kids. I don't think our readers are interested in folk music.'

'But . . .'

His phone rang, and he snatched it up. 'Peter Connelly. Hi, Ralph, what's up? Any news on the Frankie Avalon flick?'

He waved his hand at Allison, dismissing her.

Back at her desk, she considered her new assignment. Pamela ambled over. It was lucky for her that Felix

Duncan didn't work on their floor. Her orange knit dress was so snug that Allison could make out the lines of her underwear, and the thin belt drawn tightly around her waist exaggerated her ample bust and hips.

'What are you up to?' Pamela asked.

'Mr Connelly wants me to conduct an interview with Bobby Dale.'

Pamela eyes were the size of saucers. 'Bobby Dale!' she practically shrieked. 'You're going to meet Bobby Dale?'

'Shh,' Allison hissed.

Fortunately, at that moment the beauty editor stuck her head out of her office. 'Pamela!'

'Coming,' Pamela called back. Shooting one last glare of envy in Allison's direction, she took off.

Allison leaned back in her seat, bemused by Pamela's reaction. As far as she was concerned, Bobby Dale was just another teen heart-throb, one of a hundred Bobby-boys with squeaky voices who sang stupid mindless love songs and made stupid mindless girls scream. Guys who had too much publicity already.

And then there were guys like Sam, talented guys, who wrote their own meaningful songs about real life, and they didn't get any attention at all. It wasn't fair.

They'd ended up spending all of Sunday together in the Village. That evening they went back to Washington Square Park, where he played some more, and actually collected two dollars' worth of change.

Even so, Allison insisted on buying them a couple of sandwiches, and told Sam to save his money for the next day's lunch. On Monday people would be at work or at school, and he might not get any listeners at all. She could tell he appreciated her concern.

They arranged to meet up on Monday evening. Allison picked up a pizza and brought it to the apartment where he was currently crashing. It was pretty nasty – not very clean – but no one else was around, and there was a jug of cheap red wine in the refrigerator. They talked more then, and she learned a little more about him. He came from some wretched middle-class town on Long Island, from a typically bourgeois family who couldn't understand him at all. He'd escaped while he was still in high school, and he'd been hanging out in the Village for almost two years now.

Later they headed over to another coffee house, where a guy he knew was performing and they could get in without paying the cover charge. The friend called Sam up to the front of the room to play something. Sam performed a song she hadn't heard before, and this time she caught more of the lyrics. The song was about seasons, and how there were seasons for everything – a time to be born, a time to die, a time to laugh, a time to weep. It was absolutely beautiful. There wasn't much of an audience – only a dozen people – but after he sang they clapped, and she was bursting with pride when he came back to their table.

The idea, when it came, didn't burst fully formed in her head. As she went back to proofreading, it established itself as a tiny seed in the back of her mind. And as she marked punctuation errors with a red pencil, the idea grew slowly, and took on a shape and form without any effort at all. By the time she finished correcting the article on new girl singers, she knew what she was going to do.

As requested, Allison would meet with Bobby Dale, interview him and write it up. And on her own time, outside of *Gloss* hours, she would interview Sam. She'd find out what made him tick, what had drawn him to folk music. She'd learn about his inspirations, his ambitions, how he created his music.

She would write a decent article about Bobby Dale. But she'd write a brilliant article about Sam. There would only be enough space in the magazine for one interview. And if Mr Connelly had any brains at all, he would make the right choice. Teen readers would become aware that there were options in entertainment.

Sam was going to get the recognition he deserved. Allison was going to make it happen. And together they would change the world. Or at least, one boring teen magazine.♥

Chapter Nine

29 June, 1962

Summer school wasn't all that bad. For the first time in what seemed like forever, Donna had an English teacher whom she actually liked.

Miss Robertson was young, fresh out of university, and this was her first real job. She told Donna this on the third day of summer school, when the teacher asked her to stay after class.

Donna was pretty sure she knew why she'd been asked to stay. The first assignment, a book report, had been turned in the day before. They'd been told to write about a favourite book and it had been a problem for her.

Miss Robertson pulled a chair up next to her desk and indicated that Donna should sit there. On the desk lay her book report, covered in red pencil marks.

'I have some problems with this, Donna,' she said. Her voice was so gentle, Donna looked up. The teacher's eyes were kind.

'I don't read very well,' Donna said.

Miss Robertson nodded. She took a book from her desk and opened it. 'Could you read aloud for me, please? Just the first paragraph.'

Donna tried. Less than a minute later, the teacher stopped her.

'That's enough, Donna. I'm wondering if you might have dyslexia.'

Donna stared at her in alarm. 'Is that a disease?'

'No, it's a learning disability, where your brain doesn't recognize certain symbols. Now don't worry – it's not brain damage, and it's got nothing to do with intelligence, it's just a little . . . well, I'm not exactly sure what it is. A disorder, I guess.' She smiled.

'Is there anything I can do about it? Like, take a pill or something?'

'I think there are exercises you can do to improve your reading skills. I'm not qualified to diagnose this or treat you for it, but there are specialists who know how to deal with it. I'll find someone in the area who can test you.'

'How much would this cost?' she asked Miss Robertson.

'I don't know.'

More than she could afford, Donna thought. She was very sure of that.

A couple of days later, the teacher did give her some names. Donna called one and asked about fees. After that, she didn't even bother to call the others.

In the Peake household, welfare cheques barely covered necessities. But it had lifted her spirits, knowing her problem had a name. It was a comfort to

GL♥SS

realize she wasn't just plain stupid. Maybe some day, when she was out of school and working, she could do something about it.

Life in general had been better lately. Her mother was actually sober most of the time. She wanted to get back into the social scene, maybe meet a new man, and she decided she needed to go on a diet. Personally, Donna didn't think Shirley Peake was fat, but her efforts to lose weight meant that she had cut back on her drinking. And Donna could feel a lot more comfortable leaving the kids with her when she went out in the evening with Ron.

It had been over a month since that first date, and they were now going out three or four times a week. She couldn't say she was madly in love or anything like that, but Ron had a car and a job, and he didn't mind spending some of his wages on her. He picked her up when he said he would, and sometimes he would bring the little ones candy. He wasn't much of a talker, and she still didn't know much about him, just that he dropped out of high school and left a hard-scrabble life on a farm when he was sixteen. He'd come to town and took a job at one of the factories.

It didn't last long, and now he bounced from job to job. He seemed to get bored easily.

'Have you ever thought of becoming a car mechanic?' Donna had asked him once. 'I've seen ads for a training programme at a technology school downtown. You could become a qualified mechanic in less than a year.'

He hadn't appreciated the suggestion. 'Why would I do that?'

'Well, you like cars, and you could develop a real skill for repairing them. Think about what you could do with that. You might end up owning your own garage. Wouldn't you rather fix cars than pump gas?'

'Nothing wrong with pumping gas,' he'd retorted.

'Of course not, but—'

He cut her off. 'Don't bug me.'

Ron wasn't ambitious; she learned that early on. And his moods could be troublesome. He got angry easily – not at her, fortunately, but at anyone who bothered him, or even just looked at him the wrong way. But when he was feeling good, he was easy to be with, and she really had nothing to complain about.

Their dates were pretty predictable. He'd pick her up after the kids were in bed. Sometimes they just went back to the apartment he shared with a couple of other guys, and they'd watch a ball game with his roommates and their girlfriends. Other times they'd go to a particular hangout, where he'd play pool and she'd sit at the bar and watch. That wasn't much fun, especially since his pool-hall friends were low-life types, and fights sometimes broke out. But whenever that happened, he'd get her out of there, which pleased her. He never said, 'I love you,' but if he wanted to protect her, he must have some feelings for her.

Every now and then they went to the drive-in theatre. It didn't matter what was playing – all he wanted to do was climb in the back seat with her and make out. She liked the hugging and the kissing and the feeling of his body close to hers. But it usually got ugly in the end. He always wanted to take it further, and she always resisted.

He never said, 'I love you,' but . . .

'Stop,' she'd say, when he fumbled with the clasp on her brassiere, or slid his hand under her skirt.

'Come on, baby,' he'd urge.

'No!'

'Why not?'

'I'm not ready for this,' she'd tell him.

'When are you going to be ready?'

'I don't know.'

'I'm not going to wait forever,' he'd warn her.

But he kept coming around, and she was grateful for that. It was better than being alone.

Arriving home from summer school one afternoon, she found her mother in particularly good spirits.

'Look at this!' Shirley Peake called out when Donna entered the trailer. She twirled around, showing off the full skirt of a dress Donna had never seen before.

'It's a size eight,' the woman crowed. 'The last time I

bought a new dress, it was a twelve. Look!' She showed Donna the tag that still hung from a sleeve.

The tag displayed the price as well as the size, and Donna was shocked. 'Where did you get the money for this?' she asked.

'None of your beeswax,' her mother replied pertly.

Maybe she'd saved the money she used to spend on whisky and beer, Donna thought. Still, it wasn't right for her to blow it on a new dress. Kathy and Billy were growing, they needed things. Kathy had been complaining that her shoes hurt.

'I'm going to that new club on the highway tonight,' her mother announced. 'I've heard it's a real singles scene.'

'Ma! I told you, Ron and I are going out tonight. You said you'd stay home with the kids.'

Shirley's expression changed. She looked almost furtive.

'Don't worry about it,' she said, before disappearing into the bathroom. 'It's all taken care of.'

Wondering what her mother meant by that, Donna heard the sound of a car pulling up outside. She looked through the window. 'Ma? You expecting someone?'

There was no response. The car door opened, and a man got out. Donna froze. She hadn't seen him in two years, but her father hadn't changed that much.

She opened the door.

GL♥SS

'Donna, is that really you?' he asked. 'You've grown.'

She stared at him. 'What do you want?'

Her mother appeared behind her and pushed her aside. 'Come on in, Martin.'

'What's he doing here?' Donna asked.

Shirley cocked her head towards her ex-husband. 'He's taking the kids.'

'What?'

'You didn't tell her?' Martin asked Shirley.

Her mother shrugged. 'I thought it would be easier this way. Like pulling a Band-Aid off fast.'

Donna's head was spinning. 'Would somebody *please* tell me what's going on?'

Martin at least had the courtesy to look abashed. 'She should have told you,' he muttered.

'Told me what?' Donna practically shrieked.

Finally the story came out. It seemed Martin had settled down and remarried. The woman wanted children but hadn't been able to conceive. So Martin had decided to take his own back. And Shirley had agreed.

'It's better this way,' she declared. 'They've got a house and a backyard.'

'And a dog,' Martin added.

'And I'll be able to have a social life,' Shirley added happily.

Donna stared at her in disbelief. 'You're giving up

your children so you can have a *social life*? What kind of a mother are you?'

'Oh, don't be so dramatic,' Shirley snapped. 'They'll come back and visit.'

'We're just an hour away,' Martin said. 'You can visit whenever you like, Donna.' He shifted his weight from one leg to the other, and looked just beyond his eldest daughter. 'You know, Donna, I'd like to have you living with us too, but Arlene, that's my wife, she's not used to being around teenagers, and—'

'I have no desire to live with you and your new wife,' Donna declared coldly.

'And of course I'll continue to send your mother money for you,' Martin continued.

Suddenly Donna felt dizzy. She turned to Shirley. 'He sends you money?' she asked in a whisper.

Her mother's lips were pressed together tightly. 'Not that much.'

Martin went pale. 'What have you been doing with it?' he demanded.

Shirley started yelling at him. Donna backed away and went into the bedroom.

'Kids . . .'

Kathy looked at her happily. 'We're going on a trip with our daddy!'

So at least *they'd* been forewarned.

The next few minutes were like watching a movie – Donna didn't feel like she was there at all. Maybe

GL♥SS

she was in shock. But somehow she managed to help Kathy and Billy gather their things – their clothes and their pitiful toys – and place them in large bags. Then they were all outside, and Martin was putting them into the back seat of his sedan.

Donna kissed and hugged the little ones, but she tried not to make a big deal about it so as not to upset them. They were so excited about being in this nice car that they didn't seem at all aware of what was really happening.

Martin handed Donna a small card. 'This is my phone number. You call me if you need anything, OK?'

Donna shoved the card in her pocket and didn't even bother to nod.

Shirley went back in the trailer. Donna just stood there, and watched the car disappear down the road.

What time was it? she wondered. Hopefully Ron would be coming for her soon. She needed him. She needed to be held. And tonight she wouldn't care where it led.♥

Chapter Ten

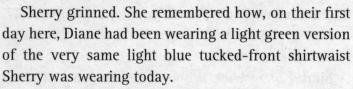

'**S**herry?'
Sherry looked up from her desk.

'Hi, Diane.'

'I *love* your dress!'

Sherry grinned. She remembered how, on their first day here, Diane had been wearing a light green version of the very same light blue tucked-front shirtwaist Sherry was wearing today.

'Great minds think alike,' Sherry quipped. 'At least, great *Gloss* minds.'

Diane lowered her voice. 'Too bad we can't say that about all the girls here,' she said pointedly.

Sherry knew who she was talking about. She hadn't missed the occasional puzzled looks Diane and Linda had cast in her direction when they saw Sherry sitting with Pamela and Allison in the Cavendish dining hall.

She shrugged, and quipped again. 'To each her own, I guess.'

'Yeah, I guess. Oh, I just remembered, I've been wanting to ask you something. Do you play bridge?'

Card games were very popular back home, and

Sherry nodded. 'I'm better at canasta, but I know bridge rules.'

'We've been playing after dinner at the Cavendish,' Diane told her. 'Me and Linda, Ellen and Vicky. But now Vicky's going out with some college boy she met, so we need a fourth. Want to join?'

It wasn't like she had anything more exciting to do with her evenings. 'Sure, glad to.'

'Great, see you later,' Diane said. She started away and then turned back. 'Ooh, where's my brain today? Caroline just told me to fetch you.'

Sherry jumped up, resisting the urge to scold her for not putting a summons from Caroline before an invitation to play bridge.

She hurried to the editor's office, where she was on the phone. Caroline beckoned for her to come in, and pointed to the chair across from her desk.

The editor's voice rose as she argued with whoever was on the other end of the line.

'No, no, no! Pink won't work at all, that's not what I asked for! This is for the September issue, I need autumn colours! What you've sent me is absolutely worthless!'

Sherry was very glad *she* wasn't the recipient of that anger. Personally she thought Caroline's tone was awfully aggressive. Mama always said a girl could catch more flies with honey than vinegar, and Sherry had always found that wheedling worked better than yelling.

She supposed a woman had to give up some of her feminine wiles to do an important job like this. Maybe that was why Caroline had never married. It wouldn't be easy for a man to have a wife who was accustomed to being a boss.

'Rust, gold, maybe a warm brown . . . yes . . . OK, send down some swatches. *Now!*'

Finally she hung up. 'Sorry about that, Sherry. Now, I wanted to get your opinion about something.'

'*My* opinion?'

Caroline ignored the surprise in her voice. 'We've never put any effort into covering the big fashion shows before. The kind of clothes they present aren't meant for our readers, and they couldn't afford them in any case.' She leaned forward, and there was a sparkle in her eyes. '*But* – why shouldn't we take a good look at what the designers are showing, the colours, the shapes, and then consider the trends in terms of how they *could* relate to our readers? So for example, if the major designers are showing empire waists, or shorter skirts, or lots of prints—'

'Then we'd look for those trends in the junior collections,' Sherry finished. 'And suggest ways in which teen girls could adapt the look.' Then she reddened. 'Sorry, I didn't mean to interrupt you.'

'No, no, don't apologize! I knew you were the girl to ask.'

There was a light rap on the door. One of the

editorial assistants stood there, with a perturbed look on her face.

'What's wrong?' Caroline asked.

'I just had a request from David for some items from the samples closet. And half of them are missing – a silk scarf, two charm bracelets, a cashmere sweater . . .'

'Did you check to see if they've been borrowed?' Caroline asked.

'Of course. But there's no record of anyone taking them.'

Caroline frowned. 'That's the third time this month.' She turned to Sherry. 'That's all for now. We'll talk more later.' She rose and left the office with the assistant.

Allison joined Sherry back at her desk.

'What was that all about?'

'Caroline thinks *Gloss* should start attending the big New York fashion shows. Ooh, maybe she'll let some of us go.'

Allison made a face. 'Do you know what some of those designer dresses cost? Thousands of dollars! And there are people right here in this city who can't even afford a place to live.'

'I still think it would be fun to go to a real show,' Sherry said mildly.

Allison brushed that aside. 'Anyway, that's not what I'm talking about. Caroline looked furious.'

'Oh, right. Some things are missing from the samples closet.'

'Does she think someone stole them?'

'I don't know.' And then, as if they could read each other's minds, their eyes turned in the direction of Pamela.

Sherry drew in her breath. 'You don't think . . .'

Allison bit her lip. 'Well, she's always talking about how she needs clothes.' Then she shook her head. 'No, I share a closet with her. I'd notice if there was a bunch of new stuff in there.'

'Unless she's hidden it all somewhere,' Sherry murmured. Then she too shook her head. 'No, that's crazy. Pamela wouldn't do that. OK, maybe she swipes an occasional lipstick, but she's not really a thief . . .' Her voice trailed off uncertainly.

'Shh,' Allison said. 'Here she comes.'

Pamela bounced over to them. 'I picked up the mail this morning in the residence lobby, and you guys have letters.' She handed each of them an envelope and moved on.

Allison looked at the return address on hers. 'It's from my mother. She probably wants to know if I'm wearing clean underwear.' She stuffed the envelope in her pocket and went back to her desk.

Sherry had a better reaction to *her* mail. There was no return address on it, but it was postmarked Washington DC. It was about time she heard from

GL♥SS

Johnny. She'd sent him a second letter the day after the movie premiere, but she'd heard nothing back.

Looking around, she didn't see Caroline or anyone else watching her, so she decided she'd take a few personal moments right then instead of waiting for the coffee break. She tore open the envelope.

Dear Sherry Ann, How are you? I'm fine. I hope you're having a good time in New York. How's the weather? Here in Washington we're having a lot of rain.

She smiled. Not very original, or personal, but about what she would expect to get from him. Writing wasn't something Johnny enjoyed. It was pure agony for him after Christmas or his birthday, writing thank-you notes to relatives.

But once the proper introductory remarks were finished, the letter actually did become personal. *Very* personal. So personal, so unexpected, so . . . so unbelievable, that she had to read it again. But not here. She needed to be alone.

Moving stiffly, she put the letter in her handbag, left the office and went into the ladies' restroom. Thank heavens, it was empty.

She unfolded the letter again, and skipped over the first paragraph.

I have to tell you something. This is really hard. The thing is, I've met someone. A girl who works in my building. I'm in love with her.

I'm really, really sorry, Sherry. I feel terrible. I know you must hate me. But I guess these things happen.

Anyway, I had to tell you. So now you know you're free to date guys in New York.

It was signed, *Your friend, Johnny.*

Her legs felt oddly weak. She sank down on one of the little stools at the counter that faced the mirror. She read the letter again. And again.

Your friend, Johnny.

Slowly it began to sink in. Her friend. The friend she'd planned to marry, raise a family with, spend the rest of her life with. The friend who was the centre of her universe.

She sat there, very, very still. Then she looked in the mirror. Had all the colour drained from her face, or did she just imagine it had? All her plans, her vision of her life-to-be. Her hopes, her dreams, everything she'd assumed, taken for granted . . . gone, all gone. Just like that.

Funny . . . she would have thought she'd be trembling, shaking. She touched her face, but there were no tears. Her eyes were dry too. Instead she felt very still, as if her body was an empty shell. No bones, no blood, no feelings.

But there must have been feelings. She just couldn't identify them because she'd never had them before.

The door to the restroom opened, and she was dimly aware of Linda walking in. She strode into one of the cubicles without speaking. But when she came out she must have caught something in Sherry's expression that made her pause.

'Are you OK?'

Sherry raised her eyes. Linda sat down on the stool next to her. Her eyes rested for a second on the letter lying on the counter.

'Bad news?'

Sherry didn't trust herself to speak. She touched the letter, and gave it a slight push in Linda's direction. Linda picked it up and read.

'Oh no. Oh, Sherry, I'm so sorry!' She leaned forward and wrapped Sherry in a tight hug.

Sherry was uncomfortable in the embrace, but she made no attempt to extract herself. Finally Linda released her and examined her face.

'You're not even crying! You poor thing, you must be in shock!'

Sherry wasn't sure what shock felt like, but she nodded.

There was a moment of silence, and then Linda asked, 'What are you going to do?'

'Mr Simpson gave me a stack of letters to file. That will keep me busy.'

'No, I mean, about your *life*! You can't go that girls' college now. What's it called?'

'Agnes Scott.' Sherry looked at her blankly. 'Why not?'

'Well, it was different before, when you had a boyfriend. How are you going to meet anyone at Agnes Scott? You need a co-ed school, with fraternities and sororities and a social life. Think about your future, Sherry!'

She could have been speaking a foreign language – her words weren't even registering. But one word did stick out, and it kept running through Sherry's head as she left the restroom and headed back to her desk. Her future. What kind of future would she have without Johnny?

Back in the bullpen, Pamela had noticed her absence. 'You sick or something?'

'No.'

But Pamela clearly wanted an explanation. 'That letter, it was from Johnny. He broke up with me.'

'Oh. Sorry about that.'

Sherry sat down at her desk and pretended to be going through the letters she was supposed to file.

'Did he break your heart?' Pamela asked.

Sherry looked up. 'Of course!'

'It's just that, well, you don't talk about him much. Were you really in love with him?'

Sherry stared at her. 'How can you ask that? He was my boyfriend!'

Allison joined them. 'What's going on?'

Pamela gave her the news. Allison, at least, had the courtesy to look more concerned.

GL♥SS

'Oh, Sherry, that's awful. He was the man of your dreams, wasn't he?'

Now Sherry stared at *her*. Had she ever thought of Johnny in those terms? She must have!

Mr Simpson approached and noticed the untouched correspondence still sitting on Sherry's desk. 'What's going on here? Don't you girls have work to do?'

Pamela responded. 'Sherry has a problem. It's one of those female things.'

Mr Simpson beat a hasty retreat, and Sherry couldn't help smiling. 'Pamela, you're terrible.'

Pamela grinned. 'It always works when you're trying to get rid of a guy.'

'He was the man of your dreams, wasn't he?'

They both went back to their own duties, and Sherry attacked the stack of letters. She was glad to have work that didn't require much concentration. On the other hand, it didn't provide much of a distraction from her own thoughts.

It didn't help when Ellen stopped by her desk, a sorrowful expression on her sweet face. 'Linda told me what happened. I'm so sorry for you.'

Sherry gave her a half-smile and a soft 'thank you'.

'The thing is,' Ellen went on, 'you have to jump right back in the saddle. You know what I mean?'

She did, but she wasn't in the mood to hear more

about that. So she simply nodded, and went back to the papers on her desk. That didn't deter Ellen.

'What about Ricky Hartnell? Didn't you go out with him?'

She wasn't about to go into that story with an intern she barely knew. 'It didn't work out,' she said simply.

'Give him another chance! I think he's working in the accounting department now. Let's see if we can find an excuse for you to go up there.'

'Not now,' Sherry said quickly. 'I really have to get these letters filed for Mr Simpson.'

Ellen took the hint and moved on. Sherry picked up the now alphabetized pile of letters, and headed to the filing cabinets. She passed Caroline on the way, and the editor stopped her.

'I've already wangled two fashion-show invitations for *Gloss*!' she announced, her eyes sparkling. 'And I've left messages with three other major designers.'

'That's great!' Sherry said, trying to match the enthusiasm in Caroline's voice. She watched as the editor headed back to her office, and again she wondered about her. The woman certainly got excited about her job, she thought. But what was her life like after working hours? Did she go home to a tiny apartment, open a can of soup and heat it up over a hotplate? And then watch television, alone? Or maybe play a game of solitaire. She thought about one of her aunts, her father's oldest sister, a spinster. She spent her evenings with enormous jigsaw puzzles. They gave her a new one every year for a gift when she came for Christmas dinner. Poor Aunt Agnes, they called her.

'Sherry?'

She hadn't even heard Michael and his mail cart approach. 'Oh, hi. How are you?'

'OK.' He pushed a lock of shiny black hair out of his eyes. 'I was just wondering – you want to take a coffee break?'

'Now?'

'Yeah, if you can leave your desk.'

'OK. Sure.' Suddenly she didn't care about Mr Simpson's filing.

They found an empty table in the cafeteria, where they could sit across from each other with their coffees.

'How's your internship coming along?' he asked.

'Good,' she replied automatically. 'How's the mailroom?'

'Boring.'

'Well, at least that gives you time to think about your novel.'

'Actually I've put the novel aside, because I had this idea for a short story.'

'Really? About what?'

He hesitated. Then he took a long sip of his coffee, as if it might give him courage. 'Would you like to read it?'

'Sure.'

He reached into the deep pocket of his work jacket and brought out some crumpled papers. 'I hope you can read my handwriting.'

She could see right away it wouldn't be easy. But days of typing up Mr Simpson's handwritten letters had given her some practice in deciphering scribbles.

'I think I can manage. Would you like me to type it up for you while I'm reading it?'

His eyebrows shot up. 'You'd do that?'

She nodded. He smiled. Was that a sparkle in those intense eyes? And those pouty Elvis lips looked even better turned up like that. At least now she wouldn't have to feel guilty for feeling that little shiver travel up her spine.

Maybe jumping back in the saddle wouldn't be that hard after all.♥

Chapter Eleven

'I was thinking,' Pamela said during lunch on Friday. 'I'll bet we wouldn't need dates to go someplace like the Peppermint Lounge. There's probably a cover charge, but maybe we could scrape up the money. And then we'd meet guys who'd buy us drinks.'

Neither Allison nor Sherry looked particularly intrigued by the notion, but Pamela persisted.

'What about tonight?'

Sherry shook her head. 'Michael is taking me to hear an author read from his work at the uptown Y.'

'I'm meeting Sam down in the village,' Allison said. 'Pam, why don't you come with me? Sam has plenty of friends – maybe you'll meet someone interesting.'

Pamela sincerely doubted that any friends of a vagabond folk singer would appeal to her. It had been, what, almost two weeks since she'd arrived in New York? And she had yet to encounter anyone who resembled the men of her fantasies. Her one date, with that so-called doctor, had been a disaster.

First off, it turned out he was only an intern at the hospital. Yes, he had a medical degree, but he wasn't making any real money yet. He didn't even have his own apartment; he lived in a residence like the Cavendish, only for hospital employees. Their double date had taken place at a boring old pizza parlour. No martinis or champagne, just beer and soft drinks.

As for the conversation, all the others could talk about was the hospital, and their patients, and the surgeries they'd watched. It was all blood and bones and guts – *not* her idea of sophisticated New York chit-chat.

She'd been so bored she invented a headache and asked to go home. Then she had to suffer his questions – where precisely was the headache? Was it a dull pain or a stabbing pain? Did she get these headaches frequently? It got to the point where she actually developed a real pain in her head.

'Pamela?'

She looked up to see Darlene, assistant beauty editor, at her desk and holding a brown envelope.

'Could you take these contact sheets upstairs to David Barnes on the thirty-first? And tell him we've ticked off the photos we want to see.'

David Barnes . . . she remembered him. The photographer who looked like Rock Hudson. She hadn't seen him since their welcome dinner, and she brightened at the opportunity.

Someone on the thirty-first floor told her that David Barnes was in the darkroom, and to wait in the reception area. She passed the time looking at the large photos of *Gloss* cover girls that were framed and hanging on a wall. There were blondes, brunettes and redheads, and they were all dressed differently, but to Pamela they all looked pretty much the same. Boring.

She saw the red light over the darkroom door go off, and a second later David Barnes came out.

'Mr Barnes,' she called.

'Yes?'

'I'm Pamela, an intern at *Gloss*.'

'Oh yes, I remember meeting you. And you can call me David.'

Encouraged, she produced one of her flirtiest smiles. 'David. That's one of my favourite names. It's so . . . masculine.'

He seemed a little taken aback. 'If you say so. Now what can I do for you, Pamela?'

Take me to dinner at Sardi's and dancing at El Morocco, she wanted to say. 'I've got some contact sheets for you, from the beauty editor.'

He took the brown envelope and glanced inside. 'Good, thanks. Oh, by the way, tell Doreen that I just had a call. Her makeover model just cancelled – she'll have to get someone else for the session.'

'OK,' said Pamela.

He started to move on down the hall.

'David?'

He stopped and turned. 'Yes?'

'I don't know this department at all. Could you show me around?'

His smile was polite, but he shook his head. 'I'm very busy right now, Pamela. Another time.'

'Or maybe we could have lunch?' she said quickly. 'You could tell me all about what goes on in that darkroom.' She cocked her head to one side and gave him a seductive smile.

Now he actually looked uncomfortable. 'Excuse me, Pamela, I have to get back to work.'

She stared after him. Never in her life had she failed to get at least a small reaction from a man after turning on the charm. She hurried into the restroom to see if she'd suddenly developed a zit or something. She looked fine, but that didn't make her feel any better.

Back downstairs, she ambled over to Doreen's office. 'I gave David the contact sheet,' she announced.

'Thank you,' Doreen and Darlene trilled in unison.

'Oh, and he said to tell you that your makeover person cancelled.'

This information elicited a chorus of shrieks.

'No, no, that's impossible!' one of them cried out. 'We have to get the shoot done today!'

'We'll never find anyone at such short notice!' the other wailed.

Pamela left them to their hysterics and went back to her own desk. There, she stared at the article she was supposed to be proofreading, not even seeing it, and wallowed in her despair. So this was going to be her summer. Days of searching for typographical errors in boring articles. Dinners in the Cavendish Residence with Allison and Sherry. Followed by evenings in front of the TV with the other residents who had nothing else to do.

'Pamela!'

Doreen was calling her back to the office.

'We've just had a fabulous idea!' Doreen announced.

'Absolutely fabulous!' Darlene echoed.

'How would *you* like to be our makeover model?' Doreen asked.

'Me?' Pamela was nonplussed. She'd seen examples of *Gloss*'s monthly makeovers in the magazine, with the 'before' and 'after' photos. They usually took some drab, childish-looking girl with a pale, clean face, limp hair and dowdy clothes. Then they put her in a modern dress, cut her hair, threw some make-up on her and in the 'after' photos, she looked . . . well, less dull.

'I can't believe we didn't think of this before,' Doreen crowed. 'After all, this is for the readers' issue. It makes perfect sense to use one of our teen interns as the model.'

Pamela didn't think this was the time to confess she'd never been a big reader of *Gloss*. Anyway, she was more concerned about what they might do to her.

'Wouldn't Donna be perfect for a makeover?'

'Who?' Darlene asked.

Pamela wasn't surprised that they didn't recognize the name. Donna had pretty much remained in the background at *Gloss*.

'Come on, Pamela, it would be fun!' Doreen declared gaily. 'And if you don't like your new look, you can always change back.'

'It's just for the one issue,' Darlene added. 'And you get to keep the cosmetics and the clothes we use.'

That could be useful, Pamela thought. She had a pretty good idea she wouldn't be crazy about the make-up *or* the clothes, but maybe she could sell them to someone at Cavendish and use the money for something else. And besides, this had to be more interesting than proofreading.

'OK,' she said. 'I'm game.'

The two editors clapped their hands in glee. Moments later, they were all exiting the elevator on the thirty-first floor. A woman escorted them into a large room where huge lights had been set up.

'This is where David will take the "before" photos,' Doreen explained.

So she would have another crack at him. And if he was taking pictures of her, he couldn't look away.

She wondered if she should try to look a little drab, to emphasize the difference in the before and after photos. 'Maybe I should go wash my face,' she suggested.

The two editors exchanged looks. 'No, you're fine just how you are,' Darlene said.

David came into the room armed with cameras in both hands. 'Hello, girls,' he said, avoiding eye contact with Pamela. 'Let's get going.'

While Doreen stood back and gave commands, Darlene gently pushed Pamela into different positions while David snapped pictures. It was all pretty simple – she faced forward, she stood in profile, she sat on a stool. Each time Pamela tried to strike a model-like pose, but Darlene made her stay as stiff as a robot.

'Don't smile,' Doreen ordered. 'You're not supposed to look too happy in the before shots.'

'That should be enough,' David said after shooting another dozen photos.

'Great,' Doreen replied. 'Has Mr Anthony arrived?'

When David nodded in the affirmative, the editors led Pamela down the hall to a room that looked like a miniature beauty parlour, with a couple of sinks, free-standing hairdryers, a table covered with brushes, combs, rollers and bottles. Mr Anthony turned out to be a thin, serious man who examined Pamela's hair in horror.

'My dear, what have you been doing to yourself?' he exclaimed.

Pamela told him she'd been doing her own hair since she was thirteen. 'I couldn't get it light enough with regular hair colour,' she explained. 'So I've been using this cream that's made for women who have moustaches.'

The hairdresser moaned. 'Do you have any idea the damage it's done to your hair?' He pulled the editors aside and they had a whispered conversation.

Then he returned.

'You must put your faith in me,' he instructed Pamela. 'Do you understand? Do not worry – I am a genius.'

She looked at him in alarm. But she knew her hair hadn't been looking its best lately. The platinum colour had yellowed from the sun. Muddy dark roots were visible and she had a lot of split ends. So she said nothing as he pushed the chair back. Now her head was in the sink and she was staring at the ceiling. She could hear him, shaking bottles and pouring and mixing, and then she felt him applying some creamy stuff to her hair. It felt pretty good, like a massage, so she closed her eyes and relaxed.

And the chair was so comfortable . . . she found herself drifting in and out of a light sleep as he worked on her. Dimly she was aware of warm water, then more stuff being massaged into her hair.

'This has to sit for a while,' she heard him say. She was jerked awake when he pulled the chair into an upright position and went to work with a scissors.

'Don't cut too much!' she said anxiously.

'Trust me,' was all he said.

'Can I see the colour?' she asked.

'Later, later,' he murmured.

Then he rolled her hair up, stuck her under a noisy dryer, and left the room.

Doreen and Darlene returned, this time accompanied by a pretty young woman wheeling a cart. Doreen spoke loudly, so Pamela could hear her from under the dryer.

'This is Melanie. She'll be doing your face.' Melanie immediately began slathering her face, including her lips, with cold cream.

Doreen and Darlene hovered anxiously as Melanie worked. The cold cream was wiped off, and other stuff went on. Brushes were swept across her face, she was stroked with cotton balls and pads, pencils and wands. Liquids, creams and powders were applied as Melanie issued orders to Pamela.

'Look up! Look down! Close your eyes. Open your eyes. Purse your lips. Smile. Stop smiling.' And all the time, Doreen and Darlene made 'ooh' sounds, and used words like 'beautiful' and 'wonderful', and Pamela began to have visions of emerging from all this looking like Kim Novak.

Finally it was over. Melanie stepped back, and Darlene moved closer to gaze at Pamela with an awed expression, as if she was overwhelmed by the beauty she was seeing. Doreen produced a large hand-held mirror.

'Take a look at yourself.'

Pamela smiled as she accepted the mirror. But as she looked at her reflection she could see the smile disappear.

She was no longer a Marilyn Monroe, Jayne Mansfield or Kim Novak blonde. No longer was her hair puffed around her face like a big platinum cloud.

She was now what people called 'dirty blonde'. Her darker hair was cut in a small bubble with wispy bangs. And her make-up – what could possibly have taken so much time? Her face looked positively naked; she could barely see any make-up at all. OK, maybe a little beige around the eyes, and her lips were vaguely pink.

She should have known this was what they would do to her. She looked like a *Gloss* girl. Boring.

'Of course, you're not finished,' Doreen said quickly. Pamela's lack of enthusiasm must have been evident. 'We have to get you dressed up. And wait till you see what you're wearing. Straight from the samples closet!'

Darlene accompanied her into a dressing room, where her bright yellow sundress and high-heeled sandals were taken away. Then she was zipped into a straight-but-not-clingy navy-blue sleeveless sheath with a little white collar. To this was added white flats, white gloves and a little white bow clipped to her hair just above her ear. Pamela wanted to die.

'Look at her, she's in shock,' Doreen exclaimed in delight.

Pamela was led to yet another room for the 'after' photos. Here the walls were covered with life-size background photos – of a classroom, a park, a window with frilly curtains. A real desk stood in front of the classroom photo, a bench by the park photo, a vanity table by the 'window'. David Barnes was already there, and this time he actually looked at her, but when he spoke, it was only to the editors.

'Very nice,' he said. 'You've done a great job.'

Pamela forced a smile and made one last attempt at wooing him.

'You like my new look, David?' she asked sweetly.

He held a camera in front of his face. 'Mm.' That was all she got from him, and he began shooting.

At one point David left the room to get another camera, and she spoke to the editors.

'I don't think he likes me very much.'

The women exchanged looks, and Doreen spoke. 'Did you try to flirt with him, Pamela?'

'Well, sure,' Pamela replied. 'Wouldn't any girl? He's very good-looking. I'm not in trouble, am I?'

Doreen hesitated. 'Of course not. But the thing is, Pamela . . . he's just not interested in women. Not that way.'

Pamela looked at her in bewilderment. Then the meaning of Doreen's words dawned on her. 'You mean, he's a . . . a . . .'

Doreen interrupted her. 'We don't really talk about it, Pamela.'

'What a waste,' Pamela murmured. At least this explained why her attempts at seduction had failed.

When Pamela returned to the editorial floor, it was quiet. The other interns had left, and only Caroline remained in her office. The woman looked up as Pamela passed by.

'Don't you look lovely!' she exclaimed.

These people had no taste whatsoever, Pamela thought dismally. But she managed a 'thank you' before taking her handbag from her desk drawer and walking out.

She had no desire to return to the Cavendish, where the other interns would first be shocked by her appearance, and then would overwhelm her with compliments – they would love the fact that she looked like them now.

Instead she walked across the street and went into Charlie's.

The tavern was busy, and her eyes swept the room, searching in vain for a place to sit. Then she spotted someone she'd seen here before.

Alex Parker sat alone in a booth, staring at what looked like a martini on the table in front of him. She'd only met the *Gloss* advertising manager once, when she'd been introduced along with all the other interns. He probably wouldn't even recognize her now.

But suddenly he looked up, and their eyes met. She caught the hint of a smile on his face, so she made her way towards him. But when she paused at his table, she saw no recognition in his eyes.

'I'm Pamela. I'm one of the interns at *Gloss*.'

He nodded. 'I thought you looked familiar.' There was a brief hesitation, and then he asked, 'Would you like to join me?'

'OK.' She took the seat across from him.

GL♥SS

'What would you like to drink?' Alex asked as a waiter approached. 'A Coke?'

She laughed lightly, as if he'd just made a joke. 'A martini. Extra dry, with a twist.'

His eyebrows went up, but he repeated her order to the waiter. 'And another for me, please. Two olives.'

The waiter left, and Alex spoke in an undertone. 'You *are* twenty-one, I presume.'

She batted her eyelashes. 'I've got an ID that says I am.'

He laughed. 'Well, I guess that's good enough. No one can accuse me of corrupting a minor.' He downed the rest of his martini, and as if on cue, the waiter reappeared with a replacement and her drink too.

'Just put it on my tab,' Alex murmured to the man.

'Of course, Mr Parker,' the waiter said, and left with the empty glass.

'Thank you, Mr Parker,' Pamela said.

'Alex,' he corrected her.

'Alex,' she repeated, and smiled.

They clinked their glasses silently, and they both took a sip.

'The waiter knows your name,' Pamela remarked. 'You must come here often.'

'Almost every day for the past few weeks,' he said. 'Ever since the wife and kids left for the summer. I hate going back to the empty apartment.'

'Where did they go?'

'Long Island. We rent a little cottage for the summer. It's better for the kids, to be out of the city. Fresh air, the sea . . .'

She supposed she should ask about his children – ages, names, that sort of thing – but she didn't. 'You must miss them.'

'I go out there most weekends.'

He hadn't really answered her. Did he *not* miss his family?

'It gets lonely during the week though,' he added.

She nodded. 'You have to fend for yourself. Do you go out for your meals?'

'Sometimes. But I hate to eat alone in restaurants. Mostly I throw a TV dinner in the oven. I have to say, I'm getting pretty tired of Salisbury steak and fried fish filets. Do you cook for yourself?'

She shook her head. 'I'm living at the Cavendish Residence for Women, and there's a dining hall.'

'How's the food there?'

'It's OK. Meat loaf and chicken pot pie.' She sighed. 'I haven't had a really good meal in a long time.'

'Neither have I,' he said. There was a moment of silence, and then he said, 'Would you like to have one tonight? We could go to a restaurant. My treat of course.'

She drew in her breath. 'Yes. I'd like that.'

'Any place in particular?' he asked.

'Sardi's?' she asked hopefully.

He smiled. 'Why not?'♥

GL♥SS

Chapter Twelve

'**R**ats,' Sam muttered.

Allison looked around in alarm. 'Where?'

'All around us,' he said sadly. 'Look at them, Allison. It's a rat race. And they're all just doing what they think they're supposed to do.'

She almost felt bad about dragging him uptown. But the evening before he'd broken a couple of strings on his guitar, and Allison had learned from Mr Connelly at *Gloss* that the best instrument-repair shop was on Lexington and 62nd. She'd given up her lunch hour to meet Sam there. The strings had been replaced on the spot, and now she was walking him to the subway station. Fervently she wished she could return to the Village with him.

'It's all about money,' Sam went on. 'Everyone's trying to make a deal, or they're looking to buy some worthless crap they don't even need. The almighty buck, that's all they care about. Like the guy in the repair shop. I can't believe what he charged you for two lousy strings.'

'I didn't mind paying,' Allison assured him. 'I felt like a patron of the arts. You know, like the Medicis.'

'The who?'

She flushed. 'This incredibly rich Italian family who supported artists like Michelangelo during the Renaissance.'

'Huh.' He considered this. 'Yeah, that's what people should be doing. Supporting artists, instead of giving money to the government to build bomb shelters.' They were just passing a building that held the sign of three upside-down triangles, indicating that there was a fall-out shelter in the building's basement. 'Like that's going to protect them. When that A-bomb drops, it's all over, babe. No hope. So what's the point?'

Sometimes it was hard to follow Sam's thoughts – he would jump from one subject to another, and the connections weren't always clear. It was like his mind was packed with so many thoughts and ideas he couldn't control them, they just spilled out. Maybe she'd just spent too many years around people who talked about trivial things. But she had to try to make some sense out of his ramblings, if she was going to write about him.

'You know,' he went on, 'in an ideal world, we wouldn't even need money. Like, that square in the shop – he should have been happy to be helping a musician. And I could have paid him with a song. It would have brought a lot more joy to his life than twenty bucks.'

A passing man moving hurriedly jostled him

slightly. 'Excuse me,' he murmured, but that didn't mollify Sam.

'What's your rush?' he yelled after him. 'Get hip to the reality, man. It doesn't matter where you're going. It's no better than where you are now.'

What an interesting way of looking at the world, Allison thought. She wished she could whip out a pen and paper and write that down.

They'd reached the subway entrance. Allison knew she should get back to *Gloss*, that she'd already used up her lunch hour, but she didn't want to leave him. She was supposed to be writing an article about him, and what did she have so far? Not much, even after spending all the last weekend with him and practically every evening this week. She needed some background about him, his family, why he left home at such an early age.

Not to mention the fact that she was hungry.

'I've got an idea,' she said suddenly. 'Let's go over to Central Park and get a hotdog.'

'I got no bread, babe.'

She linked her arm through his. 'I've got bread.'

They walked the three blocks across town to the park and stopped at the hot-dog cart on the corner.

'Hey, man, I'll play you a tune for a couple of dogs,' Sam offered.

The weary-looking vendor raised his eyes to the heavens. 'No thanks, buddy. I only take cash.'

'He's kidding,' Allison hastily told the man. She pulled out her wallet. 'We'll have two hot dogs and a couple of Cokes.'

'I wasn't kidding,' Sam told her as they left the cart with their food.

'I know, but he looked tired, and I just wanted to be nice.'

He gazed at her with those big, sad brown eyes. 'You're cute. And thanks for the grub.'

She drew in her breath and tried to keep her expression from showing her delight. Finally, a compliment!

They'd reached a bench. An old newspaper was lying on it, and Allison picked it up to make a space to sit. Glancing at the headline, she grimaced.

'Did you hear about this? The governor of Alabama tried to block integration at the state university. Isn't that disgusting?'

He made a face. 'Universities. I don't get it. I mean, what are you going to learn at a university? They don't tell you the truth. Ya gotta reach into your own soul. Everything you need to know, you can find it there.'

That wasn't her point, but she thought he'd made an interesting observation. She needed to remember it for the article.

'My parents are expecting me to go to college in September,' she said. 'But I'm not sure it's what I want.'

'Parents,' he muttered, with a face that made it clear what he thought of them.

'You don't get along with yours either?'

He took a gulp of his soda. 'They threw me out of the house when I was sixteen.'

She was shocked. 'Why?'

He pressed his thumb and forefinger together and held them to his lips.

'They threw you out for smoking cigarettes?'

'Weed.'

'Oh, of course, weed,' she said quickly. She could have kicked herself for sounding so naive. 'I can understand why your parents would be upset though,' she added. 'If you got caught, you could go to jail.'

He smiled. 'Prison. So what? We're already living behind bars.'

Her forehead puckered. What was *that* supposed to mean?

'Did you fight with your parents a lot?'

He shrugged. 'I guess.'

'What about? Other than weed, I mean.'

'The usual stuff.'

She was getting nowhere with this – clearly he didn't want to talk about his family. She decided to concentrate on his music.

'Do you write all your own songs?'

'Yeah.'

'Because you want to share your very own ideas

with the world?' She knew she was putting words in his mouth, but she needed more.

He closed his eyes for a moment. When he opened them he said, 'You share too many ideas, you're just going to lose them. The world will suck the creativity right out of you.' He hadn't answered her question, but it was yet another marvellous declaration.

'I loved your song about the seasons,' she said. 'Were you inspired by Ecclesiastes?'

'*Who?*'

'Ecclesiastes, in the Bible. I'm not religious,' she added hastily, 'but I was forced to go to Sunday School for years. And there's a verse that stuck in my head, about how for everything there is a season. Like in your song. So I was just wondering if maybe you were influenced by the Bible.'

'Never read it.'

'But the words are so similar.'

Again he shrugged.

'OK. Um . . . how did you learn to play the guitar?'

His eyes narrowed. 'You writing a book about me?'

She started. 'What do you mean?'

'You ask a lot of questions.'

'Oh. Sorry. I guess I'm just curious.' She smiled, and then with some hesitation added, 'I just want to know you better.'

She hoped he would say something like, 'I want to know you better too,' and for a moment he seemed to be pondering what she'd just confessed. Finally he spoke. 'What I sing is who I am.'

'Right.' It dawned on her that he'd never asked her anything about herself, her family, what she did when she wasn't with him. It was better that way, she supposed. His life was so much more interesting than hers.

He finished his soda, tossed it in the general direction of a garbage can and rose from the bench. 'Gotta go. You coming downtown?'

'No, uptown. But I'll come down to the Village after dinner. Will you be in the park?'

'Probably.' Then he gave her a longer-than-usual look.

'Allison . . . are you connected?'

She caught her breath. He wanted to know if she was in a relationship, if she had a boyfriend. And he wouldn't want to know unless he was really interested in her.

'No, I'm not.'

He shook his head sadly. 'You have to get connected, babe. It's the only way.'

Now she was confused. 'With what?'

'Not what, babe. Who. You gotta connect with yourself. Your spirit. You gotta feel it. And then you gotta let it go. That's the only way to be free.'

She couldn't respond, she was completely speechless. He tossed his guitar over his shoulder, turned away and ambled towards the subway.

She stared after him. What an amazing, incredible, original human being. For a moment she considered running after him, but she was late as it was. And she still hadn't come up with an excuse for Mr Connelly.

But she found one as she hurried back to Madison Avenue. Passing a newsstand, something caught her eye. It was one of those celebrity fan magazines, with Elizabeth Taylor and Richard Burton on the cover. But below their photo another story was featured: 'The Private Life of Bobby Dale'!

She snatched it off the shelf, paid for it and ran back to the Hartnell Building.

As she expected, Mr Connelly was not happy with her. 'Where have you been?' he demanded to know.

'I'm sorry, I should have told you, I've been looking for information about Bobby Dale. And look what I found!' She held up the magazine.

The editor was mildly mollified. 'Well, next time let me know when you're going to be out of the office.' He frowned as he read the title of the article. 'Damn, that was going to be our title. See if you can come up with another angle. Don't forget, this article has to be two thousand words. And get a move on – I've got a call in to Dale's manager to set up interview times. Have you gone over the biographical stuff I left on your desk? You need to be prepared with questions for him.'

'I'll be ready,' Allison promised him, and went to her desk. She took a pad of paper and started jotting furiously.

Where you're going, it's no better than where you are.

What I sing is who I am.

School doesn't teach you the truth . . . There was more to that one. She closed her eyes and searched her memory, but she couldn't find it. Hopefully it would come back to her.

But as far as composing an article about Sam, she had no more worries. She could easily come up with two thousand words writing about his talent, his songs and his brilliant original comments about life. She wouldn't even have to include information about his family and getting kicked out of the house for smoking weed. Not that *Gloss* would have let her mention weed.

Reluctantly she put the pad in a drawer and took up the magazine. *Bobby Dale may be the rising star of the music world, but his down-to-earth nature makes him seem more like the boy next door.* That was the first line, and the rest of the article was devoted to backing up this statement.

Even though Bobby has his own bachelor pad in Beverly Hills, he's more likely to spend time at his parents' home, where his mom prepares his favourite tuna casserole and he can play marathon games of Scrabble with his dad.

And later . . . *You won't find Bobby hanging out in Hollywood's fancy nightclubs Saturday nights and sleeping till noon on Sunday. He'll be up bright and early for a backyard touch-football game with his two younger brothers.*

She could just imagine what this upcoming interview would reveal. Maybe she'd come up with some startling new information, like a weekly church visit before the football game.

She was aware of a figure leaning over her desk, and looked up. An intern whose name she'd never bothered to learn was looking at the photo accompanying the article.

'Is that Bobby Dale?' she asked. 'He's so cute!'

Allison shrugged.

'You don't think he's cute?'

'Not my type,' Allison said.

The girl sniffed. 'Well, you're probably not *his* type either,' she said, and walked away.

She probably meant the comment as an insult, but Allison was pleased. The girl had just given her an idea. Mr Connelly had said he needed a new angle to the article, and now she had one.

She got up, strode over to the entertainment editor's office and rapped on the open door. Mr Connelly looked up.

'Yes?'

'I think I've got a new angle for the Bobby Dale

article. "Could *You* Be Bobby's Girl?" I could ask him questions about his ideal girlfriend, what qualities he looks for, that sort of thing.'

Slowly Mr Connelly began to nod. 'Yes. Yes! I like it, it gets the reader involved. Good work, Allison.' And he actually smiled. 'I think we just might make a *Gloss* girl out of you yet.'

It was not easy, resisting the intense desire to inform him that she had no intention of ever becoming a *Gloss* girl. But Allison had been around long enough to know when to bite her tongue. She smiled, and nodded, and thanked Mr Connelly. And held back the urge to gag.♥

> 'I think we just might make a *Gloss* girl out of you yet.'

Chapter Thirteen

From her desk, Sherry could see into Mr Simpson's office, which meant that Mr Simpson could see her too. But the door was closed, and there was no glass window through which he could peer out into the bullpen. So for the time being she was safe.

Still glancing furtively at the office, she rolled a sheet of plain white paper into the typewriter and then opened a folder to reveal Mike's short story.

'THE WHITE HORSE', she typed. And under it, 'by Michael Dillon'.

'What are you doing?'

She practically jumped out of her seat.

Allison stepped back in alarm. 'Sorry, didn't mean to scare you.'

Sherry lowered her voice to a barely audible whisper. 'I'm typing up a short story that Mike wrote. And I don't want Mr Simpson to know.'

'Why? Is it pornographic or something?'

'No! It's a beautiful story, about a teenage boy on a horse ranch out west. There's this horse that can't be tamed, and he's trying to get his father to set it free. It's all very symbolic.'

GL♥SS

'Then why are you so nervous about Simpson finding out what you're doing?'

'Because it's not *Gloss* work. I should be doing this on my own time, back in my room. I just haven't had time this week.' She sighed. 'I should never have learned how to play bridge. There's always a game going on at the Cavendish.'

Allison shook her head in disgust. 'I can't believe that's how you're spending your New York evenings. OK, I know Pamela hasn't been around much, now that she's hooked up with Mr Parker.' She wrinkled her nose. 'It's weird, calling him "Mister" when he's going out with our friend.'

What felt even weirder to Sherry was the fact that a friend was dating a married man. Helen Gurley Brown might call it acceptable, but Sherry had her doubts.

'And I know your roommate just sits in front of the lounge TV every night,' Allison continued, 'but you could always come down to the Village with me.'

Sherry smiled and nodded, but inwardly she knew this was not an option. She'd hit the Village with Allison one evening, and that had been enough for her. It was an interesting scene, but she'd found Allison's folk singer friend to be so arrogant, with all his ponderous declarations about life. Not to mention the fact that he clearly looked down on Sherry, teasing her about her Southern background and ladylike manners. For the life of her, she couldn't understand what Allison saw in the guy.

'And what about Mike?' Allison asked. 'I see you two taking coffee breaks together practically every day.'

'He spends his evenings writing,' Sherry told her.

'*Every* evening?' Allison asked sceptically. 'Even weekends?'

Sherry nodded, but she could understand Allison's disbelief. There'd been that one evening, when they went to the author's reading at the uptown community centre, but nothing since then.

One of Allison's eyebrows shot up. 'Then how come you're knocking yourself out typing up his story?'

'Because I said I would,' Sherry replied lamely. Once again she glanced nervously in the direction of Mr Simpson's office. 'But I really shouldn't be doing it on *Gloss* time.'

Allison groaned. 'Honestly, Sherry. Do you have to be Little Miss Perfect all the time? Half the interns here spend their time trying on clothes in the samples closet or looking for free make-up.'

'I know.' Sherry sighed. 'I guess it's just the way I was brought up.'

'Well, get over it,' Allison said cheerfully. 'Or, wait, how about this? Turn it into *Gloss* work.'

'How?'

'*Gloss* publishes two short stories in every issue. Why don't you submit it to the fiction editor? Or give

GL♥SS

it to the fiction intern, what's-her-name, with the short black hair and glasses.'

'Ellen,' Sherry murmured. She was one of the bridge regulars. 'Hey, that's a good idea!'

'And just think how thrilled Mike will be if it gets published,' Allison added. 'He'll fall madly in love with you. Maybe he'll even give up writing for an evening to take you out.'

'I won't hold my breath,' Sherry murmured.

Allison regarded her with concern. 'Sherry . . . you're not still torching for Johnny, are you?'

'I guess I'm still thinking about him,' Sherry admitted. 'I mean, it's only been a week since . . .' Her voice trailed off.

Allison gave her a sympathetic smile. 'I know. And he was the love of your life, right?'

'Right,' Sherry echoed.

From his office, the entertainment editor stuck out his head and bellowed, 'Allison!'

'I'd better go. We'll talk later.'

About something else, Sherry silently

hoped. One of the reasons she liked playing bridge with the other interns was the fact that Ellen knew nothing of her history, and Linda and Diane were too tactful to ask about Johnny.

Was she still 'torching', as Allison put it? She felt *something*, that was for sure. If she had to give it a name, she wasn't sure she could call it heartbreak, at least not in the way she'd seen it in movies and read about it in books. She hadn't cried herself to sleep, not even once. Was she angry? When she'd taken his picture out of the frame, she didn't crumple it furiously or tear it into bits. The only word she could think of that could describe her feelings was . . . lost.

If anyone had ever asked her how she saw herself ten years from now, she would have had no difficulty responding. She'd be in a pretty suburban home, outside Atlanta, with at least one child, maybe another on the way. Her days would be spent caring for the children, cleaning and cooking and shopping. Maybe some volunteer work for the church, and meetings of the local garden club. Johnny would come home from his job at six, and they'd have a cocktail while the kids watched cartoons. He'd tell her about his day at work; she'd entertain him with funny things the kids had said or done.

Now she wouldn't know what to say to anyone who asked that question. Hopefully she'd meet someone else who could be there for her, someone who would be the father of her children, who would support the family, who would sit at the head of the dinner table. But she couldn't give that someone else a face, and it made her feel that word again. Lost.

Get a grip, she ordered herself. She shook her head, as if the gesture would disperse all the bad feelings, and forced her mind to focus on the work at hand. What Allison had suggested, about submitting Mike's story to *Gloss* . . . well, why not?

She removed the paper from the typewriter and tossed it in the wastepaper basket. Then she took two fresh sheets, placed a piece of carbon paper between them and inserted them all into the typewriter.

It was strange – she knew Mike liked her, why else would he constantly stop by her desk and ask if they could take their coffee breaks together? And those breaks were always interesting. They talked about all kinds of things – politics, civil rights, religion. Mike did most of the talking – she still wasn't completely comfortable discussing subjects that were so off-limits back home. But she was beginning to join in and express the occasional opinion, and she enjoyed the conversations. Still, it wasn't what she'd call flirting.

As she typed, it dawned on her that there might be another reason he hadn't asked her out. He couldn't be making much money working in the mailroom, and he'd said he was saving for college. Which was another good reason for submitting his story for publication –

Gloss paid writers. Surely he'd take her out, if only to express his gratitude to her. And that could lead to a real relationship.

She started imagining a very different future – standing by Mike's side in a bookstore handing him the books to sign for his adoring fans. Books that held dedications like, 'To Sherry, my wife and my inspiration'. Hosting elegant cocktail parties, offering canapés to literary types, writers, poets, professors. It wasn't a world she'd ever seen, and not quite what she'd imagined for herself, but it could work . . .

She reached the end and separated the two manuscripts, putting one aside to give to Mike and the other in a brown manila envelope. Inserting another sheet into the typewriter, she quickly made up a cover sheet. She typed the date, and then: 'To: Martin Gold, Fiction Editor, *Gloss*; From: Michael Dillon, Mailroom, *Gloss*.' Under that, she typed: 'Attached, please find a short story I would like to submit for publication in *Gloss*. Thank you for your consideration.'

She slipped the page into the envelope, sealed it and wrote the fiction editor's name on it. Then she took it to the desk where Ellen sat. She wasn't there, so Sherry dropped it in her in-box.

She was passing Caroline's office on her way back to her own desk when the managing editor came out.

'Sherry, just the person I wanted to see! I have another favour to ask. I'm throwing a little cocktail party tonight, for a fashion editor from Paris. Normally my secretary would help me out, but she's under the weather. Do you think you could take her place?'

'Sure,' Sherry replied. 'What would I need to do?'

' I just need another pair of hands. You'd be greeting people at the door, passing trays of canapés, that sort of thing. You'll meet some interesting people, and possibly make some good contacts for the future. How about it?'

Sherry wasn't quite sure what she meant by 'contacts'. Would there be single guys there? In any case, it didn't matter. It wasn't like she had anything else to do, and she had to admit, she was curious to see how the editor lived.

'I'll be glad to help,' Sherry replied.

'Of course, I'll see that you get some compensatory time off from your internship,' Caroline added.

'Oh, that won't be necessary,' Sherry said quickly.

Caroline gave her a mildly reproving look. 'Sherry, if you're going to have a career in the magazine industry, learn to negotiate when special demands are made. Don't let bosses walk all over you.'

Sherry smiled uncertainly. Whatever gave Caroline the idea that she was seriously considering a career in the magazine industry? By now she'd realized that none of the interns was planning to go into publishing. They were here for an expenses-paid summer in New York. Maybe the editors, like Caroline, just hoped some of them would get hooked on the idea of a career.

Caroline went on, and it was almost as if Sherry had actually asked the question out loud.

'You've got talent, Sherry. I saw this right away in the review you wrote. And the piece you wrote about yourself – it's excellent.'

All the interns had been told to write a short autobiographical description that would accompany their photo in the special readers' issue. Sherry had agonized over hers.

'I wasn't sure if I should mention the Miss Teen Georgia pageant,' she told Caroline. 'I was afraid it would sound like I was showing off.'

Caroline shook her head firmly. 'No, not at all. And it's something that would appeal to a lot of our readers. I like the image of a pageant contestant who is also a serious writer, not just some shallow superficial beauty queen. And you mentioned it in a down-to-earth way, without sounding conceited.'

Sherry was at a loss for words, but she managed to stammer out a 'thank you'.

'You need to do more writing while you're here,' Caroline said. 'If you have any good story ideas, don't hesitate to propose them.'

'To you?' Sherry asked.

'No, the articles are the domain of the editors for each section of the magazine. If you want to write fiction, talk to Mr Gold. If it's a feature piece . . .'

'Talk to Mr Simpson,' Sherry finished.

'That's right. ' Caroline looked at her watch. 'I've got some calls to make.' She scribbled something on a pad, ripped off the sheet and handed it to Sherry. 'Here's my address. Can you be there around six thirty?'

'OK. Um . . . what should I wear?' In the back of her mind she saw the women her mother hired to help out at parties. They always wore a white uniform-type dress.

Caroline shrugged. 'Oh, anything you like. A little black dress always works . . .' She smiled. 'If you don't have one, borrow one from the samples closet. I wouldn't call this an extraordinary occasion, but you're doing something exceptional for *Gloss*.'

On her way to the door Caroline added, 'But make sure to sign out the dress, Sherry. We've been having some problems . . .' Her voice trailed off, and some lines of concern crossed her forehead.

'I will,' Sherry assured her.

'Oh, and if you see Donna, would you ask her to drop by my office?'

Back in the bullpen, Sherry scanned the room but she didn't spot her roommate. She *did* see Pamela, perched on another intern's desk and chatting. Sherry beckoned to her.

'What's up?' Pamela asked.

Sherry told her about going to Caroline's party. 'She says I can borrow a dress from the samples closet.

Want to help me pick something out?'

It was funny, how less than three weeks ago she would never have sought Pamela's advice on something to wear. But in the past week, ever since her makeover, Pamela's style had changed dramatically. Today she was wearing a cap-sleeved dusty-pink shirtwaist dress with neat little tucks on the bodice. And it actually covered her knees.

'I love what you're wearing,' Sherry commented as they headed down the corridor towards the closet.

'You do?' Pamela sighed. 'I don't. Alex bought it for me.'

'He bought you a *dress*? Is it your birthday?'

'No. He just wants me to look nice.' She sighed again. '*His* idea of nice. But if this is what makes him happy and he's willing to pay for it, what can I do?'

Not go out with him, Sherry wanted to say.

'You're spending a lot of time with him,' she commented as she opened the door to the samples closet.

Pamela nodded happily. 'It's been amazing! I've actually been to Sardi's, and El Morocco too! And he really knows how to treat a girl. Ooh, check out the bikinis!'

But Sherry's mind was still on Pamela's new relationship. 'Pam . . . you do remember that he's married, right?'

Pamela groaned. 'Of course I do. And don't start

GL♥SS

nagging me about that. His wife's on Long Island, he's lonely and I'm keeping him company, that's all. I'm not trying to break up his marriage, Sherry! I just want to have some fun.'

'OK, OK,' Sherry said quickly. 'As long as you know what you're doing.'

Pamela suddenly became serious. 'But listen, Sherry . . . no one can know about this, OK? I mean, besides you and Allison.'

'Because his wife could find out?'

Pamela nodded.

Sherry studied her. 'But doesn't that make you feel, I don't know . . . creepy?'

Pamela turned away. 'Let's look at some dresses.' She walked over to one of the racks. 'Now, *this* is what I call a little black dress.'

Sherry didn't have to look at it too closely – the glitter from the sequins was enough to make her shake her head. 'Think simple, Pam. What would your new man pick out for you to wear?'

With a great show of reluctance Pamela replaced the dress and looked over the selection.

'He'd like this,' she said, and indicated a simple sheath.

Whatever Sherry might think of him, she had to admit Mr Parker had good taste. She picked out two other dresses and tried them all on.

When she'd made her selection, she went to the

logbook that hung on the wall.

'What are you doing?' Pamela asked.

'Signing out the dress.' She paused, and remembered how she and Allison had wondered if Pamela might have something to do with the items that had gone missing. 'You know that we have to do that, right?'

'No,' Pamela said, 'but I haven't had any reason to borrow a dress. Hey, I wonder if going out with an executive would count as an extraordinary occasion.'

Just as they left the closet, Donna turned the corner from the bullpen into the corridor and stopped short when she saw them. For the zillionth time, Sherry had the impression of a deer caught in the headlights of a car.

'Donna,' Sherry called to her, 'Caroline wants to see you.'

If anything, her expression became even more fearful. Without even acknowledging the message, she turned and hurried back the way she had come.

'What's her deal?' Pamela asked in bewilderment. 'Why does she always look so nervous?'

Sherry shook her head. 'Search me. When we're in our room together, she hardly opens her mouth. I've given up trying to get to know her.'

Back in the bullpen, Mr Simpson was looking for Sherry.

'Did you get those letters done?' he demanded to know.

Fortunately she'd finished them before typing Mike's story. 'Yes, sir, I'll get them now.' She hurried over to her desk, snatched up the work and brought them back to the features editor.

'I'll need envelopes to go with these,' he barked.

'They're attached,' she pointed out.

'Oh yes, I see.' He seemed somewhat mollified. He went through the letters and nodded. 'Yes, these look fine.'

She decided this might be a good time to ask about writing.

'Um, Mr Simpson . . . I've had an idea for an article.'

He looked up from the letters. 'Yes?'

She took a deep breath. 'I'm wondering if readers might like to read about what goes on behind the scenes in a teen beauty pageant.'

He didn't frown, and maybe that was a flicker of curiosity in his eyes. Encouraged, she continued.

'I was in a pageant, back in Georgia, just last year. And I think I could write an interesting article about it.'

His eyebrows narrowed. 'Let me think about this,' he murmured. 'I've left an edited manuscript on your desk for you to retype.'

A shiver ran up her spine. He was actually considering it! She couldn't wait to tell Caroline. But glancing at her office, she saw that Donna was still in there. Maybe she'd have a chance to mention it tonight.

At her desk, she was typing so furiously she didn't even hear Mike say her name. When he said it again, she looked up. 'Hi!'

'Ready for a coffee break?'

She glanced at the clock. 'Not today. I've got too much work to get done.' She was rather pleased to see him looking a little disappointed. Then she remembered something that would cheer him up.

'Oh, I typed up your story,' she said, and handed him the folder.

He opened it, and his eyes widened. 'Wow. You really did it!'

'I said I would, didn't I?' She wasn't going to mention submitting it to *Gloss*. If it wasn't accepted, he'd be disappointed.

'Well . . . thanks.'

'You're welcome. It was a pleasure reading it again.' She glanced back at her typewriter. 'I'd better get back to this . . .'

But he lingered. 'I was wondering . . . if you'd like to do something tonight. See a movie, maybe? Or just get something to eat?'

She tried very hard not to look as thrilled as she felt. She wasn't even going to have to wait until the story was accepted for publication. For one fleeting second, she almost forgot that she wasn't free.

Damn.

'I'm sorry, I can't,' she said sadly. 'I have to do

something for *Gloss*. Another time?'

'Sure,' he said. 'And thanks again.'

She finished retyping the manuscript and took it to Mr Simpson's office. It was just about five o'clock.

'I'm leaving now, Mr Simpson,' she said brightly.

He tore a sheet of paper from a pad on his desk. 'Could you get one more letter typed up before you go?'

'Yes, of course.' She took the paper from him and headed back to her desk. At least it was just a paragraph – it would only take her a couple of minutes.

She inserted another sheet of *Gloss* letterhead stationery into the typewriter and turned to the paper he'd given her. The letter was going to someone named Allan Cunningham, and she recognized the name as a frequent contributor to *Gloss*. She started to type.

Dear Allan, I've got an assignment for you. Would you be interested in writing an article about teen beauty pageants? You could include interviews with contestants, and hopefully get some tips as to what goes on behind the scenes. I'd like something in the range of 2500–3000 words, with photos . . .

She stopped typing, her hands in mid-air. Her idea, her article. He was asking someone else to write it!

He was coming out of his office now, briefcase in hand, and putting on his hat. She wanted to confront him – but she couldn't move.

And what could she say to him anyway? She was

a nobody, a lowly intern. Maybe she should just be pleased that he considered her idea worthy of an article.

But she wasn't. And she was filled with feelings she couldn't recognize and didn't know what to do with.

Her idea, her article. He was asking someone else to write it!

Mechanically she went back to the letter, finished it and put it in her out-box to give Mr Simpson for signing. Then she covered the typewriter and checked to make sure she had everything in her handbag. She placed the little black dress carefully over her arm and left.

Her fury made her walk faster than usual, and she got back to the Cavendish Residence in record time. She was very grateful that Donna wasn't in the room. She wouldn't have to make her usual polite conversation.

It was already quarter to six, and she didn't know how long it would take her to get uptown to Caroline's, so she had to rush. She stripped off her clothes and went into the shower, taking the black dress with her so the steam from the hot water would hopefully erase the crease she'd made by carrying it over her arm.

When she got out, she dried off quickly, applied a

little make-up and wrapped herself in a towel. Back in the room, she was surprised to see Donna there, sitting at the desk.

'Hi.'

Donna turned slightly and mumbled a greeting. She looked even more tense than usual.

'Something wrong?' Sherry asked as she began to dress.

'I have to write something about myself for the readers' issue.'

Sherry was surprised. 'That was due on Tuesday.'

'I forgot about it. That's what Caroline wanted to see me about.' She hesitated, and then she said, 'I don't know what to write.'

'You don't need to tell your whole life's story,' Sherry told her. 'Just a little something about yourself. Like, you could talk about your family. Or your hometown.'

Donna shook her head.

'Well, how about a hobby?'

'I don't have any hobbies.'

'Um . . . you could write about why you applied for the internship at *Gloss*.'

There was no response to that, and Sherry gave up. 'Well, feel free to use my typewriter. How do I look?' she asked.

Donna turned.

'I'm helping Caroline at a party she's giving,' Sherry explained. 'She told me to dress like a guest, and she let me borrow this from the samples closet.'

'It's nice,' Donna said.

'Do you think I need a necklace? Maybe a scarf?'

Donna shook her head and turned back to her desk.

Sherry frowned. The only decent conversations they'd had were about accessories. Clearly Donna's mind was elsewhere.

Outside the residence, Sherry consulted her map. According to the address Caroline gave her, she had to get across town to the West Side, and then go up ten blocks . . . and it was already six fifteen. She checked the amount of cash in her wallet. Staying in and eating free meals every night had some benefits – she had enough for a taxi.

In the back of her mind she had a vague image of how Caroline Davison would live – maybe in one of those anonymous, sterile towers she'd passed. She imagined they held tiny boxy dark apartments where people without families lived dull, sterile lives. So she was pleasantly surprised when the taxi pulled up in front of a charming three-storey brownstone building where window boxes dripped geraniums.

A buzzer by the front door indicated three residences, with 'Davison, third floor' listed over the top button. When she pressed it, there was a noise that indicated the door had unlocked itself. Pushing it open, she climbed up two flights of carpeted stairs and rang the bell on the only door there.

It was opened by a stranger, a slightly harried-looking woman in a white apron. Sherry was confused.

'Is this where Caroline Davison lives?' she asked.

The woman nodded shortly and promptly disappeared into some other room. And Sherry entered one of the most unusual living rooms she'd ever seen. Walls were covered with framed art that looked like real paintings, not reproductions. Instead of the wall-to-wall shag carpeting that covered the floors of practically every living room she'd ever seen, there was an oriental-looking rug. Bookcases lined one wall, and shelves on another held objects that bore no resemblance to the painted plates and china figurines her mother collected. She wandered over there, and studied the brightly coloured bowls, the small statue that vaguely resembled a human being . . .

'Hi, Sherry, thanks for coming.' Caroline came into the room. 'You look very nice. Did that come from the samples closet?'

Sherry nodded. 'And I remembered to sign it out.' Something occurred to her. 'I'll bet this dress won't be featured in the magazine though. Right?'

Caroline looked at her with interest. 'And why would that be?'

'Because our average reader is between the ages of fourteen and seventeen,' Sherry said. 'And girls that age don't wear black.'

Caroline nodded with approval. 'Very good! You're catching on, Sherry.'

'My mother thinks a girl shouldn't wear black until she's twenty-one. Of course, that's a Southern perspective.'

Caroline laughed. 'True. Up here you're more likely to be allowed to wear black at eighteen. You know, that would make an interesting article, the difference between the South and the North when it comes to fashion attitudes. What do you think?'

This was her opportunity to bring up what had happened earlier, and Sherry knew she had to take advantage of it.

'I'd love to write about that,' she said carefully. 'But I don't think that's a possibility.'

'What do you mean?'

She told Caroline about Mr Simpson's response to the beauty pageant proposal. 'I guess I should be pleased that he liked the idea. But he isn't going to let me write it.'

She'd hoped Caroline would see the injustice in it, and maybe get angry. But the editor didn't even look surprised.

'Well . . .' she said, and then turned to look at the buffet table. 'I wonder if that vase of flowers would look better on an end table,' she murmured. 'Let's see.'

Sherry followed her to the table. 'Caroline . . . your position is higher than Mr Simpson's, isn't it?'

'In a manner of speaking,' Caroline said, lifting the vase. 'Managing editor is over features editor on the masthead.'

'Then, you could tell him to let me write the article.' Sherry blurted out. Even as the words left her mouth, she was shocked by how aggressive she sounded. She stepped back. 'I'm sorry.'

'Don't be,' Caroline said mildly. 'It pleases me to know you want to write it.'

It dawned on her how much she really did. 'You'll speak to him?'

Caroline gave her a slight, sad smile, and shook her head. 'In this business, Sherry, you have to choose your battles carefully.'

Sherry looked at her in bewilderment. She had no idea what the editor meant, and she wasn't going to get any explanation now. The woman in the white apron re-entered the living room.

'Shall we put everything out on the table now, Miss Davison?'

Caroline looked at her watch. 'Yes, that's a good idea.'

Another woman in a white apron appeared carrying a tray of tiny sandwiches. Caroline beckoned to Sherry, and she followed the editor into the small kitchen, where elaborately decorated trays of canapés, bowls of nuts and olives and plates of tiny pastries covered every surface.

Sherry surveyed the scene in sheer amazement. 'How did you get all this done?' A party like this would have kept her mother in the kitchen for a week.

Caroline laughed. 'I didn't. It's all from the caterers.'

Then two men arrived with boxes. Moments later, a sideboard had been set up with various kinds of glasses and bottles labelled vodka, gin and other assorted spirits. Bartenders, Caroline told her, and once again Sherry thought of parties at home, where her father spent the entire evening mixing drinks for the guests.

The doorbell rang. Caroline was with the caterers, placing small white plates on the table, and she turned to Sherry.

'Could you get that?'

Sherry opened the door to a well-dressed woman and a man in a dark suit. 'Good evening, do come in,' she said. 'May I take your hat?' she asked the man.

Caroline joined them. 'Very good, Sherry!' she exclaimed with a broad smile. 'Joan, Richard . . .' the three exchanged air kisses, and she turned to Sherry. 'This is Sherry Forrester, one of our talented *Gloss* interns.' She went on to introduce the couple to Sherry – Joan turned out to be a buyer for Bonwit Teller, one of the most chic New York stores for women, while the man was the director of an advertising agency. Sherry was only able to say a quick 'pleased to meet you' before the doorbell rang again.

Within minutes she'd opened the door at least a

dozen times, and suddenly the room was filled with elegantly dressed men and women, cocktails in hand. She recognized a few of the beauty and fashion editors from *Gloss* – but as for the others, even though Caroline made every effort to introduce them, the names, faces and titles soon became a blur. She saw two incredibly beautiful and very thin women whom she recognized from their photos modelling the latest styles in *Gloss* and other magazines. Even Miss Margo Meredith, the executive editor of *Gloss*, was there.

The beauty editor was standing by Sherry as Ms Meredith passed. 'Isn't she something?' Doreen murmured. 'Do you have any idea how hard it is for a woman to get to a position like that?'

'She's so beautiful,' Sherry said. 'Didn't she ever want to marry and have a family?'

'She tried,' Doreen told her. 'The marriage part, at least. She's had three husbands. None of them could deal with having a wife who was so successful.'

Sherry could imagine how hard it would be for a man. And she had to wonder if Ms Meredith's career had really made up for the lack of a husband.

All the people at the party seemed to know each other, and Sherry didn't even try to join any of their conversations. She was perfectly happy being an observer of a totally new scene, a party where people weren't in couples, where they didn't automatically divide themselves by gender. At the adult parties she'd witnessed back home, women huddled together discussing recipes and children while the men talked about sports. It never changed.

As she moved through the room, Sherry picked up fragments of conversation.

'. . . so I'm working on this deal which could boost circulation through the roof . . .'

'. . . have you seen the new Dior collection? I think it could have some major influence on ready-to-wear . . .'

'. . . I'm taking the morning flight to LA for the photo shoot . . .'

She was kept busy, helping the caterers replenish the trays, taking empty glasses back to the kitchen. But every now and then Caroline would motion to her, and introduce her to someone. She even made sure Sherry met the guest of honour, the editor from Paris.

Her name was Anne-Cecile, and she looked just like Sherry imagined a French fashion editor would look – incredibly chic and polished, immaculate make-up, not a hair out of place. Sherry had done pretty well in her French courses back at school, and she couldn't resist an opportunity to try out the language.

'*Bonjour, madame. Comment allez-vous?*'

Unfortunately those courses hadn't prepared her for the torrent of French that the woman uttered in response.

Caroline burst out laughing. 'Serves you right for showing off, Sherry!'

Sherry flushed. Showing off – one of the worst sins a well-brought-up Southern girl could commit. But it didn't seem to matter here. Caroline's laugh was friendly, the French editor smiled warmly. One more rule of social behaviour she could forget – at least while she was in New York.

The editor spoke English fluently, with a charming accent. 'And what do you do, Sherry?'

'I'm an intern at *Gloss*.'

'And a very talented writer,' Caroline added.

'Yes? You are writing articles already?'

Sherry could feel Caroline's eyes on her. 'I'd like to, some day.'

Caroline spoke up. 'Sherry proposed an article to our features editor today. And he liked it. Unfortunately he's assigning someone else to write it.'

'Probably because I'm just an intern,' Sherry said. 'Not really on the staff.'

Anne-Cecile looked thoughtful. 'That editor – he is a man?'

'Yes,' Caroline said.

'And he has assigned the story to . . . ?'

Caroline smiled thinly. 'A man.'

Anne-Cecile offered Sherry a sad smile. 'Welcome to our world, my dear.'

'I assume it's the same in France,' Caroline said.

'It's a man's world,' the French woman said. 'I must say though, you appear to be more progressive here in the United States.' She glanced in the direction of Ms Meredith. 'It's quite impressive that a woman holds the position of executive editor.'

Caroline sighed. 'But you can't imagine the rumours that went around when she was appointed. Some people actually thought she was having an affair with Mr Hartnell himself. They couldn't accept the idea that a woman could make it to the top on her own merits.'

The two women exchanged knowing looks. Sherry had an urge to change the subject.

'Um, do you live in Paris?' she asked Anne-Cecile. When the woman nodded in the affirmative, she added, 'I've heard it's the most beautiful city in the world.'

'And the most romantic,' Caroline added.

Sherry had heard that too. 'My boyfriend and I, we talked about having a honeymoon in Paris.'

'Then perhaps I shall see you there soon,' Anne-Cecile said.

Sherry shook her head. 'Actually, he's my ex-boyfriend now.'

The French editor shrugged. 'Well, if you stay in this business, you will certainly come to Paris some day. It is the centre of the fashion industry, you know.' She was distracted by the sight of someone she knew, and wandered off with a gracious wave.

Sherry turned to Caroline. 'What did she mean,

about it being a man's world?'

Caroline sighed. 'Well, it's not easy for a woman to make her way in this industry. We have to struggle.'

'Is it worth it?' Sherry asked. And once again she was startled by her own impulsive question. What was happening to her?

But Caroline didn't appear shocked. 'It depends on how much you want it,' she said lightly. And she moved away to bid goodbye to some guests who were leaving.

Later, Caroline saw Sherry into a taxi. 'Thanks for all your help, Sherry.'

'Thank *you*,' Sherry said automatically. 'It's been a . . . a very interesting evening.'

Caroline smiled. 'You're getting hit with a lot of new ideas, aren't you?'

Sherry nodded. 'You folks talk about a lot of things I've never thought about before.'

'Well, don't stay awake thinking about them tonight. Go home, get a good night's sleep and I'll see you in the morning.'

But it wasn't easy, not thinking. True, she'd honestly thought that Mr Simpson's refusal to consider her as a writer had to do with the fact that she was a lowly intern, not because she was female. But she wasn't as naive as Caroline thought she was. Of course it was a man's world – everyone knew that. And even though she'd never before known women who tried to make it in that world, she could imagine what a struggle it was for them.

Could *she* struggle like that? Would she even want to? How much easier it was just to leave that to the men, and put your energies into making a nice home and raising children. But bits and pieces of the evening kept flashing across her mind. People talking about their work, their business travels, plans for the future . . . there was an excitement about it all. She could practically see the exclamation points that followed some comments.

It was a lot to take in, and she was too, too . . . *something* to do it now. What *was* she feeling? Not tired. If she had drunk any of those cocktails, she'd say she was a little tipsy, but she hadn't even taken a sip. As the taxi pulled up in front of the residence, she hoped she would find a bridge game going on in someone's room. Something to take her mind off the evening.

She went directly to her own room first, to change into some dungarees and put the black dress on a hanger. Donna wasn't there – probably in the TV lounge, she thought. She noticed that there was a typed sheet of paper lying on the desk, and she couldn't resist taking a peek to see what Donna had finally composed.

She frowned as she read the brief statement. The content wasn't bad. Donna had written about her interest in style, in putting clothes and accessories together to create a complete look.

What shocked Sherry was the carelessness, the typos. Words were misspelled, punctuation was practically non-existent, sentences were in fragments, and half the time she had to read a sentence over and over before it made sense.

She wasn't just shocked, she was bewildered. If this was how Donna wrote, how on earth did she get into the *Gloss* programme? Surely her application for the internship hadn't been this sloppy, this badly written.

She could just imagine Caroline's reaction to this, and she shuddered. Maybe Donna was just a terrible typist. Up till now Sherry had been feeling sorry for her roommate's assignment at *Gloss*, being stuck filing. Now she thought maybe it was for the best.

But this . . . this could send her home. For a moment she considered going down to the lounge to find her and tell her this wouldn't be acceptable to the managing editor. Only if Donna really couldn't type, what good would that do?

She sat down at the desk and put a fresh sheet of paper into the typewriter. She concentrated on making some sense of Donna's blurb and retyped it neatly. Then she placed it on top of Donna's original version.

At least this had taken her mind off the events of the evening. And now she could go off in search of a bridge game, to keep her buzzing thoughts at bay.♥

Chapter Fourteen

9 August, 1962

Donna didn't understand how Ron could live like this. Her own trailer home was shabby, but at least she managed to keep it reasonably clean and neat. Of course it wasn't just his fault that the apartment was a mess. With two other guys living there – one of whom slept on the couch – plus an assortment of women who came and went, none of whom showed any interest in housekeeping, what could she expect?

She made some futile attempts to restore a little order to the living room. She picked up the empty beer cans and pizza cartons and brought them into the kitchen. But the garbage bin was already overflowing, so all she could do was lay the additional trash on the floor next to it.

At least she and Ron had the place to themselves for the moment. As soon as he got out of the shower, they needed to talk.

Back in the living room, she settled herself on the grubby couch and tried not to think about what might have caused some of the nasty stains on it. She heard the shower water stop, and a

GL♥SS

couple of minutes later Ron returned.

He went directly into the kitchen and opened the refrigerator door. 'Want a beer?' he called.

Almost three months together, and he still couldn't remember that she hated beer. 'No, thanks.'

'Where's the damned church key?' he barked.

She spotted it among the junk strewn over the coffee table. 'In here.'

He returned, opened his beer and flopped into a chair. She waited until he'd taken a big gulp. She'd had a whole speech prepared to lead up to her news, but at the last minute she just blurted it out.

'I'm pregnant.'

She watched him carefully, trying to read his expression. It told her nothing.

'You sure? Maybe you're just, you know, late.'

She shook her head. 'I've been to a doctor. He says I'm six weeks along.'

He took another swig of his beer, and then set it down on the coffee table. 'Shit.'

She flinched. It wasn't as if she expected him to be happy, but the word was like a slap in the face.

He said it again. 'Shit. I was careful.'

He sounded almost defensive, like it was all her fault. She didn't rise to the bait. 'Those things can break.'

He gave in. 'Yeah.'

They sat in silence for a minute. 'You tell anyone? Your mother?'

She shook her head.

'Your father?'

'Ron, I haven't seen or talked to my father since he took the kids away.'

'Well, at least no one's going to be coming after me with a shotgun,' he muttered.

'No.'

'He's still sending you money, right?' he asked suddenly.

'Yes. But it's not enough for a baby too.' She hesitated. 'Maybe if I told him . . .'

Ron shook his head and picked up his beer. He drank silently.

And then the room wasn't so quiet any more. Ron's two roommates, one accompanied by a girl she'd never seen before, charged in. They were all laughing in a way that told Donna they'd spent some time in a bar before coming home.

'Too damned quiet in here,' one of the guys barked, and turned on a radio. The room filled with the sound of the Supremes wailing 'Baby Love'. Donna stood up.

'I have to go,' she said.

Normally if she left so early in the evening, Ron would complain. And she'd tell him, for the millionth time, that she had to get up early to go to the diner. Monday, Wednesday, Friday, from six in the morning till two in the afternoon – that had been her schedule for two months now. Somehow he couldn't seem to

GL♥SS

remember. But this time he didn't say anything. She couldn't really blame him. With the news she'd just given him, he'd be happy to see her leave.

But at least he got up. 'I'll drive you home.'

'I can walk,' she said. 'It's still light out. And I feel like a walk.'

She could have sworn he looked relieved, and she assumed that was because he didn't want to talk. He did walk her out of the apartment though.

'Ron . . .'

'Yeah?'

'What are we going to do?'

He shrugged. 'I gotta think about this. I'll call you.'

She nodded. He turned and went back inside. Not even a goodnight kiss.

It was hot out, and even in her sleeveless top and shorts she could feel the sweat trickle down the side of her face as she walked.

A baby. When the doctor told her, just that morning, she hadn't known what to think. For a brief second images flashed before her eyes. A tiny, pink-and-white, soft-skinned and sweet-smelling bundle in her arms. Memories of holding the newborn Billy, just two years ago. Someone to take care of, someone to love.

But then there was the reality of the future. How would she support a baby? True, Ron had a job – for the moment – but could she count on him? Did she even want to?

She herself was making minimum wage working three shifts a week at the diner, and they probably wouldn't want to hire her full-time anyway. Besides, with a baby to care for, how could she work at all? It wasn't like there was anyone else at home to help out.

Her mother had taken off with some guy she met two weeks earlier. In a way, Donna hadn't minded. She still had the trailer, and her father's cheques paid the rent for the space in the trailer park. Funny though, how she hadn't even mentioned to Ron the fact that she was now living alone. Maybe it was because she was afraid he'd want to move in.

As she approached the trailer she could hear the phone ringing, but she didn't quicken her step. Probably her mother, she supposed as she unlocked the door. But the only reason she'd be calling would be to ask for money. It was still ringing when she entered, so she picked it up.

'Hello?'

'Hey, it's me.'

There was a slight slur in Ron's voice. How many beers could he have drunk in the twenty minutes it had taken her to get home?

'Look, I've been talking to this girl here. And she knows a doctor.'

Donna was confused. 'I told you, I've already been to a doctor.'

'Not that kind of doctor.'

A wave of nausea came over her. But of course, this would be Ron's solution. Don't deal with the situation, just get rid of it.

'But it costs,' he said. 'Three hundred. You got any money?'

'About forty dollars,' she whispered.

There was another muttered expletive. Then a sigh. 'I'll see what I can come up with.'

When she hung up the phone, she sat very still for a moment. Then, even though she wasn't hungry, she went to the refrigerator and took out the tuna salad she'd brought home from the diner. The mayonnaise was probably a bit off, but she forced herself to eat it anyway.

Then she went into the bedroom that had been her mother's and turned on the TV. She found a *Father Knows Best* episode that had just started, and she settled back to watch.

It was a re-run, and she'd seen it before, but that didn't matter. She loved the show about the Anderson family in their pretty suburban home with the white picket fence. There was the perpetually smiling mother, the wise, all-knowing father, the three kids, one of whom always seemed to have a problem. Inevitably the father provided some good advice, and the problem was resolved. The ideal family.

In tonight's episode, daughter Betty wanted to break her date for a school dance with a nice-but-ordinary boy when a better-looking and more popular boy asked her out. Even if Donna hadn't seen it before, she would know that ultimately, with her parents' guidance, Betty would realize this was morally wrong. She always ended up doing the right thing.

What if Betty had come home and announced she was pregnant? What would the parents say about that? she wondered. What kind of advice would they give? She tried to come up with a scenario that would work for the Anderson family. But in the world of *Father Knows Best*, this kind of problem didn't exist. Betty would never have sex before marriage. And certainly not with a boy she didn't even love.

At least by the time the show was over it was dark out, and she could pretend it was bedtime. But that didn't mean she'd be able to sleep.

She didn't mind the job at the diner, even though it meant getting up before dawn. It wasn't exactly a cheerful place – the boss was always yelling at the waitresses and the cook, and the smell of grease permeated everything. Lately the smell had made her nauseous, and she'd had to escape to the restroom every now and then. But the place was busy, and there was no time to think about anything but who had ordered their eggs over easy and who wanted them scrambled. And there were free saltine crackers on the tables – this was just about the only thing she could keep down in the morning. Most customers didn't take them, so it was easy for her to swipe the packets.

Something else occurred to her that next morning as she dressed for work. There hadn't been a uniform that fitted her thin frame, so she had to wear one that was too big, with a loose bib-style apron over it. Donna wasn't showing yet, and she wasn't sure when she would, but it was a comfort to know that in the weeks to come she would be able to hide her transgression, for a while at least.

On this Friday morning the diner was unusually busy, with truckers and a whole busload of tourists heading to the lakes upstate. She couldn't even take her usual lunch break, but by two o'clock her apron pockets were filled with cracker packets.

She ducked into the restroom to change into shorts and a T-shirt for the walk back to the trailer. She was very surprised, when she walked out of the diner, to find Ron waiting in his car for her. The sight of him at two o'clock on a weekday was ominous. He'd only been at this new job for a few weeks – surely he hadn't already been fired.

'What are you doing here?' she asked. 'Why aren't you at work?'

'I got the money,' he told her. 'I told the boss I wasn't feeling well so I could take you.'

For one blissful, very fleeting moment, she was confused. Then she understood. Her stomach turned over.

'How did you get the money?' she asked as she got into the car.

'Borrowed it,' he said.

She was about to ask, 'From whom?' but then she thought better of it. She had a pretty good feeling she didn't really want to know.

They drove in silence. What could she say to him anyway? That she wasn't sure this was the right thing to do? That she was scared? It wouldn't matter. This was the only way to go – that's what he would tell her. And she couldn't disagree.

He stopped at a red light and pulled a crumpled piece of paper from his pocket. 'Four-twenty West Mulberry,' he muttered.

'The doctor's office?' she asked.

'Yeah.'

But it wasn't an office building that they found at the address. Four-twenty West Mulberry was an old, rundown, four-storey apartment building. Ron parked right in front, and then he looked at the piece of paper again.

'Second floor, door on the right,' he said. But he didn't make any movement to get out of the car.

'You're not coming with me?' she asked.

He made a face. 'Look, I'm paying for it, OK? And I'll wait for you. The guy said it only takes about twenty minutes.' He took out his wallet and counted out the bills. 'Here.'

234

Silently she took the money and got out of the car.

Inside, the building looked just as bad, with peeling wallpaper and ragged carpeting. She hadn't eaten, and she was feeling weak, so she grabbed the rail as she started up the stairs. At the landing, the door on the right didn't have any sign. Maybe Ron had the wrong address . . .

She rapped at the door tentatively. It was opened by a man in a wrinkled shirt.

'Yeah?'

She wasn't sure what to say. 'I – I think I have an appointment.'

He stared at her, not blinking.

'My name is Donna . . .'

Still he said nothing.

'Ron called you . . . ?'

Finally he nodded. 'You got the money?'

She held out the wad of bills. He snatched it from her and opened the door wider. Now Donna could see the interior. It was even seedier than the hallway had been. The floor was cracked linoleum. The one window was so filthy it didn't even need the crooked and broken blinds that hung over it.

She wasn't sure what she'd expected. Something more like a hospital operating room, she supposed. Everything white and sanitary. But of course, this wasn't a hospital. This man probably wasn't even a doctor.

She stepped inside. Now she could see a table, with a sheet on it. And there was a chair, on which rested a pan filled with metal instruments. She looked away, and in the corner of the room she saw a mousetrap holding a dead mouse.

She must have gone green, because the man suddenly asked, 'Are you going to throw up?' He pointed in the direction of a yellow plastic wastebasket.

She shook her head.

'Well, I haven't got all day, lady. Take off your pants.'

She didn't move.

'Look, you want to get rid of this thing or don't you?'

This thing. That's all it was at this point, she supposed. A thing. Smaller than that dead mouse.

She turned and fled, running down the stairs so fast she couldn't even feel them under her feet. Running out the door, running to the car.

Ron stared at her. 'It's finished already?'

She shook her head. 'I couldn't,' she whispered.

He hit the steering wheel with his fist. She flinched, as if he'd just hit *her*.

'I couldn't,' she whispered again.

'Where's the money?'

She looked at him blankly.

'You gave him the money?' he asked in disbelief. A second later he was out of the car and running into the building.

Strangely, she felt calm, almost relaxed. She'd made a decision. Right or wrong, she was just going to let it happen, let nature take its course. It was out of her hands now.

When Ron returned, his face was red and he was rubbing his jaw as if it hurt. But he wasn't angry. 'I got the money,' he muttered as he climbed into the car and slammed the door. He started the engine, but just let it run.

> It was out of her hands now.

'Now what?' he asked.

She spoke carefully. 'I had an idea.'

'Yeah?'

She took a deep breath. 'I have the trailer to myself now. My mother ran off with some guy.'

'When did that happen?'

She hesitated. 'Yesterday,' she lied. 'She left me a note. Anyway, I was thinking . . . you could move in with me. Of course, once the baby comes I won't be able to work . . .'

He grimaced. 'So I'll be supporting us and the baby.'

'But you won't be paying rent any more,' she pointed out. 'That will help. And . . . and . . .' she summoned all her courage. 'If we got married, I could tell my father and he'd probably give us some money. As a wedding gift.'

She watched his expression. He was always complaining about the crowded conditions at the apartment, how his roommates got on his nerves.

Finally he spoke. 'Yeah, maybe.'

Encouraged, she went on. 'You don't have to get me a ring or anything. I'll even pay for the licence. We could go to City Hall right now and get the application. It's not far from here – you just go up Mulberry and take a right on Hawthorne Avenue.'

He didn't say anything, but he finally put his hand on the shift and pulled out of the parking space. And when they got to the end of Mulberry, he took a right on Hawthorne.♥

Chapter Fifteen

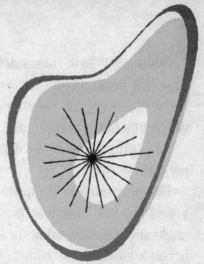

Sam had been ejected from Washington Square Park. 'They're setting up a weekend "art" show,' he told Allison, wiggling two fingers to mime quotation marks. '"Garbage" would be a better word for it. They threw us out – me and the bongo guy – and even that poor jerk who makes the balloon animals.'

'That's tragic,' Allison declared fervently. 'You're the real artist.'

'I knew we were going to be shut out for the weekend,' he grumbled. 'But this is Friday. How am I going to make it through three days with no chance to make any money?' Then his brow furrowed. 'Hey, that's right, it's Friday. What are you doing here? You get fired from your job or something?'

'It's the annual company party,' she told him. 'The big boss invited the entire staff to hang out at his fancy house with its swimming pool and tennis court on Long Island.'

'So how come you're not there?'

'Because I have absolutely no interest in seeing how rich people live,' she replied. She didn't add that she was already too familiar with big country houses, swimming pools and tennis courts.

Sam grinned and put an arm around her. 'That's my girl.'

Her heart almost stopped. *His* girl? He hadn't even kissed her yet. This was the very first time Sam had made any indication that he was beginning to consider her as a girlfriend.

'How about setting up a show on a street corner?' she suggested. 'Eighth Street has all those shops – there should be a lot of street traffic.' They started off in that direction, and she was very pleased that he didn't remove the arm that was around her shoulders. But he took it off when they passed an open garbage can on the kerb.

'Hey, look at this!' At the top of the trash heap lay a tambourine. He picked it up and gave it a tentative shake. A couple of the metal discs were missing, but it still made a sound.

'Wanna make music with me, babe?' He held it out towards her. Allison took it gingerly between her finger and thumb.

'I don't know how to use a tambourine,' she protested.

'Nothing to it,' he said. 'You just hit it in time to the music. Hey, this could be cool – girls always get more money thrown at them.'

They'd reached the corner of 8th and Fifth Avenue, which looked like an ideal location. There was space on the sidewalk, and just a few feet away there was a coffee shop with outdoor tables, all of which were occupied. They had a captive audience.

Sam opened his case, took out the guitar and threw the strap around his shoulder. Then he placed the open case on the sidewalk, and to let passers-by know why it was there, he reached in his pocket and threw a couple of coins into it. He strummed a few chords, and then went right into what Allison thought was his very best song, the one about the seasons.

He hadn't even got to the end of the first line and Allison hadn't even shaken her tambourine once when a man in an apron came out of the coffee shop.

'Beat it!' he yelled. 'You're annoying my customers.'

'You're crazy, man!' Sam yelled back. 'I'm entertaining them!'

Unfortunately a policeman happened to come along just at that moment and he offered up another objection to their presence on the street.

'Sorry, kids, you can't do that here.'

'Why not?' Sam challenged him. 'It's a free country!'

'A free country with laws,' the policeman replied patiently. 'No begging on the streets.'

'Come on, Sam, let's go,' Allison muttered, tugging on his sleeve.

But Sam was furious. 'This ain't begging, man! I'm providing a service! I'm doing these folks a favour!'

'Yeah, well, the City of New York sees it differently,' the policeman said, and it was clear to Allison that his patience was wearing thin. 'Now move along.'

'Where?' Sam demanded to know. 'Where can I legally make some music in this godforsaken town?'

'Try Carnegie Hall,' one of the customers from the coffee-shop terrace yelled, and everyone started laughing.

Now Allison got nervous. Sam's face was turning red, the anger in his expression was unmistakable and the policeman's eyes narrowed. His hand moved towards the baton that hung from his belt.

'Sam, please, let's go,' she urged.

'Better listen to your girlfriend,' the policeman said. Maybe something in Allison's frightened expression touched him, because his tone softened. 'Look, I've seen kids like you performing in the subway.'

'Is it legal?' Allison asked.

'Not sure,' the policeman admitted. 'But it'll be the transit authority's problem, not mine.'

'*You're* the problem, man,' Sam growled. 'Fascist.' But he started to walk away.

A couple of customers from the coffee shop applauded. Allison tucked her arm through his. 'Ignore them,' she said. 'Think of all the great artists who have suffered. Some day you'll be recognized.'

GL♥SS

Sam just continued to mutter about the unfairness of it all. But at least he took the policeman's advice. When they reached the entrance to the West Fourth Street subway station, he started down the stairs. Once they were on a platform, Sam went through the whole procedure again, taking out the guitar and tossing a few coins into the empty case.

People waiting on the platform glanced his way, but no one seemed particularly interested. Sam had barely strummed two chords before a subway train tore into the station and drowned out the music.

'This won't work,' Allison told Sam, yelling to be heard over the noise of the train. He agreed and they climbed back up the stairs to the entranceway. The trains running below them could still be heard, but not quite so loudly.

Once again, Sam set up his case and dropped some change into it. He began to play, and Allison began hitting the tambourine in time to the song. It was surprisingly easy. And when a couple of passing guys tossed some coins into the guitar case, she was pleased – even more so when Sam rewarded her with a smile of approval. A wonderful sense of well-being came over her. This was where she belonged – not in her parents' snotty Beacon Hill townhouse, not at the sumptuous Long Island mansion of the Hartnell family – but here, in the smelly, gritty New York subway, with a real folk-singing beatnik. Who might just be on the verge of becoming her boyfriend.

Sam finished the 'seasons' song and went into another. This one was a little harder for Allison to follow – it was a rambling ode that didn't really have a melody. Since she couldn't find a beat, she just started shaking the tambourine haphazardly. She glanced at Sam, and he nodded with approval.

Then she blinked. Was it her imagination, and the dim light in the station, or had she just recognized two figures coming through the turnstile? The closer they came, the more she kept blinking, hoping that each time she opened her eyes they'd have disappeared.

But then they were there, right in front of her – a smartly dressed woman who played canasta with her mother, and the girl who'd been president of her senior class. The girl spoke first – or shrieked, actually.

'Allison!'

Stunned, she went right on shaking the tambourine, until she realized Sam had stopped playing his guitar.

'String broke,' he muttered, and lifted the strap over his head. Leaning the guitar against the wall, he crouched down and opened the guitar case. He ignored the people standing there, but Allison couldn't.

'Hello, Mrs Gardner. Hi, Martha. What are you doing in New York?'

'Shopping,' Martha answered her, but her bulging eyes were on Sam.

Mrs Gardner, however, didn't even seem to have

noticed that Allison wasn't alone. 'Well, isn't this a coincidence! Normally we wouldn't take the subway, but it was impossible to find a taxi. We heard there was a lovely art show in Washington Square Park, and we thought it would be amusing to walk around Greenwich Village and look at all the strange people. You know, the beatniks.'

'*Mother*,' Martha hissed, and for the first time the woman realized that one of these exotic creatures was just next to Allison. And that the tambourine in Allison's hand indicated some kind of relationship between them.

Martha's mother's eyebrows rose. 'Is this a friend of yours, Allison?'

She smiled sweetly. 'More than a friend, Mrs Gardner.' She moved closer to Sam, who was still crouched by the guitar case.

'Stand up,' she hissed.

His brow furrowed, but he obliged. Allison tilted her head up, closed her eyes and puckered her lips. He'd have to be an idiot not to understand what she wanted him to do.

Sam was no idiot. Right there, in the subway station, with people all around, he wrapped his arms around her. As he pulled her close, he ran his hand down her spine, and she trembled. He must have felt her body respond, because he did it again. Then he pressed his lips against hers and kissed her so hard it almost hurt. But not in a bad way.

This being New York City, the typical subway riders passing them paid no attention. But Allison was very sure that two visitors from Boston had their eyes glued to the scene.

For once Sherry didn't care if she looked like an unsophisticated, small-town girl with limited experiences. She gazed open-mouthed at the Hartnell house in utter wonderment.

The white-columned mansion made *Gone with the Wind*'s Tara look like a cottage. The circular driveway curved through a manicured lawn that was more like a park, surrounded by perfectly trimmed hedges, dotted with flowering trees and with an enormous fountain in which massive dolphins poured forth streams of water. To one side, a beautiful rose garden was in full bloom. And the view – turning away from the house, beyond the trees Sherry could see waves crashing on a distant shore.

'This is like something out of a movie,' she murmured in awe.

Mike was shaking his head in disbelief. 'No kidding. I mean, I knew the boss was rich, but this is incredible. Do you think that's the butler?'

He was referring to a haughty, unsmiling man in a black suit who was waving the folks who had come off the bus towards the back of the house.

GL♥SS

'I don't know,' Sherry said. 'I've never seen a real live butler before.'

The man spotted them lingering and beckoned them in a way that was more of a command than an invitation. Mike suddenly went stiff and saluted. Sherry burst out laughing.

Things had changed remarkably between them over the past week. After turning him down on the evening of Caroline's party, she was very pleased when he asked her out again, and this time it was a real date. He picked her up at the residence, took her to a movie and paid for both tickets. It was a Japanese film with subtitles, the kind of movie she'd never seen before. With friends back home she saw Elvis Presley movies and beach movies, and with Johnny it was always action or horror.

They went out for something to eat afterwards, and again, it wasn't what she was accustomed to – a burger, or a pizza. Mike brought her to a Chinese restaurant, where real Chinese people served them food she'd never seen before. He'd paid the bill.

Of course that could have been just a 'thank you' for typing up his short story, so she was even more pleased when he asked her out again.

This time they went to a concert in Central Park, to hear the New York Philharmonic Orchestra. Johnny would never have taken her to hear classical music. The concert was free, but there were vendors selling food, and Mike bought enough for a picnic on the Great Lawn of the park.

She wasn't a greedy person. It wasn't that she needed or even wanted to have everything paid for. She certainly wasn't like Pamela, who demanded a sugar daddy. It was just that when a guy paid, the event became a real date, not simply two friends doing something together. And according to the rules of relationships, two dates in the space of one week meant that something was starting to happen.

And the conversations they had weren't like those she'd had with other boys – gossiping about mutual friends, complaining about school, considering the championship potential of the local sports teams. Over the Chinese food, they'd talked about the symbolism in the Japanese film. During the intermission at the Central Park concert, they talked about how a person needn't choose between popular music and classical music, that both could be appreciated.

She was liking him more and more. Which was why it bothered her a little that he'd made no effort at all to get physically close. If she counted the reading they'd gone to together a few weeks ago, then the concert had actually been a third date. But not only had there not been any necking, he hadn't even kissed her yet. OK, there'd been a peck on the cheek when he left her at the door of the residence after the last date. But nothing romantic.

Maybe that was because Mike didn't have a car, which was where all the necking went on back home. Still, she was beginning to get a little impatient. He should have at least made some show of affection by now. Which was why she was gratified when he took her hand as they obeyed the butler and followed the others around the side of the mansion. Handholding wasn't much, but it was something.

The scene was even more breathtaking at the back of the house. Mr Hartnell had gone all out for his employees. Streamers, balloons and Japanese lanterns dangled from the trees. The land, which seemed to go on forever, was covered with decorated round tables sheltered from the blazing sun by brightly coloured umbrellas. Over by the hedges that bordered the yard were long tables covered with food. A barbecue pit sent forth delicious aromas, and there were several bars set up with uniformed bartenders behind them. A live band was playing. And beyond all this, tennis courts and a huge swimming pool beckoned. There had to be at least three hundred employees from Hartnell Publications milling about, but the area wasn't even crowded.

'West Egg,' Mike declared.

'What?'

'That's what this reminds me of. Didn't you ever read *The Great Gatsby*?'

Embarrassed, Sherry shook her head. 'It's supposed

to be the great American novel, isn't it?'

'It's one of them,' Mike said. 'West Egg is what F. Scott Fitzgerald called the community on Long Island where the new millionaires in the 1920s lived. You should read it, Sherry. F. Scott Fitzgerald and Ernest Hemingway . . . they're my idols.'

'I'll read them both,' Sherry assured him. She really would too. It was something a girl had to do to make a relationship work – show an interest in what *he's* interested in. With Johnny, she'd forced herself to learn all about football. Following Mike's interest was going to be a lot more pleasant.

'Some day,' Sherry said, 'people will be talking about you the way you're talking about Fitzgerald and Hemingway. You're going to be just as successful.'

Mike shrugged. 'Who knows? I have to do a lot of struggling first.'

'What do you mean?'

'That's the way it is,' Mike said. 'Even Hemingway suffered. When Hemingway was writing *The Sun Also Rises* he was living in a walk-up apartment with no running water. If a writer's serious, he has to be prepared to live like that. It can take a long time before you make any money.'

Sherry didn't like hearing that. What did he mean by 'a long time'?

'What's the matter?' Mike asked.

'Oh, nothing,' she said quickly. 'I was just thinking

GL♥SS

about what you said. How a writer has to suffer. But what if a writer is really, really talented and gets published right away?'

'That's one in a million,' Mike said. 'Besides, I won't mind suffering for my work. It's tradition! And maybe I'll do my struggling the way Hemingway did. In Paris.'

'Paris,' Sherry murmured. The city of her dreams. Of course, *her* fantasy of Paris included plumbing . . .

'In fact,' Mike went on, 'I've been thinking. Maybe I should do that now.'

Sherry stared at him. '*Now?*'

He laughed at her shocked expression. 'I don't mean right this minute. But why should I spend the money I'm saving on university tuition? I mean, is formal education going to make me a better writer? The cost of living is a lot cheaper in France. Maybe I should move to Paris in September and just write.'

'But you need an education,' Sherry protested. 'The money you've saved – it won't last long. You'll need a job. And what kind of job could you get without a degree?'

Mike shrugged. 'I could wait tables, clean houses, something like that.'

But how could he support a wife and family that way? she wanted to know. And she gave herself a mental kick. He wasn't even her boyfriend yet, and she was thinking of him in the role of husband and father.

'Hey, folks, have you seen that buffet?' Pamela had

popped up before them. 'It's amazing!'

The plate she held was piled high with food, but that wasn't what amazed Sherry. While they'd been told this would be a casual affair, and practically everyone was wearing shorts, Pamela had taken casual to the extreme. She wore a hot-pink bikini.

'Why are you wearing that?' Sherry asked. 'There's a cabana by the pool – you could have changed there when you're ready to take a dip.'

Pamela responded with a mischievous wink. 'You think I'm going to pass up an opportunity to flaunt myself?'

Sherry didn't miss Mike's smile, and she managed a small one herself. 'Where's Mr . . .' she caught herself in time. 'Where's your friend?'

Pamela shrugged. 'I haven't seen him yet. It doesn't matter – there are plenty of fish in this sea. See you later!'

'That looked good,' Mike remarked as Pamela sauntered off.

Sherry looked at him sharply. 'Yes, Pam's cute,' she said.

'I was talking about the chicken,' he said. 'But yeah, she's a cute girl.'

Couldn't he say something like, 'but not my type'? Or 'you're cuter'? Then she kicked herself again. It wasn't as if they had any kind of commitment to each other.

Maybe it was because of a dream she'd had the other night, one that woke her up in a cold sweat. She'd dreamed of Aunt Agnes, coming for Christmas dinner. Only when the door opened it wasn't Aunt Agnes. It was old Aunt Sherry, the spinster.

Lying in bed, it had taken her less than a second to realize she'd been dreaming. But even so, she was momentarily overcome with panic. Could this be a premonition of her future?

As they filled their plates from the buffet table she scanned the crowd. The *Gloss* fiction editor, Mr Gold – he had to be there somewhere. Maybe she could arrange to accidentally-on-purpose bump into him. Find a way to casually ask if he happened to have read Mike's short story yet.

And Hartnell Publications included a book division. Mike had told her he was writing a novel. Maybe she could get him to show her a few chapters, a synopsis, something like that. She could figure out a way to meet one of those book editors, get the material into his hands . . .

With plates in their hands, she looked around for a table with empty seats. But Mike had another idea.

'I think I saw a bench by the rose garden in the front,' he said. 'Let's go there – it'll be quieter and we can talk.'

This was nice – he wanted to be alone with her.

Away from the crowd, with only the faint strains of music following them, they found the bench and settled down. Mike picked up a fried chicken leg and attacked it with gusto. Sherry poked her fork at some macaroni salad.

'So what do you think of my idea?' he asked. 'Can you see me writing in an attic in Paris?'

'It sounds romantic,' she conceded, 'but I'll bet the reality isn't so nice.'

'Probably not,' he said.

'And maybe not all writers have to suffer,' she continued.

'What makes you think I'd be the exception?'

'Because you're so good!' she exclaimed. 'That story you wrote, about the boy and the horse – I can't tell you how much it moved me.'

'Really?'

She nodded vigorously. 'And I can't wait to read your novel. Maybe I could type up the chapters as you finish them.'

His eyes widened. 'You'd do that for me?'

Again she nodded.

He gazed at her in wonderment. 'Why?'

Because I want you to be a success, she thought. Because I want you to be in a position where you can be thinking about the future, about getting married, having a family, making a living to support them.

But of course she couldn't say that, not yet. It was way too soon, she would scare him off. She looked down.

'Because . . . because I think you're a great writer. I believe in you.'

He stared at her for a minute. Then he reached over and touched her chin. She raised her face to him. He was looking at her so intently, she could practically feel his eyes. She wanted to feel more.

Touch me, she implored silently. Touch me now. All the feelings she'd been holding inside rose to the surface. A lock of hair had escaped from her headband. He reached out and brushed it away.

'You're so pretty,' he whispered, and she couldn't breathe.

He took his plate off his lap and set it down on the grass. He took *her* plate off her lap, and set it on the grass too. And then he took her in his arms and kissed her.

Pamela was puzzled. Here she was, looking so sexy in her pink bikini, and she'd barely had a glance from any of the men. She was beginning to have serious regrets about allowing her hair colour to be changed. Platinum blondes always got attention.

She spotted her bosses, Doreen and Darlene, joined at the hip as usual. They were sitting together at a table that held only other women, which wasn't very interesting. But when they spotted her and beckoned for her to come over, she had to respond.

They were whispering together as she approached, and Darlene got up to join her before she reached the table. She pulled Pamela aside to speak quietly.

'Pamela dear, this really isn't appropriate.'

Pamela looked at her blankly. 'Huh?'

'What you're wearing. It'll be OK when you're at the pool, but you shouldn't wander around in a bikini. You don't see anyone else wearing a swimsuit, do you?'

Which was exactly why Pamela wanted to wear one, so she'd stand out. 'But it's a party!'

'You need to cover up,' Darlene said firmly.

Pamela reached into her bag, took out her little dress, and slipped it over her head. 'OK?'

Darlene didn't look impressed, and Pamela could guess why. The dress was very short and very tight, and the fabric was practically transparent.

Darlene sighed. 'Better,' she allowed. 'Now come sit with us.'

It was while she was listening to the editors' conversation that she finally realized why she hadn't been getting any attention from any men at the party.

'Did you see Felix Duncan's wife? She's twice his size!'

'I like what Mr Simpson's wife is wearing. The necklace is all wrong though.'

She hadn't even noticed that there were a lot of

women here she'd never seen before, and she realized then who they were. She should have guessed that all those wives who'd been stashed on Long Island for the summer would be joining their husbands for a party on this very same Long Island. And men wouldn't flirt or even wink at her if their wives were by their side.

So when Alex finally did show up, it was no great shock to see him with a woman too. By then, Pamela was at the pool, free to wear her bikini uncovered. She had a good view of Alex and the woman she assumed was his wife as they emerged from the cabanas with their swimsuits on.

So this was Mrs Parker. Pamela had no idea what her first name was. During their evenings together Alex never spoke about her, or his kids either for that matter. All he ever really talked about was his work – how he'd snagged some account, or his efforts to get some shoe company to advertise in the magazine. It wasn't all that interesting to Pamela, but she could tell that he took a lot of pleasure in describing his job. She got the feeling that he was simply lonely, that he needed someone to talk to. And she was perfectly happy to be that person, as long as he kept taking her to nice places.

He was always a gentleman, holding out her chair for her, taking her arm when they crossed a street, that sort of thing. And he'd made no physical overtures – a kiss on the cheek at the end of the evening, that was it. This surprised her. It certainly wasn't what Helen Gurley Brown considered to be an affair.

But of course, that was how it would look to his wife, and he wouldn't want her to know about these dinners. On their first outing they'd made a plan as to how he'd explain her if they ran into anyone he knew. The excuse was that she worked in his department, and he was taking her out for her birthday. So far she'd had three birthdays, at Sardi's, Delmonico's and the Four Seasons.

She tried very hard to be discreet as she gave Mrs Parker the once-over. The woman was average height, with light brown hair, neatly coiffed in a wavy chin-length style. She carried a straw bag and wore a one-piece suit in a flowered print. It wasn't very revealing, but Pamela noticed – with some satisfaction – that she didn't have anything to reveal. Mrs Parker was thin, almost bony, and while her legs were reasonable, there wasn't much on top.

Alex didn't see *her* right away. The couple took seats on side-by-side lounge chairs. The woman took a magazine and what looked like a transistor radio from her bag. She handed the radio to Alex, who inserted the earphone. Then he lay back and closed his eyes. They didn't seem to be speaking to each other at all.

What was he listening to? she wondered. She didn't know his taste in music. She really knew very little about him.

GL♥SS

Pamela didn't see anyone she knew at the pool, and she hadn't brought anything to read. She wasn't about to jump into the pool and destroy her hairstyle. And she'd forgotten to bring suntan lotion, which meant she'd be turning red before too long. She decided to go hunt down some of the other interns.

She started to put on her little dress, and then thought better of it. Alex should see her in this pink bikini, she decided. So she sauntered alongside the pool, taking the long way around so she could pass his chair. And hers.

Mrs Parker had the open magazine blocking her view, and Alex's eyes were still closed. Impulsively she spoke.

'Hello, Mr Parker,' she chirped.

He opened one eye, then the other, and both widened. He glanced in the direction of his wife, but she was completely engrossed in her magazine and hadn't even looked up.

'Oh, um, hello.' He didn't use her name.

That didn't surprise her. Of course he wouldn't want his wife to think he actually knew her. Not when she was so much more attractive than the woman he was married to. For some odd reason, this pleased her. She started back towards the buffet table, where desserts had been laid out, but she was stopped before she got there.

'Well, hello there,' the boy called to her.

She hadn't seen him since he stopped working at

Gloss, but she recognized him immediately. Ricky Hartnell, the boss's son, the one who took Sherry to the movie premiere and tried to jump her in the back seat of the limo. She'd thought he was very cute the first time she saw him.

He was looking a little less desirable today. His hair looked like it could use a good wash, his shirt was stained and his eyes were bloodshot. As he came closer, he staggered a little, and it was clear he was feeling no pain. Then she caught a whiff of his breath, and stepped back.

'You're one of those *Gloss* girls, right?' he asked.

She nodded. 'I'm Pamela.'

'How ya doing, Pamela?'

'Just fine,' she replied.

'You *look* just fine,' he declared. 'And you look like you need a drink.'

'What makes you say that?' she asked.

'Because you don't have one.' With that, he tossed back his head and laughed uproariously. The guy was completely smashed.

He jiggled the glass in his hand. 'Let me get you one of these.'

'What is it?'

'Bloody Mary.'

Pamela looked at the remaining inch of liquid in the glass. 'It's yellow.'

He frowned and examined his glass. 'Hey, you're

GL♥SS

right.' He gulped down what was left. 'Tequila Sunrise. Want one?'

'No, thanks.'

He drew closer, and she could smell his breath. 'Sure you do.' He was slurring his words. 'You can't go through an event like this sober.'

'Why not?'

He made a face. 'Well, *I* can't. Come on, babe. Let's get drunk and go at it like rabbits.'

He grabbed her arm. She tried to pull away, but his grip tightened.

'I said I don't want a drink. Now let go of my arm.'

'Babe, don't you know who I am?'

Pamela rolled her eyes. 'Yes, I know who you are. But I still don't want a drink, and I definitely don't want to neck with you.'

It was funny in a way. When she met him on that first day at *Gloss*, she'd thought he was cool. Now, despite the fact that he was still rich, blond and tanned, he seemed kind of pathetic.

'Oh, I get it. You're playing hard to get, right?'

'Not hard to get, Ricky. Impossible to get. Now let me go.' He was really getting on her nerves now.

He didn't let her go. In fact, he squeezed harder, and it actually began to hurt.

'Let me go,' she hissed, 'or I'll scream.'

He snickered. 'Yeah, right, you're going to scream. Right here, at my home, in the middle of a party.

OK, go ahead and scream.'

Did she dare make a scene, in front of all these people? But as it turned out, she didn't have to. From just behind her, a deeper masculine voice spoke.

'Leave her alone, Ricky.'

Pamela turned to see Alex standing there. The Parkers, no longer in swimsuits, obviously hadn't stayed long at the pool.

Mrs Parker stood slightly behind him, frowning. She glanced from side to side, as if worried about who might be listening to this encounter.

Ricky glared at Alex, but he seemed to be having some trouble focusing. 'What's it to *you*?'

Pamela swallowed, and looked anxiously at Alex. Had Ricky seen them together?

But Alex didn't even glance in her direction. He kept his eyes on Ricky and spoke mildly. 'It looks to me like you're bothering one of the interns.'

'Maybe she wants to be bothered,' Ricky retorted.

'Well, let's just see about that.' Alex turned to Pamela. 'Do you want Ricky to bother you?'

Once again she noticed how he hadn't used her name. She shook her head.

'There you go,' Alex said to Ricky. 'I think you should leave her alone.'

Ricky actually released her, and he took a step towards Alex. His fists were clenched. Then, suddenly, he turned a ghastly shade of yellow-green. Pamela stepped back in alarm. It was a great relief when he staggered away.

She turned to thank Alex for his intervention, but his back was to her as he walked away with his wife. That was sweet of him, she thought. Trying to protect her like that. Was it because he cared? Or would he have done it for any of the interns? Unaccountably, under the hot sun, she shivered.

Looking around for something to distract her, she realized the band was playing more loudly now, and had switched to dance music. Right now they were doing a feeble version of 'Let's Twist Again'. She went over to the dance floor, saw some of the other interns twisting away and joined them.

'Let's Twist Again' was followed by 'Twist All Night' and then by the 'Peppermint Twist'. The other interns had clearly indulged a little at the bar, and they were giggling as they shook their bodies. Everyone seemed to be having a good time.

Except Pamela. An odd sensation was creeping over her, and she couldn't give it a name because she didn't think she'd ever felt it before. She realized that she wanted to be alone.

She left the dance floor and headed towards the house. The beach was nearby . . .

She realized that she wanted to be alone.

maybe she could walk there. She circled the house, but as she came around the side to the front she heard a woman's angry voice.

'You're a fool, Alex! Insulting Hartnell's son like that. How are you ever going to get ahead in this company?'

'I'm director of advertising, for crying out loud!'

'That's nothing. You should be a vice-president by now!'

'Phyllis, we've had this argument before. More times than I'd like to remember. I'm getting sick of it.'

'And I'm sick of reminding you that you have a family to support! I want a bigger apartment, I want our kids to go to private schools, I want our own house in the country so we don't have to keep on renting these crappy cottages! And we're never going to have any of these things if you don't start earning more money!'

'Phyllis, keep your voice down!'

'Don't worry, I'm leaving. Here's my taxi.'

From behind the hedge, Pamela could see the yellow car pulling into the driveway. Alex's wife started towards it, and Alex followed her.

'What are you doing? I've got the car – we'll go to the cottage together.'

'I think you should stay in the city this weekend and think about our future,' the woman snapped. 'And keep in mind that I have no intention of spending my life with a man who's going nowhere.'

GL♥SS

She got into the taxi and left Alex standing there staring at the departing vehicle. Pamela emerged from the hedge.

'Alex . . .'

He turned. There was a stricken expression on his face. Pamela tried to act like she hadn't heard anything.

'I just wanted to thank you for getting rid of Ricky.'

He nodded and managed a small smile. 'You're welcome.'

They stood there in silence for a moment. Finally Alex spoke again.

'Are you having fun?'

'Not really,' Pamela replied.

He cocked his head to one side and gazed at her. She got the feeling he was really looking at her, for the very first time.

'Do you want to leave?' he asked suddenly.

'With you?'

He nodded.

She moved closer to him. He continued to look at her, almost as if he was studying her. Then he reached out and touched her hair. 'You look so pretty . . .'

She smiled.

His eyes left her face and he looked around. She knew why – to make sure no one was watching. So it came as no surprise at all when he took her in his arms and kissed her.♥

Chapter Sixteen

Perched on the edge of her elegant chair, Sherry looked around at the other occupants of the room this hotel called the 'petite salon'. A third of the room was blocked off with a high opaque curtain, and she assumed that was where the models were gathered.

From what she understood, most fashion shows were held in the hotel's grand ballroom. But this show featured the work of a young, up-and-coming designer who didn't yet merit a huge room. The event was taking place a week before Givenchy, Saint Laurent, Dior and the other big names would show their designs.

But even though Rafe Bryant wasn't yet a big name, that hadn't stopped people from attending his show. There were a lot of folks there, and most of them were women. At first Sherry assumed they were society types, who bought high fashion directly from designers and straight off the runways. But then she noticed that the majority of them were wearing name tags identifying them as working for magazines and newspapers – *Vogue*, *Harper's Bazaar*, the *New York Herald Tribune*. Some of them were buyers from big stores like Bloomingdale's and Bendel's. They were

GL♥SS

career women, not rich socialites.

They were all impeccably dressed, in Jackie Kennedy suits or simple sheath dresses. Caroline had let Sherry borrow from the samples closet again, and she felt fairly secure in her white belted dress with a navy and white striped insert at the neckline. She just wished her hair was long enough to cover her name tag. With all these important women around her, the word 'intern' seemed so, so . . . *not* important.

There were some men at the show too of course. And one of them was George Simpson. She hadn't been too thrilled that morning when Caroline told her he'd be accompanying her.

'Our fashion editor is taking some vacation time before the really important shows next week,' Caroline had explained. 'And since this is the first year *Gloss* is covering the shows, I can't send only an intern. No offence, Sherry,' she added quickly. 'I'm sure you'd do just fine on your own. But if we don't have someone with a title there, it will look like we're not taking this seriously.'

Sherry wasn't offended at all. She just wished that editor would be someone other than Mr Simpson, who didn't think she was capable of doing anything more than typing his letters.

But at least she hadn't had to travel alone in the taxi with Simpson. David Barnes, the photographer, came with them.

'This is a first for me,' the handsome photographer remarked as the taxi inched up Madison Avenue. 'When did *Gloss* decide to start covering the fashion shows?'

'Caroline's idea,' Mr Simpson muttered. He looked even grumpier than usual. 'I'm only coming because what's-her-name, the fashion gal, is on vacation.'

'Belinda Collins,' Sherry murmured.

'What?' Simpson asked sharply.

'That's the fashion editor's name. Belinda Collins.' She was practically certain that Simpson knew this. After all, the magazine staff wasn't *that* big. She suspected he was just trying to appear so important that he couldn't remember everyone's name.

The features editor just shrugged, as if her comment wasn't even worth acknowledging.

David gave her a friendly smile. 'And you're coming because . . . ?'

'She works for me,' George said shortly. 'She's my intern.'

Inwardly Sherry shuddered. He made it sound like he owned her. She had an overwhelming urge to speak up for herself.

'We're not actually *covering* the shows, like *Vogue* does,' she told David. '*Our* readers aren't in the market for designer duds. But we thought it would be interesting to look at the trends in couture, and maybe come up with an article about the impact on junior dressing. Maybe a *feature* article,' she added, with a glance in Simpson's direction.

His expression was unreadable. Or maybe he wasn't even listening.

Thankfully she didn't have to sit with him in the petite salon. When they arrived, he took the last remaining seat in the front row of the semicircle. David went to the end of the runway, where other photographers were gathered. Sherry selected a seat in the third row, making sure the women in front of her weren't wearing large hats that might block her view.

The hum of conversation immediately stopped when, from somewhere she couldn't see, music filled the room. It was a bouncy tune with a rock 'n' roll beat, and Sherry noticed some raised eyebrows. She got the impression that this wasn't the usual music that accompanied high fashion shows. She took her notepad and pen from her bag, and made a note.

The first model stepped out from behind the curtain. She wore a black cocktail dress, but it wasn't the simple sheath-with-pearls Sherry had seen before. This one had a high waist, and the skirt fell in perky flounces. Teenage girls might not normally wear black, but if they did, this was the kind of dress that would suit them.

The model strode down the aisle and struck a pose at the end. In the flashes of light from the cameras, Sherry got a good look at her face. She wasn't heavily made-up at all – in fact, though she was probably a bit older, she looked like the kind of girl who posed for *Gloss*. She did a little twirl and then headed back down the aisle. Before she reached the curtained area, another model emerged and passed her.

This second girl was wearing black-with-pearls, but in a very original way. The dress itself was spotted with pearls across the bodice, making the dress look more – something. Playful, thought Sherry.

The next dress was more casual, a red sundress edged in white with tiny white polka dots. When the model turned, she saw that the back had crossed straps, like a child's pinafore. Young and breezy. Sherry could see herself in this dress at an afternoon barbecue. It was followed by another sundress, this one in sky blue with spaghetti straps and a ruched top.

By now, Sherry was writing furiously, her eyes darting up and down from the models to her notepad as she tried to catch every detail.

There was so much to take in. A series of dresses with a nautical theme emerged, all red, white and blue. An oversized white collar on this one, a print of stars on another . . . and there was a fantastic yellow taffeta party dress, with lace insets on the stiff full skirt. Oversize buttons on two-piece ensembles, kitten heels instead of stilettos. A couple of models carried shoulder bags instead of handbags. Practically everything in the collection could work in a teen wardrobe.

It was the last model who truly took her breath away. She must have had the same effect on others in the audience, because there was an audible gasp.

She wore a bridal gown, a heavenly creation, clouds of chiffon dotted with tiny rhinestones. It was unbelievably romantic, but fresh too. Like the girl had been showered with dogwood blossoms. Sherry had pored over enough bridal magazines back home to know that she was looking at something new and modern, yet still a young girl's fantasy of a wedding day.

Dimly Sherry was aware that the music had switched to a soft ballad, and maybe that was why the hush in the audience seemed so intense. The girl posed, turned and floated back down the aisle.

The music turned upbeat again, and all the models returned, walking in single file to the end of the runway and turning to walk back. This time the 'bride' was accompanied by a young man with tousled brown hair, dressed in khaki trousers and a slightly wrinkled sportscoat. The audience burst into applause, and Sherry realized that this must be Rafe Bryant himself.

The designer wore a crooked, almost bashful grin, and he took only a brief bow before following the models back behind the curtain. The show was over.

A long table laden with bottles of champagne and trays of little canapés magically appeared. The room became quickly animated as people rose from their chairs, headed to the table and formed small groups to chat. Mr Simpson joined one of these groups, and David was still huddled with his fellow photographers.

Sherry stayed in her seat and went over her scribbles, realizing she could write a really cool article about this show. It was all here in her notes – high fashion that demonstrated trends that could easily be translated into junior apparel. And with David's photographs to illustrate her words, she could create something any *Gloss* reader would appreciate.

The more she considered the possibilities, the more elated she became. And suddenly she couldn't wait to go back to the office and get started on it.

David appeared before her with a little plate of treats.

'Help yourself,' he offered, and she picked a canapé at random.

He sat down beside her and looked at the pad on her lap. 'Wow, you took all those notes for George?'

Fighting the urge to tell him they weren't for Mr Simpson, she just smiled and nodded.

'He's lucky to have you,' the photographer commented. 'I wish Caroline would give *me* an intern.'

'To do what?' Sherry asked.

'Assist in setting up equipment, maybe even learn something about basic photography so she could take preliminary shots. And it would help a lot if

GL♥SS

she knew something about styling.'

Sherry looked at him with interest. 'Styling?'

'You know, what goes with what. Adding the right accessories to an outfit, that sort of thing. Belinda gives me some directions of course, but she's not there for the shoots.'

A brilliant idea began to form. 'She wouldn't have to do any writing, would she?'

David shook his head.

'I'm going to talk to Caroline,' she told the photographer. 'There's an intern who just might be perfect for you.'

The reception was breaking up, and Mr Simpson came over to them.

'We're leaving now,' he declared.

During the ride back, Sherry tried to strike up a conversation with the editor.

'What did you think of the show?' she asked.

Mr Simpson shrugged. Either he wasn't impressed or he just wasn't interested. In any case, he said nothing and they rode in silence.

Until they reached the Hartnell building. Just as they were getting out of the taxi, Mr Simpson patted the breast pocket of his jacket, and groaned.

'Damn, my cigarette case. It must have dropped out of my pocket at the hotel.' He motioned for the taxi to wait, and turned to Sherry.

'You'll have to go back and find it.'

The dismay must have shown on her face, because he raised his eyebrows.

'Do you have something more important to do?' he asked in a tone that clearly said this wasn't possible.

'I just wanted to get started on the article,' Sherry said.

A look of disdain crossed his face. 'About the fashion show? *You're* not writing it. In fact, give me your notes now so I can decide what to do with them.'

Sherry was aware that her mouth was open, but she was speechless. She could only stare at him in disbelief.

'Your notes?' he demanded.

She took out her notebook. At least she had enough presence of mind not to hand it over. There was other stuff in it – notes on conversations with Caroline, ideas for stories. Carefully she tore out only the notes she'd taken at the fashion show and silently handed them to the editor.

'Now get back in the taxi, the meter's running,' he barked. He reached in his pocket, took out a wallet and handed her a bill. 'This should take care of the fare.'

Automatically, like a robot, she took the money and got back into the taxi. And in the back of her mind she wondered how the driver would react if his passenger suddenly burst into furious tears.♥

Chapter Seventeen

'Where the hell's that photographer?' Mr Connelly fumed.

'Here he comes,' Allison said, looking out into the bullpen from the entertainment editor's office. Seconds later, a breathless David Barnes stood in the doorway.

'Sorry to be late, folks, I was covering a fashion show uptown. Refresh my memory. What am I doing now?'

'You're going back uptown,' Mr Connelly informed him. 'Shooting Bobby Dale at an apartment on Park and 73rd.' He turned to Allison. 'This session is mainly for taking pictures. For you, it's just a preliminary meeting with the guy. You'll do the real interview in a couple of weeks, when he's back in New York. So you won't need a tape recorder today. Just take a notebook and jot down any observations you make.'

It was while she was in the taxi that Allison realized she'd picked up the notebook filled with the comments she'd been writing about Sam. Just last night he'd offered up another one of his brilliant observations, and she hoped she'd gotten it down precisely. Here in the taxi, she read it over and savoured the words.

Until we connect with the inner spirit, we're no better than robots, and our lives have no meaning.

How true, how incredibly true! She thought about her parents, their friends, their trivial, meaningless lives. She marvelled at the way Sam could capture the essence of humanity in just a few words. How lucky was she to have found a boy like this? To love a boy like this?

Love . . . she was almost certain that was what she'd come to feel for him. It was hard to be sure, since she'd never had a serious relationship before. How could she? All the boys she'd known were so shallow, so ordinary.

She hadn't used the word with Sam yet. She wanted him to say it first. But after that kiss in the subway a week ago, she'd been pretty sure there were feelings on his part too.

Since then, they'd gone way beyond kissing.

Leaning back in her seat, she closed her eyes and memories of the night before came rushing back. Having just been turned down at an audition for a gig, Sam wasn't in a very good mood. And as they were cutting through the park, a sudden summer storm broke through the clouds. They'd run under a tree, and he'd slumped against it with a grim expression. Taking his hand, she raised it to her mouth and kissed it.

He grabbed her, roughly, and then they were on the ground. In the darkness of the park, with the rain as

GLOSS

an almost musical background, they moved together in rhythm with the downpour. He didn't say anything, there were no romantic exchanges, but it didn't matter – his body spoke for him, and her body responded. She'd never felt such physical excitement before in her life . . .

'So, what do you know about this guy?' David Barnes asked.

She was about to say she thought he was amazing until she realized that of course he was talking about Bobby Dale.

'Twenty years old, born and raised in New York, now lives in Los Angeles,' she recited from memory.

'Didn't we do a piece on him last year?' David asked.

'No, that was Bobby Vee.'

'*This* Bobby . . . is he the one who sings "Blue Velvet"?'

'No, that's Bobby Vinton.'

'So this is the Bobby who's in that movie with Ann-Margret.'

'No, that's Bobby Rydell,' sighed Allison. 'This is a brand-new Bobby.' She looked back at her notes. 'Discovered on an episode of *The Original Amateur Hour* in 1961. First hit song, "Let Me Love You", went to number three on the Billboard charts. Second release, "Love Me Again", made it to number one. He's here in New York to appear on *The Ed Sullivan Show* on Sunday and to kick off a national tour.'

Her tone must have revealed her lack of enthusiasm. The photographer grinned.

'Not a big fan, huh?'

Allison shrugged. 'He's just one more Bobby.'

The taxi pulled up in front of a Park Avenue building where two doormen in uniforms covered with gold braid approached the car. One of them opened their door, while the other, clutching a clipboard, eyed them sternly. As they stepped out on to the red carpet that led under an awning to the front door, the second doorman blocked their way.

'May I help you?' he asked.

'We're here to see Bobby Dale,' David Barnes said.

The doorman eyed him suspiciously and looked at his clipboard. 'Your names?'

Allison supplied hers while the photographer handed over a business card. Finally the doorman allowed them to move down the carpet, where yet another uniformed man opened the doors into an ornate lobby whose walls were covered in gilded mirrors.

The doorman escorted them into an elevator and rode with them to the penthouse floor, where the apartment door was opened by a pudgy, harried-looking man.

'These are the people from *Gloss* magazine,' the doorman announced.

'Yes, yes, of course, come in,' the pudgy man said. 'I'm Lou Mareno, Bobby's manager.'

They entered a room that was positively palatial. From the heavy velvet curtains, the cream-coloured matching furniture and the enormous chandelier that hung from the ceiling, it screamed money and was exactly the kind of place where a filthy-rich teenage heart-throb would live. While a real talent like Sam was crashing on sofas. It was all so wrong, Allison thought.

While David busied himself setting up a tripod, the manager turned to Allison. 'This must be a big thrill for you, young lady,' he said, with a smile that was so patronizing it almost made her gag.

'I'm looking forward to conducting the interview,' she managed to say.

He looked alarmed. 'But not today! I haven't prepped him yet.'

Allison fought back the urge to smirk. Of course, the young heart-throb would have to be prepared by his manager with his answers to any questions she might ask. Most likely, the singer was an idiot who couldn't think for himself.

But again she responded politely. 'No, the interview will be in two weeks. I'm just here to observe.'

The manager was clearly relieved. 'Fine, fine. And do you have a theme for the article?'

It was embarrassing to say the words aloud. "Could you be Bobby's girl?"

The manager looked pleased. 'Excellent! Did you

come up with that all by yourself?'

She was spared having to admit she had by the arrival of the star himself.

Bobby looked exactly like his photos. Medium height, slender, wavy brown hair, perfect features, and when he smiled he revealed dazzling straight white teeth. Clean, wholesome, non-threatening. The only surprise was his eyes. She knew they were blue, but she wasn't prepared for how bright they were. In all fairness, she had to concede that Bobby Dale was extraordinarily handsome.

He turned straight to Allison. 'Hi, I'm Bobby.'

She allowed him a brief, polite and professional smile, and shook the offered hand. 'Allison.'

'You're my interviewer?' he asked.

The manager broke in. 'Not today. She's just watching you today. You don't talk to her at all.'

'Not even if I *want* to?' the boy asked. He smiled at Allison.

Oh, for crying out loud, was he trying to snow her? To get her to write a positive article?

'This is your photographer,' the manager declared. 'What's your name again, fellow?'

'David Barnes.' He put out his hand and the star shook it.

'Where do you want me?'

'Let's start over by the window, the light's good.' David positioned the singer and then moved his tripod.

Looking into the camera's lens, he frowned. 'I have to make a few adjustments.'

The manager turned to his client. 'You can go back to the bedroom, Bobby. I'll call when he's ready for you.'

But Bobby didn't budge. 'It's OK, I can wait.' He looked at Allison. 'You seem young to be a journalist,' he commented.

'Actually, I'm an intern at *Gloss*,' she told him. 'This is just a summer job.'

The manager's face went red. 'They sent an *intern*? To interview *Bobby Dale*?' From his tone he could have been saying 'President John F. Kennedy'. 'I'm calling your magazine right now.' He started in the direction of a telephone on a coffee table.

'Hold off, Lou,' Bobby said. 'They wouldn't have sent her if they didn't think she could do the job. Give her a chance.'

It was clear who called the shots around here. The manager backed away from the phone, still looking peeved.

Bobby turned back to Allison. 'So you're kind of a journalist-in-training, huh?'

'I'm not sure,' Allison replied. 'I haven't decided what I want to do.'

'Where are you from?'

'Boston.'

'How do you like New York?'

'Very much.'

'I love this town,' Bobby said. 'It's great being back here.'

Allison nodded. 'That's right, you're from here, aren't you?'

'Yeah, and I really miss it when I'm away. I like being able to look out a window and know where I am.'

'What do you mean?'

The manager looked at her sharply, and she realized her last two comments had been posed in the form of questions. She was just being polite for crying out loud!

Bobby must have caught the man's look too. 'It's OK, Lou, we're making conversation!' He turned back to Allison. 'What I mean is, New York has a look that's all its own. Some cities, they all look alike.' He sighed. 'I've been travelling so much lately, half the time I don't know where I am. It can be kind of, I don't know . . . depressing.'

Sam's words came back to her. 'Where you're going is no better than where you are,' she told him.

His eyes lit up. 'Quincy!'

'Huh?'

'Walter Quincy! You've read *The Free Spirit*.'

She shook her head.

'Wait a sec.' He left the room and returned seconds later with a battered paperback in his hand. 'One of my all-time favourite books. You sure you never read it?'

She shook her head again.

'"Where you're going is no better than where you are,"' he said. 'It's a famous line. Maybe you just heard someone quote it.'

'Maybe,' she said uncertainly.

'I've been trying to read everything he's written. He's got this way of summing up big ideas, whole philosophies, in these brief sentences.' He glanced at his manager, and lowered his voice. 'I'm not supposed to talk about this, but I've been thinking I'd like to write my own songs. And Quincy's been a real influence.'

'How so?'

Again, he looked to make sure Lou Mareno wasn't listening.

'Don't worry,' Allison assured him. 'I'm not recording this. I'm not even taking notes.'

'Well . . . you know the kind of stuff I've been recording. "I love you madly, I want you badly . . ."' He made a face. 'Quincy says, "What you sing is who you are." And what I'm singing now, well . . . it's not really me.'

Allison stared at him, and not because he was being so open with her. 'Quincy wrote that? "What you sing is who you are?"'

He handed her the book. 'Here, you can borrow this. And maybe we can talk about it when we meet for the interview in a couple of weeks.'

'OK, we can get started now,' David called out.

For the next twenty minutes Allison was only dimly aware of the activity in the room. Flashbulbs went off, David called out directions, and Bobby's manager hovered. Allison's mind was elsewhere.

So those weren't Sam's original words. Well, so what? People did that all the time. Her mother, for example. She was always saying stuff like 'A penny saved is a penny earned', and 'A place for everything and everything in its place', without adding, 'Benjamin Franklin said that.'

So Sam must be an admirer of this Quincy person. Funny how he hadn't mentioned it. But she chalked it up as just one more interesting observation that she could put in the article she would write about him. She put the book in her bag and hoped she'd find some time to start reading it tonight, if she didn't get back from the Village too late.

As it turned out, she didn't have to wait that long. Just after five o'clock, when she was on her way downtown, the train stopped between Herald Square and Twenty-third Street. The usual garbled voice mumbled something over the speaker system about a brief delay. Since everyone on the train knew it wouldn't be brief, there was a chorus of groans. Allison opened *The Free Spirit*.

The introduction was pretty interesting. It seemed that this guy, Quincy, had always been on the fast track, trying to become a big shot in his career. But even though he was pretty successful, he wasn't happy. He made a lot of money, he held a high position, but deep inside, he hadn't advanced at all.

'I see people running, rushing, trying to catch a bus or a train, trying to be first in line,' she read. 'And I want to say to them, what's your rush? It doesn't matter where you go, it's not going to be any better than where you are.'

The words rang a bell, and she realized this was something Sam had said.

There was a jerk, and then the train starting moving again. She closed the book and put it back in her bag.

Were all of Sam's profound comments taken from Walter Quincy, she wondered. It was a good thing she'd discovered this before writing the article about him and claiming all the remarks were original.

This didn't mean Sam was less than brilliant, she assured herself. He was still a deep, intellectual person. He'd have to be, to appreciate these lines.

But it was funny, to think that a shallow, no-talent, run-of-the-mill pop star would appreciate them too . . . ♥

Chapter Eighteen

Sherry was fuming. In the deserted petite salon, on her hands and knees, she searched under the chairs still in the semicircle formation. She found a comb, a freshly sharpened pencil, and a lipstick – Revlon, Cherries in the Snow. No cigarette case.

But there were still three rows to search. Gritting her teeth, she crawled around to the next level.

Damn Mr Simpson. Damn him! The show had really excited her, and she wanted to write about it. She could visualize her piece in print, in *Gloss*'s typeface, accompanied by David's photographs, read by millions of teenage girls . . .

And Simpson had taken that away from her.

She wanted to scream, she wanted to tell someone – but who? She couldn't complain to Caroline again. She would sound whiny and unprofessional. Her girlfriends back home wouldn't understand. Her intern friends – they'd be sympathetic, but they wouldn't get it either. Neither Allison nor Pamela was serious about writing. And poor Donna couldn't write at all.

*

She wondered if Mike would understand. Things had been going well for them. That first kiss, so sweet and gentle, had led to more, not as sweet or gentle, and more exciting. And just last night . . .

They'd gone to a movie, near Central Park. It was just as they left the theatre that something caught her eye.

'What are you looking at?' Mike asked.

She was almost embarrassed to tell him. She nodded toward the horse and carriage that had just emerged from the Park. He raised his eyebrows.

'OK, I know it's corny and strictly for tourists,' she told him. 'But I saw that in a movie, and it was on my list.'

'Your list?'

'Things I wanted to do in New York this summer. Take a ride in a horse-drawn carriage through Central Park. It just seemed so, so –'

'Romantic?' he asked.

She nodded.

He took her hand and practically pulled her in the direction of 59th Street, where the carriages were lined up and waiting. Moments later, they were snuggled together under the carriage roof as the top-hatted driver steered the horse down a path.

Mike had his arm around her, and she laid her head on his chest. Was it the sound of his heartbeat that made her feel so close to him? In any case, within moments they were kissing with more passion than ever before. Then she felt his hand on her breast . . .

It was too soon to get to first base, Sherry knew that. They hadn't been together long enough. But she didn't care. Her whole body was quivering, and she wanted more. She ran her fingers through his hair, and he eased her down on the seat, until he was practically on top of her.

In a way, she was lucky he'd only been able to afford a twenty minute ride. Any longer, and she just might have broken every rule in the book. And just as the horse and carriage came out of the Park, and she was tucking her blouse back into her skirt, he whispered to her, 'I think you're going to be my muse.'

Her eyes widened, and he must have thought she didn't understand.

'My inspiration,' he explained. 'Every serious writer needs one.'

Yes, Mike might understand how bad she felt about not getting to write this article. He was serious about his work, he was a real writer . . . and if she was going to be *his* muse, maybe he could be hers.

A gleam caught her eye. Stretching, she reached out under the chair and her hand rested on something metallic.

'Hello?'

Startled, she looked up and hit the underside of the chair. 'Ow!' She crawled out backwards, and rose. Rubbing the top of her head, she recognized the young man who'd come into the room.

'Are you OK?' Rafe Bryant asked.

'I'm fine, thank you,' she said automatically. He was still eyeing her curiously, and she explained. 'I was looking for something my . . .' She hesitated. She just couldn't bring herself to say 'boss'. 'Something my colleague left behind.'

His eyebrows went up and he approached her. 'You saw the show?'

She nodded. 'I'm from *Gloss* magazine.'

'I can see that,' he said. 'Sherry Forrester.'

She'd forgotten she was still wearing the name tag.

'I'm Rafe Bryant.'

'Yes, I know,' she said with a smile.

'I don't think I'm familiar with your magazine,' he said apologetically.

'*Gloss* is a magazine for teenage girls,' she told him. 'They don't usually cover fashion shows. This is a first for them. And for me,' she added.

'What did you think of it?'

Did he actually care about the opinion of a lowly intern from a magazine he'd never heard of?

'It was wonderful. I loved it.'

'Really?'

'And not just because it was my first fashion show,' she went on. Suddenly the words were rushing out. 'I was expecting terribly elegant and sophisticated clothes, like I see in *Vogue* and *Harper's Bazaar,* the kind you never see on real people walking down the street. But these were beautiful clothes that I would actually want to wear. You wouldn't have to be a society woman to look good in those dresses. Women of any age could wear your clothes!'

If she couldn't write about it, at least she could talk about the show.

And Rafe Bryant didn't seem to mind at all. 'This is exactly what I want to do, reach a younger clientele, not just society matrons.'

She had to point something out to him. 'Only how would a younger clientele afford real designer clothes?'

'Well, I've got ideas about that. I think my designs could work in ready-to-wear.'

Sherry's forehead puckered. 'I'm not sure what that means.'

'The clothes could be made in factories, in large quantities, so they could be created and sold more cheaply. Hey, would you like to go to the hotel lounge and get a coffee? I'd love to hear your thoughts about this.'

Her eyes widened. '*My* thoughts?'

'Sure, you're the kind of person I want to reach with my clothes. You give me some feedback on my ideas, and I'll buy the coffees.'

Suddenly she realized she wanted more than a coffee out of this. 'And how about if I turn this into an interview for *Gloss*?' she asked.

He grinned. 'Why not? I could use the publicity!'

Thank goodness she hadn't given Simpson her notebook. Because when she left the hotel, almost two hours later, it was packed with brand-new notes. And she was totally exhilarated, even more excited than she'd been when she left the fashion show.

Rafe Bryant's ideas were interesting, and his clothes were amazing. He had a vision of teenagers becoming the future of fashion. He thought young people were becoming more daring, more willing to be original, and that they would lead the way in creating fashion trends.

Personally Sherry wasn't completely convinced. Back home the girls weren't very bold or adventurous in their choice of apparel. It was all shirtwaist dresses, A-line skirts with flower-print tops, or madras skirts with coordinating shell tops. Winter meant a cardigan and skirt ensemble bought together so the colours matched perfectly. And everything was a proscribed length – skirts and dresses hit at the top of the knees.

But maybe that was just because she lived in a small Southern city. Here in New York she'd seen more variety. The beatnik look had caught on – Allison was a good example of that. She'd been noticing that even outside of Greenwich Village girls were doing the black capri-pants thing. She'd noticed young women on the street with hemlines creeping upward, and she'd seen

long, ankle-length skirts too. Maybe Rafe Bryant was on to something. He saw young people as being less restrictive, more open to new ideas about everything – so why not fashion too? She couldn't wait to get this down on paper, and she had a feeling Caroline would like it. And she could see *Gloss* readers devouring it.

She didn't realize how late it was until she entered the Hartnell lobby and saw people coming off the elevators and heading out on to the street. One of them was Mr Simpson.

She took the cigarette case from her bag and approached him.

'Mr Simpson?'

He stopped and turned. 'Where have you been?' he demanded. 'I had some letters for you to type.'

She wasn't going to let him kill her euphoria. She held her tongue and silently handed him the case.

'It took you long enough,' he muttered.

Not even a thank you. And just to point that out, she said, 'You're welcome,' before striding off to the elevator bank. She couldn't believe herself – she'd just been impudent! Mama would have had a fit. Sherry felt positively great.

She rolled a sheet of paper into the typewriter.

Rafe Bryant has some big ideas, so watch out, readers! You just may want a whole new wardrobe in the not-too-distant future.

She was so engrossed she didn't even hear the approaching footsteps.

'Hi! Ready?'

She tore her eyes away from the paper and looked up to find Mike standing there.

'Oh! Hi. Ready for what?'

'Dinner, remember? I've got that two-for-one ticket for the Chinese restaurant.'

She'd completely forgotten their date. 'Oh, right. Of course.' But her eyes kept returning to the typewriter.

'What's the matter?' he asked.

'I snagged an interview with a designer today. And

I think it would make a great article for *Gloss*.'

He looked at his watch. 'It's five ten. The working day is over, the prison gates are open. Time for fun.'

'I know, I know.' But she didn't move. 'It's just that . . . I'm really excited about this!'

'Why?'

'C'mon, Mike, you're a writer, you know! When you have a fantastic idea, and you want to write it immediately.'

He looked puzzled. 'A fantastic idea? About *fashion*?'

'Well, yeah. This guy has some really wild plans, and if I can describe them the right way, I just know it could be a real article. Not just a review, Mike! A real feature article in a magazine! Wouldn't you want that?'

That puzzled expression remained on his face. 'Not really. That's not why I write.'

'You wouldn't want to be published?'

'Well, yeah, sure, some day. When I've written something worth publishing. Right now, I'm writing for myself.'

'You can't make a living doing that,' Sherry pointed out.

Mike shrugged. 'I make a living doing mindless work in the mailroom. Writing . . . I can't think about writing in those terms.'

Now it was her turn to be puzzled. She'd just

assumed he thought of writing as his ultimate career. Was it just a hobby for him?

'Hey, it's OK,' he said with a shrug. 'Write your article. The two-for-one is still good tomorrow.'

'Tomorrow would be great,' she said sincerely. 'You don't mind?'

He shook his head. 'Nah, I'm kind of beat. And my mother's been complaining about how I haven't been around for dinner lately.'

She smiled gratefully, and he smiled back. Oh, those eyes . . . so deep, so sexy. For a moment, she hesitated. Maybe she could just get up early and write . . . no, she had to be strong, this was important.

He leaned over her desk, she rose, and they kissed. Which didn't make things any easier. Just that little kiss, it was so enticing.

'Tomorrow?' he said.

'Absolutely,' she replied fervently.

He started out, but he paused and looked back. 'I never realized you were so ambitious!'

'I guess I'm just, I don't know . . . excited by this. It's like . . . a challenge!'

'OK.' With a wink and a grin, he moved on.

Sherry went back to work, but Mike's words rang in her ears. 'I never realized you were so ambitious,' he'd said.

Neither had she.♥

Chapter Nineteen

16 November, 1962

At six o'clock in the morning the high school hallways were dark and silent. As Donna approached the janitorial supply room the door opened and the school custodian came out. He nodded curtly, and held the door open for her to go in.

Alone in the room that smelled of disinfectant and bug spray, she took off her coat and hung it on a hook. From another hook she took a blue smock and put it on over her clothes. At the sink she filled a bucket with hot water and added cleaning liquid. She picked up a mop, and dragged it along with the bucket down the hall to a classroom.

She dipped the mop into the bug, tugged at the mop's ringer and then pushed it along the floor. With the first stroke she winced. The bruise on her upper right arm was fairly fresh and it was bothering her. But she could only grit her teeth and get on with the work. She needed this job.

She was still getting cheques from her father, but a week after her marriage, in a rush of euphoria, she'd made a big mistake. She'd opened a joint bank account

GL♥SS

with Ron. The idea was that they'd save money, so that after the baby came they might try to get a bigger trailer, or maybe even rent a small cottage.

But in the past month Ron had started withdrawing money and spending it rapidly, mainly on poker games and booze.

It wasn't like this at the beginning. September had been an OK month. Dropping out of school was a relief. She probably could have hidden her pregnancy for a while, but what was the point? By the end of October she would have been showing and they'd make her leave anyway. She'd managed to get more hours at the diner, Ron had his work with the road crew, and while they weren't exactly living in the lap of luxury, they were managing.

And then she woke up one morning in October with terrible stomach cramps. There was blood too. Ron had to take her to the emergency room, and there she learned she had lost her baby.

Even after that, things were all right for a while. She was very sad of course. She'd lost a lot of blood, and had to stay in the hospital for two nights, but when she came home Ron was kind and took care of her.

Then one day he'd shown up at work drunk, and he was fired. Then, just as she was feeling strong enough to go back to work, the diner caught fire and burned down. There was no job waiting for her there.

Or anywhere else. Those cheques from her father became their only support, and that was when Ron started withdrawing money from their joint account. When she found out and confronted him, he was drunk, and he hit her. And so began a new and horrible phase of their relationship.

In desperation she went to an agency that supplied cleaning workers to businesses. The only position they had for her was at her old high school. So here she was, back at the place she thought she'd escaped from. And it looked as if she'd never be able to make another escape.

At seven o'clock she started on the restrooms. She had just begun cleaning the four sinks when the restroom door suddenly opened. Four laughing girls, all clad in cheerleading uniforms, burst in. Three of them ignored her and went directly into the stalls. But one remained outside by the sinks.

'Well, hello, Donna.' Sandy Clement exclaimed. 'I wondered what happened to you. When you didn't show up in homeroom this year, I missed you.'

Sure you did, Donna thought grimly. You missed having someone to pick on. She concentrated on an imaginary stain in the sink and rubbed harder with her sponge.

Her silence didn't bother Sandy. 'So you left high school for a career! How exciting for you. Maybe you can be a real janitor some day.' She peered over

GL♥SS

Donna's shoulder into the sink. 'I think you missed a spot.'

When Donna still didn't respond, she must have gotten bored, because she called to the others, 'Girls, come on! We're here for practice, remember?'

Finally three toilets flushed and the others came out of their stalls. They all went to the sinks to wash their hands. Sandy remained by the sink Donna was scrubbing.

'Excuse me, Donna, I'd like to wash *my* hands.'

Donna pressed her lips together tightly and stepped aside. Sandy made a big deal out of washing her hands, using a lot of soap so the scum would remain in the bowl. When she finished, she took a paper towel from the machine on the wall and dried her hands, before dropping it on the floor.

Donna couldn't hold back any longer. 'You couldn't put that in the bin?' she asked.

A silence fell, and the other cheerleaders looked at Sandy expectantly.

Sandy smiled. 'I'm doing this for you, Donna. If we didn't dirty up the restroom, you wouldn't have a job!' There was a chorus of giggles as she led the group out.

It wasn't the worst nasty crack she'd ever received. But Donna found herself gripping the edge of the sink so tightly her hand hurt.

Mechanically she resumed her work. In the first toilet stall she discovered a magazine lying on the floor, maybe left by one of the cheerleaders. It was a copy of *Gloss*, and it immediately brought back memories of cutting out pictures to make paper dolls for her little sister. She stuck it in her smock pocket. There was no one to make paper dolls for any more, but this would give her something to look at when she took her break.

The break came at seven twenty. She headed back to the janitor's closet, retrieved the baloney sandwich she'd prepared that morning, and took it next door to the school supply room to eat. The scent there was less pungent.

As she opened the copy of *Gloss*, a manila envelope slipped out. It wasn't sealed, so its contents fell out too. She picked them up.

The first page was some kind of form. It took her a while to read it, but eventually she realized that it was an application for something called an internship. She didn't recognize the name of the person who'd filled it out.

Curious, she persevered and read on. By the time her break was over, she'd managed to figure the whole thing out.

It appeared that *Gloss* magazine invited readers to apply for summer internships at the magazine's offices in New York. They wouldn't be paid a salary, but they would be flown to New York and given a place to live there for the summer. All they had to do was fill in the form and attach something they'd written.

This applicant – Mary Something – had filled out the application form and attached a neatly typed three-page story about a trip to Disneyland. She'd already addressed the envelope too.

Donna knew what she should do with this. There was a lost-and-found box just outside the principal's office. When this girl, Mary, realized she'd lost her application, that was where she'd go to see if someone had turned it in.

But an idea had begun to take shape in Donna's mind. It was crazy. It was completely insane. It probably wouldn't work. And it certainly wasn't right.

It was a possibility, however. A chance to escape. A slim chance, to be sure, but a chance nonetheless.

On one of the shelves in the supply room there was a row of small black and white bottles bearing the label Liquid Paper. She took one, shook it and unscrewed the cap. Dipping the tiny brush in the white liquid, she scraped it along the side of the bottle to lose the excess. Then carefully, very carefully, she applied the liquid and covered the name and address of the applicant. Afterwards, she blew on it so it would dry. Touching it lightly to make sure it had set, she then took a pen from a shelf, and wrote over the new blank spaces.

LAST NAME: Peake
FIRST NAME: Donna♥

Chapter Twenty

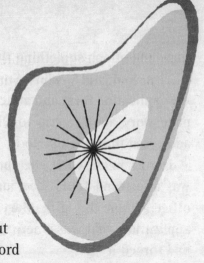

I t had been almost a week since Sherry had left her article on Caroline's desk, but Caroline hadn't said a word about it. She didn't even know if the woman had read it, or if it was now buried under the piles of paper in her in-box.

She knew the managing editor had been unusually busy this week. Some executive editor on an upper floor had suddenly resigned, and Caroline was constantly called out of her office for meetings upstairs. Then her assistant had been rushed to the hospital for an emergency appendectomy.

So Sherry had been busy too, because Caroline had asked her to fill in for the ailing assistant. For the first couple of days she'd been asked to look over articles and check the grammar and punctuation. But while she was reading, Sherry hadn't been able to resist adding a few notes about improvements she thought could be made in the text. Caroline had liked her suggestions. And now Sherry had more articles to read.

That wretched Simpson had objected of course,

when Sherry wasn't available to do his scutwork, but Caroline had mollified him with the services of another intern.

Working for Caroline was entirely different. There were deadlines that had to be met. And if Sherry hadn't finished with something by five o'clock, she didn't leave the office until she had.

Mike didn't approve of this. 'She's using you,' he'd warned her. 'You're just an intern – you're not even being paid.'

'I don't mind,' Sherry had assured him. Strangely enough, the more she worked, the more she enjoyed herself.

On this particular morning she arrived at her desk to find a stack of files with a note from Caroline on top.

Sherry, these are unsolicited article ideas that have been submitted. Could you take a quick glance, decide if any of them have potential and pass the promising ones on to the appropriate editors? Give the rest to my secretary, and tell her to send out standard rejection letters.

Sherry was thrilled with the assignment. Just a few weeks ago she would have been typing those standard rejection letters for the articles turned down by Mr Simpson. Caroline was actually asking for her opinion. She was doing something real, something that would have an impact on the contents of *Gloss*. And the feeling this gave her was something she couldn't even put into words.

She started going through the files, making notes on them, organizing them into piles on her desk. The next time she looked at the clock, an hour and a half had passed and she'd barely made a dent in the stack. Just then Caroline came into the offices, with the harried expression she'd been wearing so much lately. As she passed Sherry she made the waving gesture that Sherry had come to recognize. It meant that Sherry was to follow her into the editor's office.

Caroline sank into the chair behind her desk. 'First off, I took your advice about Donna. I've sent her upstairs to meet with David Barnes this morning. I just ran into him on the elevator, and he thinks she's going to work out fine.'

'That's great!'

'And another thing – that interview you did with the designer, Rafe Bryant – it's very good.'

Sherry drew in her breath. 'Really?'

'It needs some work,' Caroline went on. 'You'll need to lose about three hundred words, and cut about a hundred exclamation points as well.'

'I guess I went a little overboard,' Sherry acknowledged. 'I was so excited by what he was saying.'

Caroline smiled. 'Your enthusiasm shows, and that's good. That's our style here at *Gloss*. But can you tone it down just a little?'

'Sure,' Sherry said, and looked at the editor questioningly.

Caroline nodded. 'I think we can use it.'

Sherry's eyes widened. 'It's going to be published in the readers' issue?'

'Actually I think I'll hold it for the issue after that, our special fall-fashion one. So of course you'll be paid for this, at the rate we pay all our contributors.'

The thrill she felt from these words sent her flying. Getting paid for an article . . . and it wasn't just the money, it was the fact that she was being treated like a real writer, a professional writer.

Caroline eyed Sherry keenly. 'Sherry, what are your plans after this internship?'

The question brought her back down to earth. 'I'm going to college in Atlanta.'

'Will you be able to study journalism there? Because I think you have a real future in this business.'

'I don't know,' Sherry replied. She was suddenly embarrassed to admit she knew very little about the college. 'It's where my mother went to school, so . . .' Her voice trailed off.

'Well, maybe you should look into this. You need to think about your future.'

My future, Sherry thought as she left the office. That vague, fuzzy thing that used to be so clear. There was the future she thought she had with Johnny, the future she was beginning to imagine with Mike. And now a very different possibility, one that she'd never considered at all . . .

She arrived back at her desk to find Mike standing there waiting. Glancing at the clock, she saw that it was coffee-break time.

'Mike, hi! Listen, I'm sorry, but I'm swamped.' She indicated the stack of files on her desk. 'I've got all those to get through.'

'I need to talk to you,' Mike said. 'It's important.'

She actually looked at him, and she was alarmed by the expression on his face.

'Well . . . OK.' She picked up her purse and followed him to the exit.

She was still drifting on the euphoria of Caroline's news, which might have been why Mike's silence in the elevator didn't bother her. It wasn't until they were settled at a corner table in the cafeteria that she gave him her full attention. That was when she noticed he'd been carrying an envelope, which he then slapped down on the table.

'I got this today,' he said.

The envelope had already been ripped open, and Sherry extracted the paper inside. Opening it, she could see that it was on *Gloss* stationery, with the magazine's name embossed on the top.

Dear Mr Dillon, Thank you for your submission to Gloss. While your short story was read with interest, we regret that we are unable to accept it for publication.

However, we believe that your work shows great promise and we encourage you to submit future work.

'Did you have something to do with this?' Mike asked.

She sighed. 'When I typed up your story, I made a copy and gave it to the fiction editor. Oh, Mike, I'm sorry.'

'Sorry for what?'

Startled by the coldness in his voice, she looked up. His face was positively stony.

'Sorry my story wasn't accepted? Or sorry you submitted it? Because you had no business doing that, Sherry.'

He didn't look at all the way she'd expected him to. He wasn't disappointed. He was *angry*. And she was confused.

'I thought you would want to be published.'

'I do, some day. When I'm ready. When I feel like I've written something I want people to read. But this story . . . this was something I wrote for myself.'

'Oh.' She was still puzzled.

'And I certainly wouldn't want my first publication to be in some stupid girly fashion magazine,' he added.

Sherry frowned. '*Gloss* isn't stupid. OK, maybe it's not exactly an intellectual literary magazine, but we publish some good fiction, we've got the largest circulation in the field and we're moving in very interesting directions.'

'*We?* You're talking like you actually work here!'

She ignored that. 'And it would be so good for your future, to get published now. It could be the beginning of a real career!'

'A career? I'm only eighteen! I'm not even thinking about a career yet. I just want to write.'

'But you could be a successful writer,' Sherry argued. 'You'll need to make a living if you want to get married, raise a family . . .' she stopped. Mike had gone positively white.

'Good grief, we've only been seeing each other for a few weeks, Sherry.'

Hastily she amended that. 'I wasn't talking about marrying *me*, having a family with *me*. I'm just speaking generally.'

But it was too late. 'I gotta get back to work,' Mike mumbled. And without even meeting her eyes, he was gone.

She stared after him in disbelief – a disbelief that was directed more at herself than at him. She'd just committed the cardinal sin – she'd been pushy.

And she was pretty sure she'd just been dumped.

For a moment she sat there and tried to collect herself. Within thirty minutes, she'd gone from the highest high to – what? She couldn't honestly say it was the lowest low. It certainly wasn't the kind of blow she'd experienced when Johnny ended their relationship. Still, she'd invested some time thinking

GL♥SS

about a future with Mike, and now those dreams were shattered too.

Oddly enough though, she didn't feel the need to immediately seek out an empty restroom and feel sorry for herself. Possibly shed a few tears. Maybe she was just too stunned. It would probably hit her later, and the restrooms would still be there.

Work turned out to be her consolation. She got so caught up in the files she didn't even seek out Pamela and Allison to share her new tale of woe, and when they came by to get her for lunch, she asked if they could just bring her back a sandwich to eat at her desk. At six o'clock, long after the other interns had left for the day, she closed the last folder.

Was now the time to hit the restroom and mourn her loss? No, she decided, she might as well wait till she got back to her room. Donna would probably be eating dinner, and she'd have the place to herself.

Sure enough, the room was empty when she arrived. She lay down on her bed, buried her face in the pillow and waited to feel really sad.

But the feelings didn't come. She rolled over and stared up at the ceiling for a while. Then she got up, went to her desk and took out her stationery box and a pen. She'd write a letter, that's what she would do. She'd write her girlfriends back home and tell them about her latest heartbreak.

In the process of opening the box, she managed

to knock the pen. It fell on the floor and rolled under Donna's bed. With a sigh, she reached under the bed with one arm and felt around on the floor. Her hand touched something. It wasn't a pen, but she tugged on it anyway.

It was a scarf, a beautiful silk scarf, in a blue and white print. She'd never seen Donna wear it, and she was surprised to find she had something so nice.

She reached under the bed again, and this time pulled out a bright red patent-leather pump, brand new and shiny. She looked at it in wonderment and something clicked in her memory.

Using a coat hanger, she poked deeper under the bed. Slowly she pulled out more items – a soft cashmere sweater. The other red pump. Two charm bracelets. And finally something she recognized immediately – the black quilted Chanel handbag that Caroline had shown them that very first day at *Gloss*.

The door to the room opened, and before she could even turn to see Donna, she heard her roommate gasp.

'What are you doing?' Donna whispered.

'Donna. These are the missing things from the samples closet.'

Donna didn't deny it. Slowly she made her way to her desk and sat down on the chair.

'Donna, you stole these!'

The girl nodded.

Sherry was stunned. 'Listen, I know you don't have many clothes, but–'

Donna interrupted her. 'I wasn't going to wear them.'

'Then why did you take them?'

Donna hesitated. Then she gave an odd sort of shrug, like someone who'd just given up. 'I thought I could sell them on the street. Or maybe to a store. I need money.' After a few seconds she added, 'For a bus ticket.'

'A bus ticket,' Sherry repeated. 'To where?'

This time Donna gave a shrug. 'Anywhere.'

Sherry gazed at her in bewilderment. 'I don't understand.'

There was a moment of silence. Then Donna began to talk.

She spoke in a monotone, and Sherry listened to her story in horrified fascination. Of course she'd known people who had family problems, who didn't get along with their 'These are the missing things from the samples closet.' parents. But she'd never heard anything like this before. The father who left, the mother who drank. A little brother and sister who were taken away. Getting pregnant, marrying a man who didn't care about her, who hit her. Losing the baby. It was unbelievably sad.

When Donna got to the part about forging the application for the *Gloss* internship, Sherry could totally understand her action. She herself would have done anything to escape.

'I can barely read or write,' Donna said. She offered a half-smile. 'You already know that, don't you? I never thanked you for fixing that autobiography note for me.'

'That's OK,' Sherry murmured.

'But I know someone at *Gloss* will find out the truth about me sooner or later,' Donna went on. 'And I'll have to take off.'

'Would you go back to your husband?'

Donna shook her head vigorously. 'Never. And he can never know where I am. Before I left I wrote my father and told him to stop sending cheques. I'm sure Ron's ready to kill me by now.'

Sherry shuddered. After a moment she said, 'Now that you're working for David, you probably won't have to do any writing.'

Donna nodded, and almost smiled. 'It's a good job for me. I mean, I've only been with David for a day, but I like the work. And I'm learning about photography . . .' Her voice drifted off, and she gazed down at the items from the samples closet.

'I've never stolen anything before,' she whispered. 'OK, the application . . . but nothing valuable. I just didn't know what else to do.' She looked at Sherry. 'I guess I have to give them back, huh?'

Sherry nodded.

'And I'll be fired from the internship,' Donna said.

She was right. Sherry couldn't imagine Caroline keeping an admitted thief in the programme. But what she said out loud was, 'Maybe not.'

Donna looked at her wonderingly.

'If you could get the stuff back into the closet without anyone seeing you . . . no one would know who took them.'

She couldn't believe these words were coming from the lips of Sherry Ann Forrester, Little Miss Perfect, the goody-goody who couldn't even tell a lie or use a four-letter word.

She took a deep breath. 'I'll help you.'♥

Chapter Twenty-One

The Copacabana!

In all of her many fantasies about life in New York, Pamela had never entertained the idea that she might find herself in the famed eastside nightclub, the swankiest of them all.

Walking under the red awning, descending the staircase and entering the huge, tropical-theme room, with columns that resembled enormous white palm trees, she tightened her grip on Alex's hand. A red-jacketed waiter led them through a jungle of round tables decorated with little lamps and populated by dressed-up men and women.

'It's beautiful,' she breathed.

'You fit right in,' he whispered.

Actually, she had to admit she did. The strapless beige gown was sleek and simple, and as sophisticated as anything else she saw in the room. She'd gone to Caroline and pleaded for the opportunity to wear something from the samples closet. Lately Caroline had become even more rigid than usual about borrowing clothes. But when she heard where Pamela would be going, she'd agreed to let her choose something. Of course, she didn't know who would be accompanying Pamela to the Copa.

She'd managed to keep Alex a secret from everyone at *Gloss*, except Allison and Sherry. And now she was wishing she'd never told them either. They were starting to fret about the relationship.

'Aren't you seeing an awful lot of him?' Allison had asked. And Sherry, with her ladylike concern, had wondered if maybe Pamela wasn't getting too 'involved'.

'I'm just having fun,' she'd assured them both. 'We're not lovers.' But she silently added, 'Not yet.'

It would happen though, and very soon, she thought. Because it wasn't only being in the most famous, most glamorous nightclub that had her so wildly happy. It was also being in love.

She hadn't expected this. It wasn't part of her plan. She'd only wanted to have fun, to experience the New York she'd seen in movies, to live the *Sex and the Single Girl* fantasy for a summer. Alex would be her escort, someone to get her into the best places, pay her way and show her a good time.

To her immense surprise, he'd become more. Much more.

It all began to change with that first kiss, in front of the Hartnell mansion on Long Island. Had it really been less than two weeks ago? It seemed like a lifetime. They'd gone back to the city together, and for the very first time he took her to his apartment.

It was a nice place. Nothing like those neat bachelor digs she'd seen in movies like *Sunday in New York* and *Boys' Night Out*. But it didn't seem like a family home either, not like the kind she'd known. Maybe because all she saw was the living room and the guest bathroom. He didn't even give her a tour of the other rooms, which was fine with her. She really didn't want to see evidence of his kids, and he didn't seem eager to share anything about them with her.

But he did talk about his wife, Phyllis. He'd mixed them a couple of martinis, they'd sat on the sofa and he told her all about his life with her. How they'd married just after college, how they lived in a tiny walk-up, how Phyllis had worked as a secretary while he'd struggled to make a living as a low-level adman in a small agency. Then he got a job at Hartnell Publications, his salary had gone way up and they bought this place. Phyllis had been able to quit her job, and she got pregnant.

For a while, all was well. He rose up in the company, Phyllis had a second child, he was in a position to send them to the country every summer. But one day it wasn't enough for Phyllis.

'She started meeting people with real money,' he told her. 'People with bigger apartments, and country homes. Their kids had nannies and went to private schools. The husbands drove big cars, the wives wore mink coats, and they took holidays in Miami Beach

GL♥SS

and Las Vegas. She wanted those things too, and she wanted me to get them for her. And when I couldn't, she made me feel . . .' He was struggling for the right words, and Pamela provided them.

'Like you weren't enough of a man?'

He nodded.

Right then and there, she wanted to cry for him. Either that, or find Phyllis and knock some sense into her. Alex was such a lovely man, so handsome and kind and generous. He deserved to be appreciated. He deserved to be *loved*.

She could love him.

They'd kissed again that night, several times. And then, like the perfect gentleman that he was, he brought her back to the Cavendish Residence.

They'd been together every evening since then, even over the next weekend, because he didn't go to Long Island. After work she'd dash back to the residence to change her clothes. Alex couldn't pick her up there – another intern might recognize him – so she'd take a taxi and meet him at the apartment. Sometimes he still took her out to one of the fancy restaurants she'd heard about. But that wasn't so important to her any more. She was happy to stay at the apartment, where Alex would mix martinis. She'd put potatoes in the oven to bake and fix a salad while he grilled a couple of steaks. Sometimes they talked, sometimes they watched TV. Always they kissed and necked on the couch.

Tonight was the first night in over a week that he'd taken her out somewhere special. There was a reason for this.

Earlier that day at *Gloss* she'd had an inter-office memo from him. *Dress up tonight*, he'd written. *We're celebrating.*

She was excited, but puzzled too. What were they celebrating? Was it his birthday? No, that wasn't possible. She'd asked him once what his sign was, and he'd told her Aquarius. That was a winter sign.

She couldn't resist indulging in the wildest possible fantasy. Alex had realized he was madly in love with her. He'd told Phyllis he wanted a divorce, and he was going to ask Pamela to marry him. But that was absolutely ridiculous, too far-fetched to even contemplate. It was more likely to be something like his getting a raise in pay, or securing a new account for *Gloss*.

Still, she was in high spirits all day, and now, watching Alex quietly speak to a waiter, she wondered when she'd find out what they were celebrating.

She looked around the room and tried to take mental photographs so she could remember every detail about this place. Way over at a corner table there was a couple who looked like Sandra Dee and Bobby Darin. Was that possible? She'd have to find an excuse to walk around at some point. She could just imagine telling the folks back home that she'd been hobnobbing with movie stars.

The waiter returned with a bucket, out of which rose a bottle of champagne. Pamela was practically giddy with excitement now. She'd never had champagne before in her life.

The waiter expertly popped the cork and poured the champagne into tulip-shaped glasses. When he left the table Alex picked up his glass, and Pamela did the same. She started to bring it to her lips, but he shook his head.

'I want to make a toast,' he said.

The bubbles from the champagne had tickled her nose, but she resisted the urge to rub it.

'Happy anniversary,' Alex said.

She stared at him. 'Huh?'

'It's August 10, Pamela. It was exactly one month ago that we had our first drink together. Don't you remember? Charlie's, across from the Hartnell building?'

She nodded.

'Martini,' he said. 'Extra dry, with a twist.'

'I can't believe you even remember what I ordered!'

'I remember everything,' he said. 'You've made me very happy this month.'

It wasn't her wildest fantasy, but it was pretty damned close. 'You make me very happy too,' she whispered.

They clinked their glasses and drank their

champagne. Then there was dinner. Alex ordered duck à l'orange, something else she'd never had. Flaming crêpes for dessert. Then there was a show, with dancing girls and a singer she'd actually heard of. And then there was dancing – not the Twist or any of the other new dances, but slow dancing, and Alex had held her close.

It all passed so quickly, and when she caught a glimpse of Alex's watch she was shocked.

'What's the matter?' Alex asked.

'It's after curfew,' she told him. 'And I forgot to ask someone to stick a brick in the back door to hold it open.'

He smiled. 'Don't worry. You won't be sleeping on the streets.'

She smiled back. She had a pretty good feeling she'd be seeing that master bedroom tonight. And now, she was ready.♥

GL♥SS

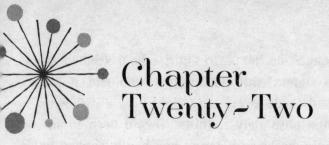

Chapter Twenty-Two

'Donna, I'll need an exposure meter for this next shoot,' David Barnes said.

'OK, I'll get one.'

'And two medium umbrellas,' he added.

'They're already set up,' Donna told him.

He smiled at her in approval. 'You learn fast.'

That was the first time anyone had ever said that to her.

Was it possible for a person's entire life to change overnight?

One day ago, at precisely this hour, she was filing letters in a cabinet and fervently hoping no one would be looking for these letters in the near future. Because, given her reading skills – or lack of them – she was very sure that many of these letters had not been precisely alphabetized.

Twenty-four hours ago she was a criminal, with a stash of stolen goods under her bed. Technically she'd probably still be considered a criminal, but at least the evidence of her crime was gone.

Just yesterday she didn't have a friend in the world. Now she was thinking that maybe she did.

She still couldn't believe how Sherry had

come through for her – this girl who'd seemed so perfect to Donna, this golden girl who had it all, who seemed to do everything right . . . a girl who owed Donna absolutely nothing. They'd been room-mates for six weeks and Donna had barely spoken to her.

She hadn't spoken to anyone, for fear she might reveal something about herself. She wouldn't have blamed Sherry for despising her, and not just for being so unfriendly. For being what people called 'trailer trash'. And for being a thief.

But Sherry had listened to Donna's story, this wretched tale populated by the kinds of people Sherry would never know, and she hadn't been repulsed. She not only listened, she offered to help. Having never encountered someone like this in her life . . . well, it was another first for Donna.

She'd wondered, the night before, if Sherry had been as frightened as she was when they approached the Hartnell building. She didn't even know how they'd get in. But because Sherry had been working late several nights recently, the night watchman recognized her. Sherry came up with some cock and bull story about needing some papers for an early-morning meeting. With her sweet face and Southern accent, she charmed the man into letting them in.

'How are we going to get into the closet?' Donna had wondered when they got off the elevator.

'Caroline keeps a key in her desk drawer,' Sherry told her.

'But how are we going to get into Caroline's office?'

It turned out that Sherry had been doing a lot of work for Caroline, and Caroline was out of the office so much she'd given Sherry a key.

It all went off without a hitch. The scarf, the sweater, the purse, the red pumps, the bracelets . . . everything back in its place. Then they'd gone back to the residence and stayed up talking half the night. They talked about their lives, their families, their relationships. Their hopes and dreams. Or lack of them.

'I have to come up with a new plan,' Donna told Sherry. 'I think I'll be OK till the internship is finished. But now I need to think about what I'll do after that. What are you going to do? Do you have a plan?'

'Oh, I've got plans,' Sherry had replied. 'I've got my whole life planned.'

'Lucky you,' Donna said.

Sherry had smiled, but she shook her head. 'I'm not so sure any more.'

Donna wanted to ask her more. She wanted to make up for six weeks of loneliness. But

'I've got my whole life planned.'

by that point they were both exhausted and needed to sleep. Still, at least she'd made a start at friendship, and it felt good.

And today, only her second day working with David, she thought she just might be making a start towards a future. She was fascinated by his talk of lighting, exposure, composition. And Donna, who'd never been much of a student, was picking it all up and remembering it.

'You know, I think you may have a talent for this,' he remarked that afternoon. 'Have you ever thought about a career in photography?'

She couldn't tell him she'd never thought about a career in anything.

'Women can do that?' she asked cautiously.

'Sure, why not? There are plenty of women photographers. In fashion, news, art . . .'

'How do you become a photographer?'

'Different ways,' David said. He was adjusting a camera on a tripod at the moment, so he couldn't see her incredulous expression. 'Some people study at schools. Others learn by jumping in, learning on the job, working with a photographer . . .'

Like she was doing right now, with him.

'Oh, I almost forgot,' David said. 'Can you schedule the interns for their shots this week?'

'Their shots?' She was confused. Were they all going to be inoculated against something?

'For the issue,' David said. 'Caroline's putting the readers' issue to bed end of next week, and I need to have all the interns' photos ready.' He misunderstood

GL♥SS

Donna's sudden change of expression and he grinned. 'Yep, your pretty face is going to be in *Gloss*, for all the world to see.'

As the words sunk in, Donna's head began to spin. Her face. For all the world to see. And Ron was in that world.

No, Ron didn't read *Gloss*. But other people did, and some of those people had to know Ron. And all it would take was one, one person who could show Ron the magazine and say, Hey, isn't this your wife? The woman who ran away, who cut off your income?

She made a supreme effort to keep her voice from shaking. 'David, when will the readers' issue be on the newsstands?'

'Last day of the month,' David said. 'No, wait, that'll be a Saturday. So it'll come out on 30 August.'

30 August. Two weeks from now. How long would it take Ron to get himself to New York to start looking for her?

It was funny in a way. She'd been thinking how amazing it was to have her life change in twenty-four hours, to find herself as close to happiness as she'd ever been. And now, less than an hour later, she was in an even worse place.♥

Chapter Twenty-Three

Over her coffee in the Hartnell cafeteria, Allison tried not to appear shocked as she absorbed Pamela's news.

'You're *living* with him?'

Pamela rolled her eyes. 'Allison, I haven't slept in our room for a week. Where did you think I was?'

'I figured you were staying with him,' Allison admitted. 'But I didn't think you'd moved in!'

Pamela nodded happily. 'You didn't notice that all my stuff was gone? I'll bet you haven't even missed me. But you have to be happy to have all that closet space.'

'I don't care about closet space,' Allison said. 'Pamela, I hate to remind you, but . . . he's married.'

Sherry arrived at the table. 'Hi, what's up?'

'Pamela's moved in with Alex Parker,' Allison announced.

'Hey, that's *my* news!' Pamela declared.

Allison could see the concern on Sherry's face. 'Really?' Sherry sat down. 'What does his wife have to say about that?'

'Yeah, that's just what I was wondering,' Allison said.

'She's on Long Island, remember. I told you guys that.'

'But just for the summer,' Allison noted. 'Which is very soon to be over. He's got kids, right? School starts just after Labor Day, and that's just two weeks from now. She'll be back before then.'

She wasn't pleased to see the small smile that crossed Pamela's face.

'Not necessarily.'

'What do you mean?' Sherry asked.

'They had a big fight at the Hartnell party, and they haven't seen each other since. Why are you looking at me like that?'

Sherry seemed upset. 'I'm just remembering something you said when we first met, about having affairs with married men. You thought it was OK, as long you didn't take it too seriously. You said you weren't planning to break up a marriage.'

Pamela looked down and stirred her coffee. 'Things have changed.'

'How so?' Allison wanted to know.

'I'm in love with him.'

Allison had never seen her roommate look so serious, and she was alarmed. 'Is he in love with you?'

'He's crazy about me,' Pamela said. 'I make him happy.'

'But is he in love with you?' Allison pressed.

Pamela shrugged. 'It's the same thing. And hey,

since when are you such an authority on love? Has Sam ever said, "I love you"?'

'Not exactly. But that's different.'

'Yeah? How so? He's never even given you anything.'

Allison glared at her. 'Pamela, true love doesn't require presents. Sam and I have a deeper connection. I know him. I know about his past, his dreams, his philosophy, and that's what's important. Don't you agree, Sherry?'

Sherry seemed to be paying undue attention to her food. Allison's direct question forced her to look up.

'OK, I get that you know Sam,' she said carefully. 'But does he know you?'

'What do you mean?'

'Like, does he know about your family, your problems with them?'

Allison brushed that side. 'I don't want to bore him. That's not interesting stuff.'

'If he loves you, he'll find it interesting,' Sherry said.

Allison didn't agree. But glancing at the clock on the wall, she saw she didn't have time to argue the subject.

'I have to go. I've got my interview with Bobby Dale.' She got up. 'Talk some sense into my roommate, OK? Moving in with a married man is just not cool.'

Sherry nodded, but it seemed to Allison that she was distracted, like she had a lot on her mind. How those two had changed, she mused as she hurried back to the office. Sherry, who had looked so confident and self-assured when she first arrived at *Gloss*. Pamela, who had been so cocky, who was more interested in good times than falling in love. Allison herself was the only one who hadn't changed, not a bit.

Back upstairs, she went directly to the entertainment editor's office to pick up the tape recorder. Peter Connelly was waiting for her.

'Look, there's been a change,' he said.

She groaned. 'Oh no. Don't tell me the manager has cancelled again.' The interview had been postponed twice, and the issue would be closing in just a few days.

'No, no, it's just a change of venue. There's a car service waiting for you outside. Just give him this.' He handed her a slip of paper, along with the tape recorder, and she took off.

Outside the building, she got into the car and showed the driver the paper.

'I have to take you to *Queens*?' he complained.

'I guess,' Allison replied. She hadn't even looked at the address.

Muttering and grumbling, the driver started the engine. Allison reached in her bag and took out the copy of *The Free Spirit* that Bobby had lent her. She'd just started the chapter called 'Making Connections'.

'You go through life trying to connect. We want to

make connections that will bring us into a satisfying romantic relationship. We want to make connections that will improve our status in society, that will get us a better job, But we ignore the most important connection we can make.

Before you connect with anyone else, you have to connect with yourself, with your inner spirit. Until you connect with the inner spirit, you're no better than a robot, and your life has no meaning.'

She frowned. Sam had said that too. In fact, she'd found just about all of Sam's profound comments in this book. In another chapter, Quincy had talked about people living as if they were behind bars, in prison. And elsewhere, he'd talked about how the best education couldn't be found in universities, but in your own soul. But he'd never even mentioned this book.

She glanced out the window. They were on 59th Street now, heading east, and she could see that they were approaching a bridge. Closing her eyes, she lay back in her seat and tried to go over the questions she'd be asking Bobby.

But she found her thoughts kept going back to Sam. And to what she'd just said to Pamela, about the approaching end to the summer. It was something she had to think about too.

In two weeks the *Gloss* internship would be finished. She wouldn't be able to stay any longer at

GL♥SS

the Cavendish Residence, even if she could talk her parents into footing the bill for a while. She'd been surprised to learn that all the rooms were booked.

She wasn't all that disappointed about this. The residence wasn't the perfect place to live, with all its rules like curfews and no men allowed beyond the lobby. But where could she go if she was planning to stay in New York?

Maybe, if she could get a job right away, she could rent a room and Sam could crash with her. She smiled as she imagined the reaction of her parents when they learned she was living in sin with an impoverished folk singer.

She wasn't worried about supporting Sam forever. He'd never take a regular job of course – his philosophy wouldn't allow for that. He was perfectly content living off the pittance he collected from playing in parks and on streets and in subways. But there were ways he could make a little more money without giving up his principles. He was bound to get a paying gig for his music. And that song he wrote, the one about the seasons – it was as good if not better than any folk song she'd heard before. Maybe he could record it . . . or sell it, to someone like Bob Dylan!

'What's that street number again?' the driver asked.

She glanced at the paper she was still clutching, and told him. Looking out the window, she found it hard to believe they were only thirty minutes out of

Manhattan. It was a completely different scene here in suburbia. Modest two-storey houses set back from the street, with tiny but well-kept lawns. On the sidewalk there were people walking dogs, wheeling baby carriages. Kids on bikes and roller skates whizzed by.

The driver pulled up in front of the house. Turning, he handed her a card.

'Call this number when you're ready to leave and the service will send a car for you.'

'It won't be late,' she told him. Sam was doing another open mic at a folk club, and she planned to meet him there at seven.

Holding on tightly to her handbag, now heavy with the addition of the tape recorder, she moved up the paved walkway to the front door. Suddenly she became a little nervous. Had Mr Connelly given her the wrong address? This did not look like the residence of a pop star. No guards, no doormen . . . she gave a tentative knock.

Bobby Dale himself opened the door.

'Hi, Allison. Come on in.'

He remembered her name. That was nice, and unexpected. But she reminded herself that his manager had most likely prepared him.

She was ushered into a living room that was a far cry from the Park Avenue penthouse where she'd last seen him. Fat, overstuffed furniture, a worn but bright braided rug, an old-fashioned bookcase filled with knick-knacks. A counter held a TV, a radio and a record player. There was a piano, but not a grand, just an ordinary upright. On a coffee table, a vase held flowers that looked like they'd been plucked from a garden, not arranged by a florist.

Definitely not a teen-idol abode, and maybe that was the point. 'Is this where you hide from your fans?' she asked him.

'It's where I live,' he said simply.

Allison recalled her research. 'I thought you lived in Los Angeles.'

'This is where I grew up,' he told her. 'After my first record I moved my parents and my sisters to LA. They like the weather. And the swimming pool. But when I'm in New York, this is still home.'

'What about the apartment on Park Avenue?'

'You thought I lived there? With velvet curtains and chandeliers?' Bobby shuddered. 'That was Lou's place.'

A plump, grey-haired woman bustled into the room. 'Bobby, haven't you offered your guest any refreshment?'

'I was just about to, Nana. Allison, this is my grandmother. She's the only one who refused to move to Los Angeles.'

'Who wants to live in a city with one season?' the woman asked. 'And I don't swim. Bobby, you haven't even asked your guest to sit down!'

'I'm not really a guest,' Allison explained. 'I'm

interviewing Bobby for a magazine.'

'Well, if you promise you'll only write nice things about my grandson, there's a chocolate cake in the fridge. Now, I'm off to my garden-club meeting. You young people behave yourselves.'

'Don't worry, Nana. I'll keep my hands off her.'

His grandmother made a 'tch tch' sound. 'Don't you sass me, young man. It was lovely to meet you, Allison.'

'Nice to meet you too,' Allison murmured. She had the strangest feeling, like she'd just stepped into one of those wholesome family situation comedies on TV.

She turned back to Bobby. 'I need to plug in the tape recorder.'

'Let's go in the kitchen,' he suggested.

It was another cosy room, all yellow and white. Chintz curtains with a floral print framed the window, shiny brass pots and pans hung from hooks on the walls. She and Bobby sat down at a round wooden table, and Bobby indicated the electric outlet.

'I suppose your manager told you what kind of interview we're doing,' she said as she carefully wrote BOBBY DALE on a label and stuck it on the frame.

'Probably, but I forget. Just between us, half of what Lou says goes in one ear and out the other. Hey, that thing's not on yet, is it? I wouldn't want Lou to hear that.'

Allison shook her head. 'No, but here goes.' She

pressed the two buttons and cleared her throat. 'Testing, one, two, three. Testing, one, two, three.'

She thought she sounded pretty professional, and Bobby must have thought so too.

'I guess you do this a lot, huh?'

Allison wanted to maintain her professional air, but she made the mistake of looking up and into his disarming blue eyes. She was beginning to see what made him so irresistible to his legions of fans.

'Actually I heard a journalist say that on a TV show,' she confessed. 'And it's the first time I've ever used a tape recorder.'

'Could've fooled me,' he said.

She hit the 'rewind' button, and then 'play'. What came out sounded like squealing tyres.

'I think you hit "fast forward",' Bobby said kindly. He came around behind her and leaned over her shoulder to press buttons. He smelled nice, she thought. Like minty soap. Sometimes, she wished Sam would smell a little . . . *fresher*.

Now she heard, 'Testing, one, two, three. Testing, one, two, three.' She grimaced.

'Ick, do I really sound like that?'

'Nobody sounds good on a tape recorder,' Bobby assured her. 'You should see what they have to do to voices in recording studios to make them sound good.'

'Is that why so many singers just mouth the words to their records when they sing on TV?' she asked.

He nodded. 'I had to do that the other day in Philadelphia when I was on *American Bandstand*. It's because they don't have a band there. But it still makes me feel like I'm cheating.'

Now *that* was interesting, and she looked to make sure the little wheels were turning on the machine. But Bobby looked uncomfortable. 'Uh-oh, I don't know if I'm supposed to say that. There might be kids who think we're really singing on that show.'

'Do you want to check with your manager and find out what you're allowed to say?'

He stared at her for a minute. 'It's not what you think. I just don't want to disappoint anyone.'

'And in concerts, do you just move your lips to recorded music?'

He shook his head firmly. 'Absolutely not. I have a back-up band that tours with me.' He frowned. 'Is this what the interview is going to be about? Lip-syncing?'

'No, I was just making conversation,' she said. 'The title for this article is "Could You Be Bobby's Girl?"'

He nodded seriously. Then he crossed his eyes and made a face.

She couldn't help herself – she burst out laughing. She wished David Barnes was there – this would have made a great photo.

'I know, it's pretty silly,' she said. 'But it's what the readers want to know.'

His face went back to normal. 'Do you really believe that?' he asked.

'No,' she said promptly. 'But that's what the *Gloss* editors think readers want to know. Maybe they're right. The magazine has a big circulation.'

'Yeah, but what kind of choice do the readers have?' Bobby asked. 'The teen magazines, they're all pretty much the same, aren't they? Kids don't have any choice.'

Allison cocked her head to one side and looked at him with interest. 'You think they'd rather read something else?'

'I don't know,' he admitted. 'I mean, it's like TV. Everyone watches these stupid game shows or the detective shows or the medical shows because that's all there is. And the shows are all alike!' He was getting excited now. 'Like, take the detective shows. There are always two detectives, one good-looking sidekick, a pretty secretary. And the medical shows – one young handsome passionate doctor, one older wiser doctor . . .'

'And a pretty nurse,' Allison finished.

'Exactly!'

'You could say the same thing about popular music,' Allison ventured. 'Singers like Bobby Vee, and Bobby Vinton, and Bobby Rydell, and . . .' she hesitated.

He finished the sentence for her. 'And me. We're all singing the same garbage.' Then he clapped a hand over his mouth and looked at the tape recorder. 'Uh-oh. Look, this can't be part of the interview, OK? The record company would kill me.'

'Don't worry,' Allison assured him. '*Gloss* would never publish it anyway.' But she was curious. 'Do you really think your music is garbage?'

He shrugged. 'It's OK. Like they always say on *American Bandstand*, it's got a good beat and you can dance to it. But it's not really my kind of music.'

'Then why do you sing it?'

He gave her an abashed smile. 'So I can get myself in a position where I *can* sing my kind of music. If I can become important enough to the record company, they'll have to let me record what I really want to sing.'

'And what kind of music is that?'

He looked at her thoughtfully for a moment, as if he was trying to make a decision. Then he stood up. 'C'mon back in the living room.'

There, he picked out an album from the bookshelf, and then very carefully he slid the record out from the sleeve. Holding it delicately, as if it was fine bone china, he brought it to the record player.

'Listen,' he said.

It was a voice she'd never heard before, sort of gravelly and with a twang. The man sounded a little like a hillbilly, or how she thought a hillbilly would sound. She could almost picture him, sitting on a porch, strumming his guitar, singing to himself.

The song was about a house in New Orleans, called the Rising Sun, and someone who got in trouble there. It sounded vaguely familiar. And when the song ended, and Bobby lifted the needle, it came back to her.

She snapped her fingers. 'That's on Bob Dylan's album!'

'Yeah, he recorded it too,' Bobby said. 'This is Woody Guthrie. He was singing it long before Bob Dylan.'

Allison was shocked. 'You mean, Bob Dylan stole the song?'

'No, this is a real folk song. Nobody knows who wrote it.'

'My boyfriend's a folk singer,' Allison announced.

'Yeah? Is he playing anywhere?'

'Well . . . mainly on street corners. That's where people are, right?' She was aware that she was sounding defensive.

'Absolutely,' Bobby assured her. 'But I want the kids who listen to me now to hear this kind of music. And the way I figure, if I'm famous enough and popular enough, I might be able to get them to listen.'

He went to the piano, sat down and began to play. She recognized this song immediately – 'This Land Is Your Land.'

Bobby sang it beautifully, simply and clearly, without any fancy flourishes. And she realized it wasn't just a pretty song about America, but a song full of longing, a song about people yearning to feel that this country belonged to them.

When he finished, she wasn't sure whether she should clap. He didn't seem to expect that.

'Does your boyfriend sing that song?' he asked.

She shook her head. 'He only sings songs he wrote himself.'

Bobby's eyebrows went up. 'Really? That's odd.'

She stiffened. 'Why?'

'Because there's so much wonderful folk music already out there. I mean, it's great he writes his own stuff too,' he added hastily. 'Woody Guthrie wrote "This Land Is Your Land". Joan Baez writes songs too. But they all sing other stuff as well. I just don't think a folk singer should limit himself.'

Allison could only shrug. She wanted to defend Sam's point of view, but she wasn't sure how.

Bobby seemed to sense that she was uncomfortable, and he changed the subject. 'Tell me about you.'

'*Me?*'

'Yeah. Why not?'

'Because this isn't a social visit, it's an interview!'

He really had a lovely grin, boyish and easy. 'But I'm curious. Come on, we've got time. I think you told me before, you're from Boston, right?'

She nodded. 'I just graduated from high school there, and I'm here in New York for this summer internship at *Gloss*.'

'Do you want to be a journalist? Wait, I asked you that before, didn't I?'

'You did, and I still don't know,' she admitted. 'I don't even know what I'll be doing two weeks from now when this internship is finished.'

'You're not going to college?'

She hesitated. 'Probably not.'

He nodded understandingly. 'Money, huh? I remember when I was looking at colleges and universities a couple of years ago, before I got the recording contract.' He whistled. 'Those tuitions can be outrageous.'

She wasn't sure why, but she had a sudden desire to be honest with him. 'It's not the money. My parents . . . well, they can afford it.'

'You're lucky,' he said. 'I had a fantasy about going to one of the Ivy League schools. You know, like Harvard or Yale. I had good grades, and I think I could have gotten in. But I didn't even bother to apply. There was no way my folks could swing it financially.'

'I've been accepted at Radcliffe,' she told him. 'That's the women's college at Harvard.'

'Wow!' he exclaimed. 'That's fantastic!'

She didn't know what to say, and then she looked at her watch. 'Gosh, look at the time. We have to get going on this interview.'

'And we need some of my grandmother's chocolate cake,' Bobby declared.

Moments later they were back at the table, with huge slices of cake in front of them. Allison noted with some dismay that she hadn't turned off the machine before going into the living room. She could rewind it, but there still seemed to be plenty of tape left, and she was kind of hoping the tape had picked up Bobby singing 'This Land Is Your Land'.

'Can you be Bobby's girl?' Allison said loudly. 'OK, Bobby, what would you look for in a girlfriend?'

Bobby grinned. 'Shall I tell you the truth or what your editors think your readers want to hear? No, don't worry, I know what to say. I could even write it for you!' He took a deep breath and began to recite.

'Do you like nature and the outdoors? Because Bobby loves hiking, camping and toasting marshmallows over an open fire. And he loves seeing animals in their natural habitat.

'Bobby likes good conversation. He's interested in current events, and any girl who wants to snag Bobby should be reading a newspaper every day.

'Bobby likes girls who are down-to-earth, who don't wear a lot of make-up or worry about the latest fashions. He's not interested in fancy food. Do you like hot dogs, hamburgers, pizza? Then you and Bobby will get along just fine!'

It was a good thing the tape was running and she didn't have to take notes. Her mouth had dropped open. This was exactly what *Gloss* expected her to write.

He continued.

'The kind of girl Bobby likes is close to her family. Bobby thinks family is really important. Sure, everyone disagrees with their parents once in a while and maybe they feel the need to rebel. That's normal. But in the long run, family counts. Friends come and go, and so do romances. But families, they have to love you, no matter what you do!'

The tape was running out, but that was OK. He'd given her enough for a typical *Gloss* celebrity interview. All she had to do now was type it up, add a little description, and Mr Connelly would be satisfied.

'OK?' Bobby asked.

'OK.'

'How about another piece of cake?'

She looked at her watch and gasped. She'd told Sam she'd be at the open mic in fifteen minutes. 'I have to go. Can I use your phone to call the car service?'

He walked her outside to wait for her ride.

'How did I do?' he asked.

'Just fine,' she said. She couldn't resist asking, 'How did *I* do?'

He smiled. 'Listen, I've had a gazillion interviews with magazines. And that was the best.'

'But I think you interviewed me more than I interviewed you.'

'That's what made it the best. Hey, have you got a pen or a pencil? And some paper?'

She was able to provide both. He scribbled on her pad. 'That's my phone number. In case . . .'

'In case what?'

'Well . . . maybe you'll think of something else.'

'To ask you?'

'Or to tell me.'

The car appeared, and she stuck the paper in her pocket. Before the driver could get out, Bobby opened the door.

But before she could get in, he said, 'Hey, one more question. Do you like the outdoors? Hiking, camping, toasting marshmallows over an open fire?'

'I've never done that,' she replied.

'Think you might like to try?'

He was standing so close to her now, she could smell him. Was it that fresh, minty scent that gave her this sudden, crazy urge to kiss him? Which was absolutely ridiculous, of course. She had a boyfriend, how could she have thoughts like that?

'Where to, lady?' the driver asked.

She gave him the address of *Gloss*, and got into the back seat. Bobby closed the door, but he stayed there, with that questioning look still in his eyes. But all she could do was smile before the car took off.

Feeling just a bit rattled, she leaned back in her seat. That hadn't gone exactly the way she'd thought it would. It dawned on her that Bobby probably knew more about her now than Sam did. Much as she hated to admit it, when they talked at lunch Sherry had been right. Sam never asked her questions about her life.

Sam never talked about the future either. Which was totally cool, she assured herself. That was so conventional, making plans. It was the kind of thing her boring brother did.

Still, maybe they needed to talk just a little bit about the future. It was less than two weeks away. Tonight, she decided. She'd bring it up casually, without a lot of fuss. What was going to happen to her – to *them* – when the summer was over?

'Could you drop me in the Village?' she asked the driver.

There was a lot of traffic, and getting back into Manhattan took a lot longer than she'd expected. With a sinking heart she realized she'd probably miss Sam's performance. She just hoped she could get to the club before he left, since she had no idea where he was crashing tonight.

In the Village, they got stuck in a jam on Sixth Avenue, and it was already eight thirty.

'I'll get out here,' she told the driver. She ran down 8th Street, and bumped into Sam and his pals. When Sam saw her, he scowled.

'You missed my set.'

'Which was just as well,' one of Sam's pals said. It occurred to her that she didn't know this guy's name, or any of the others' for that matter. Sam never bothered with silly things like introductions.

'Why?' she asked.

'He got booed.'

She was shocked. 'No!'

'He forgot the words,' one of the girls said.

'How could you forget the words to your own song?' Allison asked him.

He looked at her coldly, and she quickly changed her tone. 'Listen, I'm so sorry I missed it. I got stuck at work.'

'Work,' the other boy repeated, in a tone that made it sound like a dirty word. The others laughed.

Allison linked her arm with Sam's. 'Let's get out of here,' she whispered in his ear.

'We're having a party,' Sam told her. 'At the new crash pad.'

She couldn't argue with him, not after what he'd just been through at the club. With her arm firmly linked through his, she walked with the group.

'I can't believe they booed you.'

'Jerks,' Sam muttered. He pulled her closer. She appreciated this, but at the same time, she harboured a hope that this new crash pad might have shower facilities available. Sam didn't seem to have indulged in a good wash recently. She wished she knew the name of that nice minty soap Bobby Dale used.

The group turned into an alley that was lined with trashcans. Allison had to hold her breath. At a metal door, one of Sam's friends fiddled with a padlock hanging from a chain, and the door opened.

She let out her held breath, but the smell inside wasn't much of an improvement over the alley. In darkness, they all filed down some creaking stairs. At the bottom someone clicked a switch on the wall, and a naked bulb hanging from the ceiling emitted a dim light. Allison was actually grateful for the limited illumination. What little she could see looked pretty dismal – a grimy cement floor, with three bare mattresses.

'You sleep on that dirty mattress?' she whispered to Sam in horror.

He gave her a look she'd come to recognize. Great, profound words of wisdom were about to come.

'If you're comfortable with yourself, you can be comfortable anywhere.'

'Walter Quincy!' she exclaimed. '*The Free Spirit*!' She reached in her bag and pulled out the book.

He stared at her with something like alarm. Suddenly, Mr Comfortable didn't look quite so comfortable any more.

One of the boys opened a paper bag and took out a large bottle. A girl went over to a corner of the room and returned with three grimy glasses.

'We'll have to share – these were all I could find,' she announced.

'Why don't I wash them first?' Allison suggested brightly. 'Is there a sink?'

Someone muttered something, and it sounded like 'bourgeois'. For once she didn't care. There was no way she was drinking out of those disgusting glasses.

Gathering them up, she found a tiny bathroom, just a toilet and sink. So Sam wouldn't be taking any showers here, she thought sadly. It was too bad really, she thought as she tried to rinse out the glasses in the trickle of brownish water. She had that lovely shower back at the Cavendish, but she couldn't get Sam past the lobby. Things would be different when she got a real apartment.

Opening the door, she heard some scratchy-sounding voices, and they weren't the voices of her companions. Approaching the group, now sprawled across the mattresses, she was horrified to see that one of the girls was fooling around with her tape recorder.

'Hey, what do you think you're doing?' she exclaimed. 'That's mine!'

'Whoa, she's the possessive type,' a guy said. 'Better watch out, Sam.'

Sam uttered a short laugh. Meanwhile Allison tried to get the machine away from the girl. By now the faint but audible sound of 'This Land Is Your Land' could be heard.

'Who's that?' Sam asked.

Allison had managed to get the recorder from the girl, who fell back on the mattress and started giggling hysterically.

'Who was that on the tape?' Sam asked again.

'Bobby Dale,' Allison muttered as she put the machine back in her bag.

The non-giggling girl let out a shriek. 'Bobby Dale? You know Bobby Dale?'

Her boyfriend looked at her in disgust. 'Don't tell me you like that crap!' He turned to Sam. 'Did you hear that? Your girlfriend's carrying a tape of Bobby Dale.'

Allison tried to defend herself. 'It was for my job.'

'*Job*,' the guy muttered, in the same tone he'd used for the word 'work'.

'Bobby Dale,' the girl cried out again. 'He's so cute!'

Allison got a good look at her for the first time. She couldn't have been more than fourteen years old.

Now she was really uncomfortable, and she wanted to get out of there. Not to mention the fact that she needed to get Sam alone, so they could talk. She turned to him.

'Sam . . .'

But Sam was too preoccupied to look at her. He had a little plastic bag in his lap. 'Who's got the papers?' he asked.

Someone tossed him a packet. Sam deftly began rolling some of the bag's contents into a small rectangle of paper. Then he twisted the ends, held it to his lips and struck a match.

'Hey, man, you got weed!' one of the boys exclaimed in delight.

Sam took a long drag, and then passed it to the guy. Allison caught a whiff of something she'd frequently smelled in Washington Square Park. Combined with the mouldy smell of the basement room and the cheap wine, she suddenly felt nauseous. She was going to have to suffer the little toilet room again.

It was while she was in there that she heard a pounding sound. And then a muffled but audible voice.

'Police! Open up!'

She froze. Through the bathroom door she could hear girls shrieking and the sound of heavy shoes coming down the stairs. There were loud cries of protest. Then someone was banging on the bathroom door.

'Police! Come out now!'

With a trembling hand she opened the door and faced the uniformed man. He was holding her handbag.

'Is this yours?' he demanded to know.

She nodded.

From the pocketbook he pulled out the little bag of marijuana.

'But that's not mine!' she cried out.

'Sure,' he said, shaking his head wearily, and took her arm.

'You're under arrest.'♥

GL♥SS

Chapter Twenty-Four

n her room at the Cavendish, Donna sat at her desk and studied the contact sheets David had given her. 'Look them over carefully,' he'd said. 'Then pick the one you think is best of each intern.'

Donna had been taken aback. 'You want *me* to choose the pictures for the magazine?'

'Why not? You've got the gift, Donna. A good eye. And you know these girls, I don't. So you won't just pick the prettiest photo – you'll choose the one that best reflects the girl and her personality.'

Donna just stared at him. He thought she knew these girls. In reality, she could barely attach names to the faces.

He misread her reaction. 'You don't have to stay here and do it,' he assured her. 'Wow, it's almost seven. I've kept you too late already.'

'I don't mind,' she said.

He shook his head. 'I'm going to take off now, and I don't feel comfortable leaving you here on your own. Did you hear about the stuff that was stolen from the samples closet?'

Donna managed a thin smile. 'I heard it was all replaced.'

'Yeah, but even so, who knows what kind of people are hanging out here after hours.' He put the contact sheets in a large envelope and gave her a magnifier loupe so she could examine them back in her room.

Now, moving the loupe from photo to photo, she realized the only person she felt she knew at all was her roommate, Sherry. Looking at Sherry's photo now, she could see warmth and openness, but confusion too.

With the special marking pen David had lent her, she checked Sherry's best photo and moved on to the girls she knew at least slightly. Allison . . . she was an interesting girl, but puzzling. Her family had plenty of money, she'd been accepted to a top college – and yet she was a rebel and misfit. Donna didn't get it. But who was she to pass judgement? Maybe a girl could have it all and still have problems.

And then there was Pamela, who looked like a real tart when she first arrived at *Gloss*. She'd seemed like a happy-go-lucky type, without a care in the world, and determined to have a good time. But appearances could be deceiving, Donna thought. Pamela looked more conventional now, and most people seemed to think this was an improvement, but gazing at her photo, Donna could see a tension and an uncertainty that hadn't been there before.

She realized she knew nothing about any of their lives, not really. She didn't know their stories any more than they knew hers. For all she knew, they could all be like Sherry, with anxieties and issues and all kinds of mixed-up feelings going on beneath their oh-so-normal *Gloss* exteriors.

As for her own photo . . . she went through the proofs and searched for the one that looked least like herself, a photo that was totally unrecognizable. But David was just too good a photographer. Every picture was a clear image of Donna Peake.

Or maybe not. Scrutinizing each picture through the magnifier, she got the feeling that maybe she didn't look exactly like the girl who'd arrived here less than two months ago. Something was different. Not her hair, not her eyes, nose, mouth . . . it was something in the expression.

She'd always hated having her picture taken at school. When she brought the pictures home, her mother would laugh and say she looked like a deer caught in the headlights of a car. She always looked frightened.

She didn't look so frightened in these pictures – in fact, she looked calm. Which was strange, since she had more reason than ever to be frightened now. In less than two weeks this picture would be in one of the most popular magazines in the country, on news-stands all over. Someone was bound to bring it to Ron's attention.

Donna didn't know the laws of marriage, but she assumed that as her legal husband Ron had rights.

She had memories of her mother talking about her marriage to Martin Peake, how he'd bossed her around, controlled their money, told her what to do. Never get married, she would tell Donna. A husband owns you, and you'll lose your independence.

She imagined Ron tracking her down in New York, claiming her, taking her back to the trailer. Forcing her to call her father and demand that he start sending cheques again. Oh yes, she should be afraid, very afraid.

But she didn't see fear in the photos. She turned to the mirror and examined her reflection. No, she couldn't say she saw fear there either.

Something had changed over the course of the summer. Maybe it had something to do with the way she'd faked her way through the internship. Or the fact that once she started working with David Barnes she'd discovered that she could do something well, that she had value. That maybe, just maybe, she could survive in the world on her own.

Sherry came into the room and flung herself on her bed. 'I'm beat. I finally finished revising the article about the designer, and Caroline's happy with it.'

'Great!' Donna exclaimed. 'You must be starving. I figured you wouldn't be back until after the dining hall closed, so I brought something back for you.' She handed Sherry the neatly wrapped sandwich.

'Thank you,' Sherry said with feeling. She started to

unwrap it, but she didn't get far. There was a knock on the door and then a voice.

'Sherry Ann Forrester? There's a call for you.'

Sherry let out a heartfelt groan. 'It's got to be my mother. She's the only one who would ask to speak to Sherry Ann. Coming!' she called out, and got off the bed. For a moment she just stood there, looking grim.

'You think something's wrong?' Donna asked.

'She must have received the letter I wrote.'

Donna knew about the letter, and she looked at Sherry with sympathy. 'This isn't going to be easy, is it?'

Sherry shook her head. 'But I'm going to have to deal with it sooner or later. Wish me luck.'

'Good luck,' Donna said as her roommate started towards the door, looking for all the world like a soldier going into battle.

Donna watched her in sympathy. For all the good things she had going for her, Sherry had problems too. Probably every girl in this residence had some problem or another, something she had to face and conquer. Maybe that's what had changed for Donna.

She had her problems, but she wasn't alone.

Pamela turned on Alex's television. It was a game show, where a contestant was screaming hysterically because she'd just won a new refrigerator. She turned the dial to the next channel, and saw the comedian

Red Skelton. He could usually make her laugh, but she didn't feel like laughing tonight. She turned the dial again. *Make Room for Daddy* – one of those happy-family shows, with a mother and a father and two kids. No, she wasn't in the mood for that either, and she turned off the set.

She didn't really feel like watching TV at all. She'd only turned it on because it was so quiet in the apartment. Maybe music would help. She turned on the radio.

The sound of a popular crooner filled the room, Steve Lawrence singing his big hit of the summer, 'Go Away, Little Girl'. It was about an older man in love with a much younger girl, and he was telling her to leave because the relationship could never work out. Immediately she switched off the radio. This was definitely not something she wanted to hear at this point in time.

She looked at the clock on the mantle and saw that it was already after nine. Where was he? She tried not to fret, or conjure up images of accidents and hospital emergency rooms. He'd been working late a lot.

Pamela couldn't understand why he wasn't more anxious to get back to her. After all, he'd invited her to stay here. True, it was supposed to be for that one night, after they'd gone to the Copa, when it was too late for her to get back into the Cavendish. And she couldn't help recalling that surprised look on his face when she showed up the next evening with a suitcase.

But that expression hadn't lasted long. She'd smothered him with kisses, and then, while he was mixing their drinks, she'd disappeared into the bedroom and changed into a red negligee that she'd bought for the occasion.

That was the first night they made love. She couldn't say it was a wonderful experience. It hurt, and it was all she could do to keep from crying out. She'd thought he'd be pleased, realizing that he was her first, that she'd saved herself for someone like him, but he seemed uncomfortable, almost reluctant. He didn't say so, but she could sense it. Afterwards she wanted to talk about it, to talk about *them*, but he apologized and said he was just too tired, he needed to sleep.

He hadn't touched her since then, not really. Even his kisses changed – they became little pecks that didn't last very long. For the past four nights she'd cuddled up to him in bed, but he didn't respond. Maybe he thought she needed time to recover from that first night. Maybe he was just tired – he'd been working late every night. Problems with a new account, he'd said. She wasn't sure she believed him.

Maybe he just didn't like coming back *here*, she thought. Wandering through the apartment, it occurred to her that his wife, his soon to be ex-wife, had probably decorated the place. The woman was usually responsible for that sort of thing. Most likely it was Phyllis who had picked out the colour of the walls, chosen the furniture. The dishes and the silverware – they were probably wedding gifts. And there were framed photos all over the place – Alex and Phyllis and . . . She didn't even know the names of his two little boys.

This was why he didn't want to come home, she decided. Too many memories. It was a relief to have figured this out, and now she could think of a way to deal with it. There was an easy solution, she thought. A new place! An apartment that *she* could decorate, a place where they could make their own memories.

When she finally heard his key in the door she rushed to open it before he could. He bent down to kiss her – it was a brief kiss, but she thought she could smell alcohol on his breath. The guys from the office must have gone out for a drink . . .

But when she wrapped her arms around him, she smelled something else.

'Shalimar.'

He moved past her and set his briefcase on the coffee table. 'What?'

'I can smell Shalimar on you. It's a perfume. Were you with someone who wears Shalimar?'

He shrugged. 'Maybe in the elevator.'

'It must have been awfully crowded for the scent to rub off on you like that. And you must have been in the elevator for a long time. Did it get stuck between floors or something?'

She spoke lightly, as if she was joking, but he frowned. 'Do you want to check for lipstick on my collar too?'

'I'm teasing!' she protested.

He ran his fingers through his hair. 'OK, OK.' Then he noticed something on the coffee table, and he frowned. 'What's that?'

'A vase,' she told him. 'I passed a stoop sale on the way home, and I got it for a dollar. Isn't it pretty?'

'Don't start bringing stuff here, Pamela. You might forget to take it with you.'

'Take it with me . . . when?'

'When you leave.'

She still didn't understand. 'Why would I leave?'

'When the summer's over, when your internship's finished. You'll be going home to New Jersey, won't you?'

'Pennsylvania,' she corrected him automatically.

He went to the liquor cabinet. 'And you'll have to be out of here before Phyllis and the kids come back of course.'

'Phyllis and the kids,' she repeated faintly.

'Do you want a martini?' he asked as he took out a bottle. He wouldn't meet her eyes. 'Actually . . . you'll have to go back to that residence before that. Phyllis is in town this weekend. We have theatre tickets.'

'Phyllis . . . is coming here? But . . .'

'But what?'

'It's over between you! You don't get along, you don't even sleep with her any more – you told me that!'

He still wouldn't look at her. 'Look, Pamela . . . I'm sorry if I gave you that impression. Phyllis and I do fight a lot, but . . . well, we've got kids and all.'

'But you don't love her! You love me!'

He finally turned in her direction. 'I never said that.'

'But you don't love her! You love me!'

Her heart was beating so fast she thought she might faint. Her eyes went to the bedroom door.

He sighed. 'We were just having fun, Pamela. That's what you said you wanted, right? See New York, have a little fling . . .'

'But I love you,' she whispered.

He was dropping ice cubes in a glass, and he didn't say anything. Maybe he hadn't heard her.

'I love you!' she said more loudly. Actually she was speaking a lot more loudly than she meant to. In her own ears it sounded more like a scream. And from the expression on his face, she had a feeling it sounded like that to him too.

GL♥SS

Allison had never been so frightened in her life. The police station was like something out of a nightmare. A handcuffed man was shouting incoherently as he was led down the hall. Three scantily clad women were yelling obscenities. Another, older woman was wailing incessantly.

'You're making a big mistake,' Allison kept saying to the policeman who still gripped her arm. 'The stuff you found in my bag, it isn't mine!' The officer didn't even respond. He led her to a desk, where a bored-looking uniformed man was sitting.

'Last name.'

'What?'

'Give me your last name.'

'Sanderson.'

'First name.'

'Allison.'

'Date of birth.'

Was she being booked? she thought wildly. Would she be fingerprinted, searched, thrown in a cell? Scenes from TV detective shows came back to her.

'Hey, don't I get a phone call?'

'Date of birth!' the man demanded.

She told him. The man grimaced.

'Seventeen, huh?' He turned to another officer. 'Take her to make a phone call.'

Another officer took over and led her to an office.

He pointed to a phone on the desk. 'One call. Local, not long distance.'

Allison's hand trembled as she lifted the receiver. Who was she going to call? Her mind was a blank, she couldn't even remember the number of the Cavendish Residence, or the payphone on their hall.

Suddenly she remembered a piece of paper in the pocket of her pants. She fished it out and looked at it. No, this was crazy, she barely knew him, why would he help her out?

Then she recalled those bright blue eyes, the dazzling smile, and more than that – the way he'd looked at her when he put her into the taxi. And the way that look made her feel.

She began to dial.

'Sherry Ann, you're talking nonsense.'

'Mama, it's just an idea. I haven't decided anything. It's something I'm thinking about.'

'Well, you can stop thinking about it right this minute, young lady. We've already booked your ticket to Atlanta, and Daddy's taking the day off to meet you at the airport. Actually I was thinking I'd come with him, and we could have a day of shopping. You still need some things for college, don't you?'

'Mama, haven't you heard a word I said? I might not go to Agnes Scott after all. They don't have journalism there.'

Her mother went right on as if she hadn't spoken. 'And there's something else, honey. I wasn't going to tell you this because I didn't want you to get your hopes up. I ran into Johnny's mother last week at the beauty parlour. Guess what she told me? Sherry Ann? Are you there?'

Sherry sighed. 'I don't want to guess, Mama. Just tell me.'

She couldn't miss the note of triumph in her mother's voice. 'That business in Washington DC, with that . . . that *girl*? Well, it's all over. It was just some silly little fling. And I don't think she was very nice, if you know what I mean. Now, I know you must still be very angry with him. But you know, sugar, this is how men are. They can be tempted, and some of them stray. That's just their nature. You can forgive him, can't you?'

'Mama, it's not a question of forgiving . . .'

But the woman kept right on talking. 'I have a feeling he's going to be very happy to see you when you get home. You two will make up, you'll go to Atlanta in September like you planned, and everything will be just fine.'

'Mama, you're not listening to me!'

Just then another voice broke into the conversation. 'This is your operator speaking. I have an emergency call for this line.' She rattled off the number of the payphone. 'Will you hang up, please?'

The notion of an emergency wasn't pleasant, but Sherry was glad to have a reason to end the call. 'I'll call you back later, Mama,' she said, and hung up. She waited by the phone uncertainly.

The phone rang, and she picked it up. 'Hello?'

A man spoke. 'I need to speak to Allison Sanderson.'

'I'll see if she's in,' Sherry said, though she doubted she would be. Allison spent every evening down in the Village. But she ran down the hall and banged on the door. When there was no response she went back to the phone.

'She's not in. Can I take a message for her?'

There was a moment of hesitation, and then the man spoke again. 'Is this one of the *Gloss* interns?'

'Yes, this is Sherry Forrester.'

'Well, this is a little awkward . . . I have one of your . . . your colleagues with me, and she's a little upset.'

Now Sherry could hear someone sobbing in the background.

'Is this Mr Parker?' she asked sharply.

He didn't answer. 'I'm bringing her over to the Cavendish Residence now, and I was wondering if you or one of the other interns could help her.'

She could feel anger rising in her, but she kept her voice even. 'I'll meet you outside.' She hung up the phone and ran back to her room.

Donna came down to the lobby with her. They

stood by the window, and a few minutes later a sedan pulled up to the kerb. Sherry recognized the advertising director at the wheel.

'Isn't he going to bring her in?' Donna wondered when the car just sat there.

'He's probably afraid of being seen,' Sherry said grimly. 'Come on, let's go get her.'

They went out to the car. When Alex Parker saw them approaching he got out and looked around, as if he was afraid someone was watching. Then he went around to the passenger side of the car and opened the door. By then the girls were by his side, and they could see Pamela.

She didn't look like she was crying now, Sherry thought. She looked stunned.

Her face remained blank as she stepped out of the car. Mr Parker went into the back of the car and dragged out a suitcase. Donna took it from him.

'You'll get her back to her room?' the man asked.

'Yes,' Sherry said. She put an arm around Pamela. The girl was shivering. She glanced up at Alex with wide eyes.

'I'll call you,' he said, and got back into the car.

'Don't bother,' Sherry whispered as he took off. 'Come on, Pam.'

They went back into the Cavendish and up the stairs. Sherry fumbled in Pamela's handbag and found her keys.

Once inside the room, Pamela's mask came off. She didn't speak, but tears were streaming down her face. Sherry sat her down on a bed and sat down next to her.

'I'll get her some water,' Donna offered, and went into the bathroom.

Sherry put an arm around Pamela, and the girl leaned on her shoulder. As Sherry murmured soothing words her eyes went to a book on the bedside table. Pamela's bible, *Sex and the Single Girl*. With her free hand, Sherry picked it up.

'Damn you, Helen Gurley Brown,' she muttered. And she tossed it in the direction of the wastebasket.♥

Chapter Twenty-Five

When Donna opened her eyes, she didn't need to check the calendar on the wall to know the date. It had been imprinted on her mind for weeks now. Friday, 30 August. For some, it was the beginning of a weekend. For Donna, it was possibly the end of the world.

Friday, 30 August. The day the special readers' edition of *Gloss* arrived in mailboxes and hit newsstands all over America.

It was ironic in a way. She'd managed to get through this entire internship without getting caught as a fraud. Today she should be congratulating herself on her success. Instead she found herself in more danger than she'd been in since she arrived.

She lay in bed and considered the plan that had been evolving in her head since she first learned her picture would appear in the issue. It would mean humbling herself, doing something she'd promised herself she would never do. But it was the only way.

Sherry came out of the bathroom wrapped in a

towel. 'Morning, sleepyhead,' she said. 'The shower's all yours.'

Donna sat up. 'I don't think I'll be going into the office today.'

Sherry paused in the midst of dressing and looked at her in disbelief. 'Donna, it's the last day of the internship! You can't miss it – there's going to be a party.'

'I'm not feeling too good. My stomach's upset. Maybe it was last night's meat loaf.'

'Want me to run to the pharmacy and get you something?'

'Oh no, that's OK,' Donna said quickly. 'I think I just need to take it easy.'

'OK.' Sherry was now preoccupied with the buttoning of her shirtwaist dress. 'Damn, I've put on a couple of pounds. I can't fasten this middle button.' She took it off and pulled something else from the closet. 'Hey, you're thinner than I am. You could wear that dress.'

Donna was barely listening – her mind was on her plan. But Sherry misunderstood her silence.

'Look, it's not charity, Donna. It doesn't fit me, and I doubt I'll be losing this weight any time soon. By the time I can get into it, it'll be out of style.'

Donna managed a half-hearted smile. Her plan for the day already committed her to losing pride. Why not accept Sherry's offer?

'Thanks,' she said. 'If I feel better later, I'll wear it to the party.'

As soon as Sherry left, she got out of bed and took a quick shower. When she came out of the bathroom she took a good look at the dress Sherry had left for her. It was really cute, peach-coloured, with a slightly flared skirt and deep pockets. And Donna was so sick of her own two dresses, both of which had been washed so many times they were completely faded. Plus, there was the confidence a nice dress might give her. She'd need all the confidence she could muster for what she was about to do.

The night before, Pamela had distributed a massive pile of make-up samples she'd amassed in her work as the beauty editor's intern. Donna poked through the tiny lipsticks and miniature eyeshadows, and for the first time that summer she actually applied some make-up. When she finished, she pulled back her long hair and with the help of some bobby pins twisted it into something resembling a chignon.

She had to admit, her reflection pleased her. And it gave her a boost. Stop thinking this is the end of the world, she ordered herself. It's a new day, a new beginning. A new you.

From the back of her dresser drawer she drew out her secret stash. All summer long she'd picked up coins she spotted on the street, coins she'd found in public telephone boxes. At work David frequently sent her out with money to buy both of them coffees or sodas. She'd buy one for him, and pocket the money her own would have cost.

She had a pile of change now, and it filled the pockets of her dress.

Leaving the room, she went down the hall to the payphone.

She was grateful for the fact that she had a good memory. Months ago, when he came to get Kathy and Billy, her father had told her the name of the company he worked for. It was easy to call four-one-one for the information operator, and she got the phone number.

Inserting more coins, she dialled zero for the regular operator, and placed a long-distance person-to-person call for Martin Peake. She could hear the phone ringing, and the hand that held the receiver began to hurt as the tension filled her.

She knew there was a way people could send money quickly around the country. Just last week, Vicky had run out of money and her family in California managed to get money available for her through Western Union the very same day. She'd ask her father to do the same. She hadn't taken money from him for almost three months – he owed her. Or he could treat it as a loan, she didn't care. She just needed enough to get out of New York, fast, before Ron could find out where she was.

Finally she heard a female voice answer the ringing phone with the name of the company her father worked for.

Her operator spoke. 'I have a person-to-person call for a Mr Martin Peake.'

'Mr Peake isn't here at the moment. Would you like to leave a message?'

'Caller, would you like to leave a message?' her operator repeated.

'Yes, would you ask him to call Donna?' She rattled off the Cavendish Residence number, and hung up.

Now what? She couldn't go to the dining hall or watch TV in the lounge – she had to stay in her room where she could be found when her father called back.

She tried to amuse herself by poring through the rest of the cosmetic samples, but they weren't very distracting. There was too much running through her mind. The interns had to be out of the Cavendish by Sunday, so she had to have money by then to buy a bus ticket. But to where? And to do what?

The room intercom buzzed, and she jumped up. Thank goodness, Martin Peake was responding. She rushed to the wall and pressed the button. 'Yes?'

'Donna? There's a gentleman in the lobby who wants to see you.'

Her stomach dropped. How was this possible? Had the magazine come out earlier in the Midwest? Had Ron discovered where she was some other way?

'Donna? Did you hear me?' the receptionist enquired.

'Oh, yes. I'll be right down.'

She lifted her shaking finger from the button and tried to stop the panic from totally overwhelming her. She couldn't think – but she *had* to think. Taking deep breaths, she considered her options.

The building had a back door – but the only way out to the street from there meant going around to the front of the building, and anyone in the lobby could see her through the window.

Window . . . the window in the bedroom looked out on to a side alley. And there was a fire escape.

Tossing her things into her backpack, she put it on over her shoulders and went to the window. The Cavendish was air-conditioned, and the window hadn't been opened all summer. It took some effort to unfasten the latch that held it closed, and pull it open. Then she perched on the sill, swung her legs over the ledge and settled them on to the metal steps.

Slowly, clinging to the sticky, dirty handrail, she made her way down the stairs. Only the fire escape didn't go all the way to the ground. It ended around the top of the first floor, and she had to jump the rest of the way. She landed on her rear end.

Her first reaction was relief that she'd made it without injury. Her second thought was for the pretty dress that surely had to be smudged now. And her third sensation was shock – to see David Barnes standing at the end of the alley, just a few yards away, staring at her in disbelief.

He strode forward. 'Are you OK?'

She stood up and made a futile attempt to brush the dirt off her dress. 'Yeah, I'm fine.'

He shook his head in bewilderment. 'What were you doing?'

It was amazing, how quickly she was able to fabricate an excuse. 'Um, my door was stuck.' And before he could question that, she came up with her own demand. 'What are *you* doing here?'

'Looking for you. I was waiting in the lobby, and then I saw you coming down the fire escape.'

Funny how she'd never noticed that one of the lobby windows faced the alley.

'Can we go inside?' he asked, wiping a bead of sweat from his brow. 'It's hot out here. You'll want to wash your hands, and tell that janitor about the stuck door.'

Now that she realized it hadn't been Ron who was waiting for her, she agreed. But there was something that still puzzled her.

'Why did you come looking for me?' she asked David as they entered the lobby together.

Before he could respond, the receptionist called out to her, 'Oh, there you are! Donna, you have a phone call. It's from your father.'

She hesitated. How could she talk to Martin Peake

in front of David Barnes? The receptionist must have noticed her discomfort.

'If you need some privacy, just go pick it up on the hallway phone.'

'I'll be right back,' she told David, and hurried through the swinging doors.

'Hello?'

'Hello, Donna, it's your father, returning your call. How are you?'

'Fine, thank you,' she said automatically. And then, 'No, I'm not fine.' She decided she might as well get right to the point. 'I need some money.'

'Where are you?' he asked.

'I'm in New York, it's a long story. But I need to get out of here. I left Ron, you know.'

'Yes, I know. He called me two months ago, looking for you.'

'Well, I think he may know I'm here, in New York, and I'm afraid he'll be coming after me.'

There was a moment of silence and then her father said, 'That's not going to happen, Donna.'

'How do you know?'

'Because Ron is dead. He was killed in a car accident. He was driving drunk.'

After a moment of silence he asked, 'Donna? Are you still there? Have we been disconnected?'

'No, I'm here.' Her head was spinning. Had she ever loved Ron? She'd made love with him, she'd almost had his baby. Was it shameful for her to now be feeling an enormous wave of relief?

'About the money . . .' her father began.

She was grateful for the change of subject. 'I can stay here in New York and start looking for a job,' she said. 'I just need enough to get through a few weeks until I find something.'

He mentioned a sum of money that she thought was more than generous and told her he could wire it to a Western Union office in New York.

'Thank you,' she said softly. 'How are the kids?'

'Doing well,' he told her. 'They ask about you. Maybe, once you're settled and in a job, you could come out and visit. I could help with the airfare.'

He was trying to make amends for not having been there for her, she could see that. And although at an earlier date she would have rejected these efforts, now she actually sensed in herself the ability to forgive, and move on.

'Maybe,' she said cautiously. 'I'll write you with my new address.'

After hanging up the phone she stood there for a moment and tried to absorb all the news. Then she remembered David Barnes. She still didn't know why he'd come looking for her.

He was still there, waiting patiently in the lobby.

'I was worried when you didn't come in this morning,' he told her. 'I was afraid you were leaving early to go home. I've got an offer for you.'

She looked at him blankly and repeated his words. 'An offer?'

'A couple of weeks ago I asked the personnel department if I could get approval for a new position. And this morning I got their answer. I can offer you a job at *Gloss*, to work as my assistant. Are you interested?'

Would her head ever stop spinning today? How many emotions had overwhelmed her in the past hour? Fear, relief, shock, gratitude . . . and now this. But at least this news could be met with a single word.

'Yes.'♥

Chapter Twenty-Six

Never in a million years did Allison think she'd be spending her last night in New York at the Copacabana nightclub. She was surrounded by rich people, ostentatious décor, ridiculously expensive food and drink, everything she despised.

But she couldn't say she was miserable. She was with friends, and she wasn't in jail.

The friends were certainly far from miserable.

Sherry was looking around with avid interest. Donna was clearly in awe.

'I've never been in a place like this before,' she murmured. 'Do I look OK?'

'More than OK,' Allison assured her. Donna had gone through a complete metamorphosis. With some of the money her father had sent, she'd bought some clothes and she'd had her scraggly hair cut. Tonight she was wearing a straight, fitted sheath in sunny yellow that brought out unexpected gold highlights in her now fashionable brunette flip. But the greatest change of all came from her demeanour. She was talking, she was smiling, and she no longer had the expression of a scared rabbit. And she was clearly thrilled to be at a famous nightclub.

Allison had been a little worried about bringing Pamela here. The last time her roommate had been in the Copacabana, it was with that jerk Alex Parker.

But Pamela wasn't showing any grief. In fact, it was hard for Allison to believe this was the same girl who'd sobbed for hours in their room less than a week ago, and wouldn't go back to *Gloss* the next morning. Allison had assumed she'd planned to spend the day crying in bed. But she'd been wrong. When Allison returned from *Gloss* at six, she found that Pamela had spent the day in a beauty parlour, getting her hair dyed back to platinum blonde. She'd also taken all the clothes Alex had bought her to a consignment shop and traded them in for the tight orange pencil skirt and the *very* tight jersey top in hot pink that she was wearing tonight.

She was probably still harbouring some sad feelings, Allison thought. But on the surface, Pamela had bounced back.

Even Sherry was looking at her with approval. 'You look great, Pamela. That *Gloss* makeover was never right for you – I can see that now.'

Pamela nodded in agreement, and then, for a brief moment, a wistful look crossed her face. 'It's funny, in a way. If I hadn't had that makeover, Alex would never have noticed me. And I wouldn't have gotten myself in that mess.'

'Oh, I don't blame you,' Sherry said quickly. 'It was all his fault. He took advantage of you.'

Pamela shrugged. 'Maybe. But I was looking for trouble. Remember how I said I wanted a sugar daddy who would take me to fancy places?'

Allison remembered. 'Yeah, you really were an idiot,' she said cheerfully.

Pamela grinned. 'Look who's talking. At least I got to go to some great restaurants. *You* ended up in jail.'

Sherry sighed. 'I guess none of us were too successful, romantically speaking. I mean, look at me and Mike.'

Allison looked at her curiously. 'Why *did* you two break up? I never heard the whole story.'

'He was searching for a muse and I was searching for a husband,' Sherry replied.

'Are you still?' Allison asked. 'Searching for a husband?'

Sherry looked thoughtful. 'Not at the moment,' she said finally.

'Good,' Donna said. 'Because they're not all they're cracked up to be.'

The others gazed at her respectfully. Now that they all knew about Donna's past, they could understand why the girl had seemed so odd. And now the girl who wasn't even supposed to have been there for an internship, who hadn't shown any interest in the magazine, was actually going to be working there.

'What about your new love?' Sherry asked Allison. 'You think there's a future?'

Before Allison could respond, a waiter rolling a cart appeared at their table. On the cart lay a bucket filled with ice and a bottle of champagne.

'Compliments of Mr Bobby Dale,' he announced.

As her friends gasped in unison, and the waiter placed special champagne glasses on the table, Sherry's question rang in Allison's ears. A future with Bobby Dale? It was hard to say. But thinking back to the past week, she had to admit to herself that she wouldn't write off the notion.

When she'd called him from the police station, he didn't ask a million questions. He sent his lawyer there, and the lawyer had arranged bail. By the next day, the police had interviewed the others who had been in the basement, and one of the girls admitted that she had seen Sam put the bag of marijuana in Allison's purse.

She and Bobby had been together almost every evening since then, at his grandmother's house in Queens. Of course, she'd been enormously grateful to him, but she'd been a little worried that he'd expect a real show of appreciation – a physical one. But even when his grandmother wasn't around, he'd been totally respectful. They'd talked a lot – about their lives, families, their hopes and dreams.

Each night, as he put her in the cab to take her back

GL♥SS

to the Cavendish, he'd kissed her. And each night, the kisses became longer and more intense. But it wasn't until last night that things began to happen.

She'd told him all about Sam. Then he told her all about a girl in Los Angeles. He'd thought they were in love, until he realized she was just using him to get into the music business herself. They'd talked about what fools they'd both been. They'd ended up in each other's arms, at first murmuring words of comfort, then moving on to other words, then moving on to silence.

It was nothing like her make-out sessions with Sam. Every touch, every caress, went way beyond anything she'd felt with Sam. With Bobby, it wasn't just electricity. He made her heart sing. And her body yearn for more.

The pop of the champagne bottle brought her out of her reverie, and she was startled by the way the other girls were grinning at her. Everything she'd been thinking about must have shown on her face.

'Yes, I'd say there's definitely a future,' Pamela declared.

'Well, not right away,' Allison said. 'He's leaving tomorrow to go on tour.'

'Will he be coming back to New York soon?' Donna asked.

'Maybe. But I won't be here.'

The others looked surprised. 'I thought you were

always planning to stay in New York after the internship,' Sherry said.

Allison was almost embarrassed to tell them her new plan. 'Well, I started thinking about how maybe I'm not really ready for that. I mean, I've been pretty naive about the world, right?'

She was a little annoyed by how fervently they nodded in agreement, but she couldn't really blame them. 'Anyway, I hate to give in to my parents, but . . . I've decided to go back to Boston. I'm enrolling at Radcliffe next week. I'm going to be a college girl, just like Sherry.'

Sherry bit her lip. 'Actually . . . my plans have changed too. I'm *not* going to be a college girl. Not this fall, at least. Caroline offered me a job at *Gloss*, and I'm going to take it.'

'This is incredible,' Allison exclaimed. 'Look at how we've all changed! Donna was a runaway. Sherry was the good girl who did what she was supposed to do. I was the rebel. And now, we're all – well, not who we were.'

'But you're still wearing black,' Sherry pointed out.

Allison laughed. 'I still love the beatnik look. But I know I'm different inside. We all are.'

'Except for me,' Pamela interjected. 'I'm going to do exactly what I'd planned to do when the internship was over. I'm going to secretarial school.'

'But you've changed too,' Sherry said quietly.

'Maybe even more then the rest of us.'

Pamela was silent for a moment. 'Yeah, maybe you're right. I may not be much older, but I'm definitely wiser.'

The waiter had finished pouring the champagne, and Sherry held up her glass. 'We should make a toast. To us?'

'To Bobby Dale?' Donna suggested. 'It was awfully nice of him to give Allison tickets for all of us.'

'To changes,' Allison said. 'To growing up.'

'To all of the above,' Pamela declared. And they clinked their glasses.

The lights went down, and a voice from somewhere echoed across the packed room.

'Ladies and gentlemen, the Copacabana is proud to present the sensational Bobby Dale!'

There was massive applause, a few whistles, and a couple of squeals as the lights came up over the band and Bobby ran out on the stage.

'He's really cute,' Sherry whispered in Allison's ear.

There was no denying that, Allison thought. Not *her* type, of course. Too clean-cut, too classically handsome, too normal. But even so, a little shiver went up her spine.

The band struck up the opening to Bobby's latest

hit, 'Let Me Love You', and the crowd went wild. It was odd, Allison thought – she'd heard that song a million times, it was always on the radio, and she'd chalked it up as typical teen drivel. But it sounded better to her now. Maybe it was just that Bobby's voice live was clear as a bell, sweet and full of feeling. The lyrics were still pretty silly, but he invested them with what sounded like real emotion. Or maybe it was because he made eye contact with her, and she swore she saw him wink.

From there, he went right into more hits, and thirty minutes flew by. Then, just before he took his break, he spoke to the audience.

'You all know me as a rock and roll singer,' he said. 'But I'd like my fans to know there are other kinds of music out there. And I'd like to close this half of the show with a very special song, written by Pete Seeger, one of America's great folk singers.'

Allison had heard of Pete Seeger, of course, though she couldn't recall any particular song of his. But she recognized this one immediately.

'To everything, turn, turn, turn, there is a season, turn, turn, turn . . .'

If there was any last little spark inside her, one that still bore a fond memory of Sam, it flickered and went out. He really was one-hundred-per-cent fraud.

For some bizarre reason, an image of her mother came to mind. She had this annoying habit of tossing

GL♥SS

out proverbs and so-called 'words of wisdom' at every opportunity and whenever she wanted to teach Allison a lesson about appropriate manners and morals. One of the woman's favourites was 'You can't judge a book by its cover.'

So corny. But for once Allison had to admit there just might be a tiny element of truth to it. Sam, the beatnik, the non-conformist, the rebel – he was a total phony. Bobby Dale, the pop star, the teen idol, was – well, she wasn't completely sure what he was yet. But she definitely wanted to know more.

And Boston was one of the cities on his tour.♥

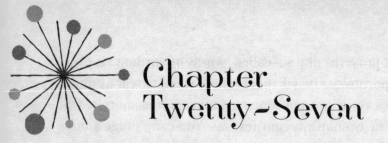

Chapter
Twenty-Seven

On Monday morning, 9 September, Sherry took her seat behind her new desk, which was identical to her old desk. The only difference was the location – she was now at the other end of the bullpen, just outside the office of the managing editor.

This desk too held a typewriter, a phone, in- and out-boxes, a Rolodex and a jar holding a variety of pens and pencils in different colours. But something new was about to be added.

'Mail,' came the call from the boy in an oversized Hartnell jacket who pushed the cart. It wasn't Mike of course. Mike had left his summer job in the mailroom right around the same time the internships had finished. This new, sandy-haired, gangly boy paused by Sherry's desk.

'I guess this is for you, right?' he asked, offering her an oblong metal object.

'Thank you, Larry.' She took the nameplate and examined the white letters on the black background. S. A. FORRESTER, EDITORIAL ASSISTANT. Then she placed it on the far right corner of the desk, with the name facing outward.

GL♥SS

Stopping at her desk, George Simpson didn't notice it.

'I need to have these letters typed,' he told her. At that very moment Caroline Davison came out of her office and overheard him.

'I'm sorry, George, the interns have left. Didn't you get my announcement memo? Sherry is on staff now. You'll have to give those to your own secretary.'

His brow furrowed and he didn't look happy. There was no 'Congratulations' or 'Welcome to *Gloss*', but at least he turned and strode away. That was enough for Sherry, and she smiled at Caroline.

Caroline smiled back, and she noticed Sherry's nameplate. 'Well, you're official now. How does it feel?'

How could she possibly describe the feelings she'd been having for over a week now? Besides, she was a working girl now. There was no time for chit-chat.

'Fine,' was all she said, and Caroline gave her a brisk, pleased nod. Then she dropped some folders into Sherry's in-box.

'This is the last of the unsolicited article submissions. I can't believe you've managed to get through them so quickly. You're going to be a real asset, Sherry.'

'I'll do my best,' Sherry replied.

Caroline gave her another nod and a smile and moved on.

Sherry took the top folder and opened it. It was

so hard to believe it had only been a week since she became S. A. Forrester, editorial assistant. A week that had started with bidding farewell to new friends, exchanging addresses and promises to stay in touch. Then filling out countless forms – personnel, tax, social security, all the stuff that would turn her into a real working girl. And then there were the hysterical phone calls from her parents, the letters she had to write to friends and to the college she wouldn't be attending. Not this fall at least. Maybe not ever. When she was ready to go to university, she'd find one with a journalism department. Right now, she was exactly where she wanted to be.

When Caroline had made the offer on the last day of the internship, to stay here at *Gloss* and work full-time, she'd been stunned by how easily she'd said yes. The managing editor then called the Cavendish Residence and pulled some strings. She and Donna could stay in their room for another six months.

Of course they'd have to pay for the room now, but they both had salaries. And during the six months they'd be very careful and save money, so they could afford a small apartment to rent together. Donna used the money her father sent to buy a small TV for the room, and Sherry had come up with enough cash for a hotplate, so they could boil water for coffee and tea. She felt reasonably sure that eventually Mama would come around to accepting her decision, and she'd send Sherry her things from home.

She was halfway through the stack of files when the phone on her desk rang, for the very first time. Feeling terribly important, she lifted the receiver.

'Sherry Forrester.'

There was a moment of silence before she heard a voice.

'Hey, Sherry.'

It had been a while, over two months, but she recognized the voice immediately.

'Johnny?'

'Yeah, it's me. How are you?'

'Fine,' she replied automatically. 'How are you?'

'Fine. I'm in New York.'

'Really? What are you doing here?'

He didn't answer the question. 'Um, could we meet?'

'Now?' She glanced at the clock on the wall.

'Well, sometime today?'

'I've got a lunch break at noon. We could meet then.'

'OK.'

She gave him the name and address of a coffee shop nearby on Madison. Hanging up, she stared at the phone for a minute. She supposed she shouldn't be so surprised to hear from him. Mama would try anything to get her back home.

An hour later she stuck her head around Caroline's

door and told her she was going to lunch. She was running a little late, but she still couldn't resist taking a moment to duck into a restroom and check out her reflection. In her own eyes she looked just as she had two months ago. Her light brown hair was still in its chin-length flip and she was still wearing the same shade of pink lipstick. The dress she was wearing was something she'd worn back in high school. Johnny would see the same girl he'd known for so long. Even if she wasn't.

He was already seated in a booth when she arrived. Seeing him, for a moment her heartbeat quickened as the memories flooded back. Cheering him as he made a touchdown on the football field. Kissing in the back row of the movie theatre. Prom night, getting to second base . . .

He looked up and their eyes met. She strode forward and came to the booth.

'Hey, Johnny.'

'Hey,' he replied, but his eyes seemed focused over her head.

The waitress appeared, slapped two plastic-coated menus on the table and left.

Johnny looked down at the one in front of him. 'What's good here?'

'Johnny!' she exclaimed.

He looked up. 'What?'

'Look, you just turn up, out of the blue, and you're

wondering what to eat? Don't you think you might tell me why you're here first?'

He had the courtesy to look a little abashed. 'I guess I just feel kind of weird. It's been a while. And I've never been in New York before. I can't stay long – I've got orientation at Tech in a couple of days.'

'Johnny,' she said patiently, 'why are you here?'

'I've come to get you back,' he said simply.

She smiled. 'My parents sent you.'

'They're pretty upset,' he said. 'About you deciding to stay in New York.'

'I'm sorry about that,' she told him, 'but they'll come around.'

The waitress reappeared. 'You folks ready to order?'

'Can we just have a couple of Cokes for now?' Sherry asked.

After she left, Johnny's eyes roamed the room for a few seconds before he spoke again. 'That's not the only reason I'm here,' he blurted out. 'I made a big mistake, Sherry. I was really stupid. I never should have broken up with you.'

She struggled to come up with an appropriate response. 'Well, these things happen. People change.'

He took a deep breath. 'I still love you, Sherry.'

It was odd, she thought. Suddenly she couldn't remember him ever actually saying those words before. Maybe he never had.

But now that he'd got them out, he kept on talking.

'We need to be together. I mean, we were all set, remember? I'd go to Tech, you'd go to Agnes Scott. As soon as I pledged a frat, I'd give you a lavaliere. We'd get pinned junior year, and then we'd get engaged after we graduate.' His voice went up on the last word of each sentence, almost as if he was posing them as questions, trying to find out if she remembered.

'I guess you like city living now, right?' he went on. 'So we could live in Atlanta after we're married. I'll get a job, we can start a family . . .' His voice trailed off. He was waiting for her to say something, but she couldn't think of anything to say.

The waitress plunked the sodas on to the table. They each took their time, removing the straws from their wrappers, putting the tubes into the glasses, taking a long drink.

'So, what do you say?' Johnny asked. 'Will you come home?'

She shook her head.

He scowled. 'Look, I said I'm sorry. Can't you forgive and forget?'

'It's not that, Johnny.'

He stared at her. 'Oh, wait, I get it. You've met someone else.'

She shook her head again. 'It's not that either.'

'Then what?' His eyes widened, as if the unthinkable had just occurred to him. 'You don't care about me any more?'

She didn't want to hurt him, and she spoke carefully. 'I'm just not sure what I want any more. I thought I knew, but now I'm thinking there might be something else . . .'

He stared at her in complete and utter bewilderment. He didn't get it, and she wasn't sure she did either.

His voice hardened. 'I'm not going to beg.'

'I'm not asking you to.' She reached across the table. 'We can still be friends.'

Almost involuntarily he drew back, and she knew why. Boys and girls couldn't just be friends. Not after they'd been something else. That was one of the rules.

He finished his Coke and pushed the glass aside.

'Do you want to eat something?' she asked.

He shook his head.

'I should go,' she murmured. 'I've got a lot of work to do.'

He shrugged.

She went into her purse, took out some money and put it on the table. 'Goodbye, Johnny.'

Back out on the street she started walking rapidly, almost as if she was running away. But that wasn't how she felt. She couldn't even begin to identify the emotions that filled

She was frightened and excited and confused.

her at that moment. A little bit of sadness, a little relief . . . she was frightened and excited and confused. All she knew for certain was that she had just made a choice. When she wasn't even sure there were choices to be made.

But she was aware of an extraordinary lightness in her step as she sailed down Madison Avenue on her way back to work.♥